SHE looked about the apartment they had furnished with so much love and hope and courage, and everything in it brought some stabbing memory. How little any of it meant with Chris gone!

There was no false pride left in her. She knew now that the fault had been hers. She had said unforgivable things for which she must now ask forgiveness. If only it wasn't too late!

Ever After

Phyllis A. Whitney

FAWCETT CREST • NEW YORK

EVER AFTER

THIS BOOK CONTAINS THE COMPLETE TEXT OF THE ORIGINAL HARDCOVER EDITION.

Published by Fawcett Crest Books, a unit of CBS Publications, the Consumer Publishing Division of CBS Inc., by arrangement with Houghton Mifflin Company.

ISBN: 0-449-24128-9

Printed in the United States of America

12 11 10 9 8 7 6 5 4 3

Ever

After

1

Through a Revolving Door

There was a little square of park across the street on her left, nestling comfortably down among surrounding sky-scrapers. There were bushes there, and bright new spring grass and benches that invited.

The girl with the red feather on her hat paused and looked yearningly at the park, while the crowds divided and walked around her, jostling her elbows, annoyed because she fitted into neither stream. Someone who was going neither east nor west, downtown nor uptown, had no business on a New York street.

There were freckles on the girl's nose and she had shoulder-length brown hair that waved just enough, a determined chin, and brown eyes that were a little frightened. Under one arm she held an artist's portfolio with the name "Marel" lettered across it, and beneath the name the words "Oak Park, Illinois."

On her right the revolving door of a big office building completed its circuit again and again while the girl named Marel hesitated. Then the jaunty red feather and the determined chin won out. She turned her back on the park that meant a temporary escape at least, and entered a section of the door behind a tall young man, who put more energy than was necessary into the act of going through a revolving door.

She catapulted into a long corridor practically on the young man's heels. He turned and put out a long arm to stop her before she bumped into him.

"In a hurry?" he asked.

She looked up into a nice sort of face. Not the movie star kind she was always trying to put into her drawings, but a face with interesting planes that caught an artist's attention and was somehow satisfactory in all its parts. All except the eyes. The gray eyes were laughing at her. She didn't like to be laughed at.

The red feather on her hat bobbed indignantly. "I'm not in a hurry," she told him. "Do you always go through revolving doors like that?"

"Always," he said, "when it's ten o'clock of a spring morning."

She turned away to study the big rectangular directory that listed the many offices in the building, and the young man went on toward his elevator, still smiling.

E. Eakins, Edwards, Elston, *Embree*. Embree Studio, room 918. That was it. The elevator had gone when she turned toward it again and she waited a little nervously for the next car.

This was the moment she'd been looking forward to ever since her train had pulled out of Chicago a week before. This was the moment she'd been moving toward ever since she took her first step in Grand Central Station. Oh, long before that, really. She'd been waiting for this time when she'd be an honest-to-goodness professional artist ever since art school in Chicago. And now that the moment was really here, her heart was thumping under her ribs and the palms of her hands were damp with nervousness. Her mother and father had been awfully decided about her career. She might have one year in New York with Aunt Peg. A year in which to prove she could earn her living in her chosen field. After that home again if she couldn't make good.

She was in the car now and she heard herself say, "Nine, please," in a voice that broke unexpectedly in the middle, and she stepped out of the elevator into another long corridor. This wouldn't do—damp palms and a quavery voice. She spied a door with the word "WOMEN" lettered in gold and hurried through it. There was no one in front of the mirror, thank goodness, and she could take thorough stock of herself in the glass.

She looked all right. Quite nice, in fact. Not terrified practically out of her wits. The forest-green suit Aunt Peg had helped her choose looked very New Yorkish, and of course the green hat with its bold red feather was a dream. It ought to be—a Peggy Pope original and a gift right out of her aunt's shop. No, there was nothing to worry about as far as her appearance went. She didn't even need a dab of powder on her nose. Powder never hid the freckles anyway. And probably Fran Embree would hardly look at *her*. It would be the drawings in her portfolio Miss Embree would want to see.

Well, no more postponements. All she had to do was keep her chin up at a jaunty angle that matched the lift of the feather and walk down the corridor into the Embree Studio looking as if she knew the world belonged to her. Nobody needed to guess by looking at her what her tummy was doing under the neat green jacket.

So down the corridor she went to room 918. Outside, she paused for a last deep breath and then opened the door and went in. There was someone ahead of her in the small waiting room—the gray-eyed young man who took revolving doors so furiously in his stride. She was sorry to see him there because his presence made her bluff that much more difficult. She could recall uncomfortably that he had seen her in a hurried and flustered state just a few moments before and would probably not be impressed at this late date by an air of self-possession.

He looked, unreasonably, pleased to see her—as if they were quite old friends.

"Hello, Marel from Oak Park," he said.

She gave him what she hoped was a haughty nod and looked about her uncertainly. There were just three chairs in the room. One of them held the revolving-door man and the other two were heaped with magazines. There was a low round table. piled with books, and on the walls were hung a fascinating array of art work. Across the room —all of three steps away—was a window, with a desk and chair behind it, presumably for a receptionist. But at the moment the window was empty. Marel went over and stood beside it, not too hopefully. Somehow the entire place had an air of being not at all interested in the fate of a girl from Oak Park, Illinois.

"No use standing there," the young man informed her. "Pearl's off again. Her oldest kid's got measles. That means she won't be back till the two others have 'em too. And that'll make a long wait."

Marel looked around at him in annoyance. "You're very helpful. What do you think I'd better do? I'm sure there are people here. I can hear them."

She could certainly hear them. A pair of feminine voices were carrying on an argument about—of all things!— elbows. How elbows looked and how they didn't look. Another voice, apparently talking to itself, was bewailing a delay in delivering finished drawings for something re- ferred to as "the truck book."

"You'll have to make more noise than they're making," the young man told her, "or they'll never know you're here. Have you got anything you could break?"

"Very funny," Marel said, and turned her back on him.

"It wasn't, was it?" He sounded surprisingly contrite. "That's what spring does to me. Sort of busts out all over and deludes me into thinking I'm a wit. Fran knows I'm here. She's on a long-distance call to Philly right now. Wait, I'll fix you up."

He came over and put his head through the receptionist's window. "Hey, Gail! Customers!"

"I'm not," Marel protested. "I'm not even one cus- tomer."

He winked at her. "That's the way to get attention. See? Here she comes."

The discussion about elbows broke off, and a tall, rather brassy-looking girl came to the door of the waiting room. No hair could ever have grown that color, but it was beautifully, sleekly combed and certainly eye-taking. She'd have been quite pretty except for the hard lines about her mouth and the suspicious way her blue eyes regarded the world. In one hand—a hand with the longest, most brilliantly lacquered nails Marel had ever seen—she held a paint brush with a dab of ocher on its tip, and over her black dress she wore a paint-smeared yellow smock.

"Hi, Chris," she said, addressing the young man. "Customers?"

He nodded at Marel. "Over there."

The blue eyes that took in everything and gave out nothing examined Marel critically, coveted her hat and came wearily to rest when they reached her portfolio.

"Oh," she said. "One of those. Just out of art school, I suppose?"

Marel summoned all the dignity she could manage under the circumstances. "I'm Marel Gordon. I have an appointment with Miss Embree. She's expecting me."

The other girl's attention shifted back to the hat. "Oh," she said. "You're Peggy Pope's niece. No wonder." She sighed and turned away, disappearing into another room.

"Just by way of keeping the record straight," the young man said, "that was Gail Norcross, one of the fixtures around here. Fran's assistant, and a good painter in her own right. I'm Chris Mallory, no fixture anywhere at the moment, but with prospects. Now if you'll just tell me what Gail meant by 'no wonder,' and how you got the name of 'Marel,' I'll be practically content. Here, sit down," and he cleared one of the chairs of its load.

There was no resisting his friendliness. He wasn't being fresh, the way she'd thought at first. He was just taking her in and making her feel at home, in spite of herself.

She sat down on the edge of the chair, expecting that she'd need to jump up any minute. "I imagine the 'no wonder' was because of my hat," she explained. "She wondered how a poor art student happened to be wearing a Peggy Pope. And she was right. I wouldn't be if it weren't that Peggy Pope is my aunt."

"Mm," he said. "I don't know much about hats, but I like that feather. Now about this Marel business."

She found herself telling him. "It's really Margaret Elizabeth. But my aunt is Margaret and my mother is Elizabeth, so they didn't want to call me either. I chopped the names off myself when I was too little to say so many syllables and turned it into Mar-el. And I've been called that ever since."

"Now I feel better," Chris said. "You look like Margaret Elizabeth. Marel had me worried."

She thought about that. "You mean a Marel would never have freckles on her nose, but a Margaret Elizabeth would?"

"That's it!" He had a nice sort of laugh. Not a polite, held-back kind, but a laugh that came right out in the open and made you laugh too.

While he was laughing, Fran Embree came in, and Marel knew right away she was going to like her. She was small and dark and vibrantly alive. Watching her, you had a sense of a high tension wire kept well under control. A wire charged with purposeful power. Everything about her was quick and to the point, but it was a friendly sort of quickness and you knew the point would never be meant to carry hurt.

"Hello," she said. "Wish I had time to hear the joke. It sounds like a good one. Chris, the author biogs you've done for the catalogue are tops. I read them with one eye while I was bawling out Philly over the phone. You needn't change a period. I'll get the stuff off to the printer right away and my check will be along for you in a day or two. I'll call you the next job I get."

"Thanks, Fran," Chris said. He had risen when she came in and Marel hoped he would go away. No matter

how friendly he had been, she was experiencing dismay at
the thought of exhibiting her drawings. They had looked
so wonderful back in Chicago. But now in this professional atmosphere, she was remembering their flaws. She
knew suddenly that they were kid stuff, art-student stuff.
They'd never get her a job in a place like this, no matter
how kind Fran Embree was. It was going to be bad
enough showing them to her, but it would be worse to
reveal her awkward efforts to this Chris Mallory too.

Fran sat herself in the chair Chris had vacated and
reached briskly for Marel's portfolio. Marel clung to it
just an instant before she gave it up; an instant long
enough for Chris to note. He had been standing beside
them, watching with lively interest, showing no sign of
leaving, but somehow Marel knew that he sensed her
hesitation. Without comment he walked to the opposite
end of the small room to look with absorbed interest at
the array of pictures on the wall. Apparently he wasn't
going off entirely as she wished he would. But at least
he wouldn't embarrass her further by looking at her
drawings. She liked him for understanding.

One by one Fran Embree turned them over, regarding
each with a professional eye that sent Marel's heart sinking to her toes. They were even worse than she remembered them. How could they possibly have looked good
to her teachers in Chicago? How had they ever looked
good to her?

There were a few scenes, a still life or two, but mostly
they were pictures of babies and small children. She had
worked so hard drawing them, so lovingly. And now they
seemed a waste of time. Fran made no comment, just
turned the drawings over one by one, and Marel did not
dare look toward the tall young man so interested in pictures across the room.

"Your aunt tells me you want to try your hand at illustrating," Fran said when she was nearly at the end of the
collection.

Marel said, "Yes," in a very small voice.

"Illustrating books for children—that was it, wasn't it?"

"Yes," Marel echoed again. "That's why I sort of specialized in drawing babies and small children. They *are* bad, aren't they?" She wanted to say it herself. Say it before Fran said it and Chris Mallory heard.

"No," Fran shook her head judicially. "They're not bad at all. For a student they are very good indeed."

"But not for a professional," Marel said quickly. "I'm not ready. That's what you mean, isn't it?"

The older woman ruffled through the drawings again, and Marel had an uncomfortable feeling that she was searching for words. She did not need to look at the pictures again to make up her mind.

"You needn't try to be kind," Marel told her. "You can say what you think."

"Good," Fran said. "Then I will say what I think. It's true that you aren't ready yet. I act as agent for a good many artists. Especially in the juvenile field. Though we're more than agents. Sometimes we see a book through from start to finish when a publisher wants to leave it in our hands. But I have to be able to recommend each artist on my list, and——"

"And you couldn't recommend me," Marel said. She reached for the drawings, began to stuff them untidily back into the folder.

Fran stopped her. "No, wait. Look here, I want to show you. This little girl throwing a ball. Her dress is sweet. But she's all dress. There isn't a real little girl inside that pretty design. You've been working at home, haven't you? Drawing children the way you remember them? Or getting your ideas from fashion magazines. Isn't that it?"

"Well—yes," Marel admitted. "Oh, some of them were done in class from models, but we had to work so fast then, and——"

Fran selected one of the drawings. "This was done from

a model, wasn't it? It's not so stiff as the others. Hurried, perhaps, but more natural. Do you see what I mean?"

"But even it isn't good enough," Marel said. "I guess you don't hold out much hope for me?"

"Of course there's hope. You have an eye for composition and color. And you catch design detail. But your children don't have an authentic appeal. That you'll need to get by working on it. Come back and see me when you think you have it. Maybe in a few months, maybe in a year. Who knows?"

Fran stood up and her expression was kindly and sorry at the same time. Marel caught up her folder without bothering to fasten it. All she wanted was to get out of the studio quickly. Away by herself where Fran Embree and Chris Mallory wouldn't know how she felt. Maybe months. Maybe a year. But a year was all she had.

She brought her chin up once more to match the brave angle of the red feather on her hat. "You were awfully good to look at these," she told Fran. "Thanks a lot. I—I guess I'll run along."

Chris was still studying the pictures and he had not turned around.

"Good-bye, Mr. Mallory," she said, and hurried out the door without waiting for an answer.

It was a relief to be out of the studio, but she would not feel really safe till she was downstairs and away from the building. The elevator was taking forever and her eyes felt blurry. She mustn't cry. She wasn't a baby. She should have had better sense than to pin all her hopes on this interview with Fran Embree.

The elevator gate slid open and she stepped in and moved to the back. But before the gate closed, a man came running down the corridor in time to catch the car. People shifted to let him in and he turned around to face the gate, so she could not tell whether Chris Mallory had seen her or not. She hoped he hadn't. She didn't want him to feel sorry for her. Didn't want to answer any more questions he might ask. She wanted to get away by herself and face the sickening sense of disappointment that filled her.

But it was hard to hide with a red feather on your hat. He was waiting for her when the car emptied at the main floor. She glanced up at him once and then quickly away. At least he didn't look pitying.

"That was tough," he said. He sounded casual and not at all as if he knew her whole world had practically come to an end. "What's your next move?"

She had no answer for that. "I guess there isn't any next move. Miss Embree would know whether I'm any good or not. If she says I'm not, I expect I'm not."

"You mean this is the end of you as an artist?"

She stopped just before they came to the revolving door and turned to face him. The tendency to tearfulness was gone now.

"Of course it's not the end of me. I'll get there some day, no matter how long it takes. It's just that I—I don't know what to do next."

"That's more like it," he approved. "Let's get out where we can talk this over."

It was amazing the way he seemed to have taken her in charge and how natural it was that a perfectly strange young man should be interesting himself in her problems. She went through the door ahead of him and he followed decorously this time without setting it whirling with spring exuberance.

They cut through the two-way stream on the sidewalk and reached the comparative calm of the curb's edge.

"Now then," he said, "the first thing I'd recommend is that you follow Fran's advice."

"But she said my children were no good. She said——"

"No. She only said they weren't real and that you'd have to find out how to make them real before you come back to see her."

Marel must have looked her bewilderment, for he was

wearing that disarming grin again.

"Why don't you get out and draw kids?" he asked. "Draw 'em from morning to night right from life the way she said to do it."

"But how?" Marel demanded. "I've only been in New York a week. I don't know any children. How would I find models?"

"Come along," he said, and guided her across the street by one elbow. She went, unresisting, curious now, and with an odd surge of hope rising in her.

They were heading for the green oasis of the little park, set down in the desert of tall bare buildings. Pigeons thronged the walks, scarcely moving their plump little bodies out of the way of passing feet as they pecked greedily at peanuts being doled out by a small boy. Chris led the way to an empty bench, dusted her place off with his handkerchief, and sat down beside her.

"Got anything to draw on?" he asked.

She shook her head. "I didn't bring my sketch book."

He clicked his tongue against his teeth disapprovingly. "An artist without a sketch book is as bad as a writer without a notebook. Oh, well—use the backs of your drawings. I suppose you have a pencil?"

She found one in the depths of her purse and then opened her folder of drawings. Somehow she did not mind now if he saw her awkward efforts. She selected one of the least promising and turned the paper over.

"That's the stuff," he said. "And there's a model for you." He nodded toward the small boy with the peanuts. "Get busy."

She smiled her thanks. "This is a wonderful idea. I expect there will be children playing here all day."

"Sure," he said, "and you can come here every day and draw. You'll find other places, too, where children go. I don't know anything about drawing. In fact, that stuff of yours looks pretty good to me. But it seems reasonable that if you put in some intensive work, maybe a bit of drudgery even, you ought to be able to straighten out some of the kinks. Well, I've got to be on my way. I've got an appointment to try for a job myself."

Somehow she didn't want him to go. He was the first person her own age she had met in New York and she liked him better every minute. Now he'd go off and be lost in all those millions of people and she wouldn't see him again. But there wasn't much she could do about it.

"I thought you had a job," she said. "Aren't you doing some work for Fran Embree?"

"Those are just odd jobs. I can't eat on them."

"What do you eat on?"

"Writing. Stories mostly. For the pulp magazines."

"Oh, my!" she said. "A writer! I've never known a writer before."

"I've never known an artist before, either," he told her, and put out his hand.

They shook hands gravely and then laughed together.

"What kind of job is it?" she asked. "If you have time to tell me."

He pointed toward a tall building rising beyond the park. "That's where I'm going. It's a store, and they have an opening in the advertising department. Maybe I'll get a chance to write for regular pay. Eating is easier that way."

"But what about your story writing? Isn't that more important?"

"Sure, it's important. But I'm not good enough at it yet. Just the way you're not good enough at drawing to go out and get a regular job. When we're starting in, we have to get bread-and-butter jobs and keep at our other work in our spare time."

Marel sighed. "I suppose that's what I'll have to do too. I had a rosy little dream about earning my living as an artist right away. Now I suppose I'll have to get a job selling notions or something."

"Not notions. If you get into selling, you'd better

connect it in some way with your art work. You're set on being an artist, I suppose?"

"With every bit of me," Marel said solemnly. "Drawing is like breathing to me. I couldn't do without it."

He stood up. "You'll get there. Some day when you have your name on a book, I'll go around telling people I knew you when you used to sit on a park bench. Well— so long."

"Thank you," she said. "You've helped a lot. More than you know. Good luck on the job. I hope you do better than I did."

He gave her a wave of his hand and turned away. But before he had taken three steps, he swung about and came back.

"Look," he said, nodding toward the big building again. "See that row of windows going up the middle? Wider windows than the others?"

She nodded. "I see them."

"That's where the stairs are. Count up to the fourth window. Got it?"

"I've got it," she said, wondering what he meant.

"Maybe you'll be here awhile drawing," he said. "If I get the job, I'll come down to that window and wave my handkerchief. I won't be able to pick you out, but you can see something white moving from here. Then you'll know if your wishing me luck did any good."

"That will be fun," she said happily. "And I *do* wish you luck."

He went off then, and she watched his tall figure wind its way among the shrubbery along the paths until he disappeared from view. Even if she never saw him again, she was glad she'd know how he came out on his job. Not to know would be like dropping an interesting story right at the climax.

The small boy had run nearly out of peanuts, and he was regarding the pigeons that still flocked about him with an air of indecision. You could tell what he was thinking. He wanted awfully to feed those birds. But he wanted equally to finish the last of the peanuts himself. If she could just catch that expression on paper——

But she couldn't. The moment was too elusive and she lacked the skill. Instead, she took to sketching parts of him. Knees and solidly planted feet, the hand clutching the paper bag, the mop of hair over his forehead. A nurse came along wheeling a baby carriage and holding a little girl by the hand. The little girl had a ball, and when the nurse settled down on a bench, the child began to bounce it and chase after it as it rolled away.

Ruefully Marel compared the wooden ball thrower of her own drawing with the lightness and life of this little girl. Miss Embree had certainly been right. Her pictured children weren't real at all. She struggled to capture that real child on paper, but nothing came right. Her pencil moved stiffly, the results were discouraging, but she kept at it doggedly. Maybe it would be drudgery some of the time. Chris Mallory was right. But this was the way. She knew it was the way.

Every now and then she glanced up at the tall building across from the park and counted to the fourth window. After a few times she knew where it was without counting. But each time it was blank and empty and she began to worry a little. She was remembering things about him now. His shoes had looked scuffed and worn under their brave coating of polish. And there had been frayed threads about the buttonholes of his suit.

She found herself wondering about him as her pencil moved automatically on paper and her eyes studied the romping children before her. Did he belong in New York or had he come from outside too? Where did he live? Would she ever run into him again?

And then she looked up just in time to catch a flutter of white behind the glass of the big window. To the astonishment of the nurse across the path, Marel climbed on a bench and waved one of her drawings wildly in the air.

Probably he wouldn't see it, but she had to try to let him know how glad she was for him.

Queer to be so happy about a job landed by a man she had never seen before that morning.

It was nearly lunchtime, and she gathered up her folder and started back for the crowded streets and her aunt's apartment building. Spring in New York was wonderful. It had got into her step somehow, so that she almost skipped as she walked. She did not feel a bit like a girl who had been turned down on a job. She felt like a girl who was sitting on top of the world. That wasn't sensible, of course. But when had spring ever been a sensible season?

2

Story Hour

A week of living in a penthouse apartment had not lessened the thrill for Marel. It was still exciting to step into the softly lighted, luxuriously carpeted elevator, and be whisked away to the very roof of the world. It was exciting to put her own key into the door and let herself into the perfection of Peggy Pope's apartment.

Nothing could be farther removed from the rambling old house in Oak Park where she'd lived all her life. Nothing had been perfect about that. The furniture was shabby in spots and had been collected not too thoughtfully over the years, so that it seemed thrown together any old way. Summer after summer the sun had beaten against the living-room windows until the draperies had faded to a nondescript color. Wherever you looked, something new was needed, but the purchase of a new article always seemed a drop in the bucket compared to all the things that were needed.

Aunt Peg's apartment had been put together by an interior decorator and everything in it belonged. The beige carpet, that would have been mud-streaked in a week in Oak Park, seemed always bright and fresh. Venetian blinds let in just the wanted amount of sunshine, and each chair, each picture, each vase, seemed the one perfect choice for the spot it occupied.

"Hello, hon!" That was Aunt Peg's voice from her bedroom. "Maggie says luncheon is ready. Hurry and wash, so you can tell me about your morning."

Peggy Pope's smart little hat shop was just around the

corner, so often, when she had no other engagements, she came home for lunch. Marel breathed another little "thank you" to Chris Mallory while she washed. If it had not been for Chris, it would have been awfully hard to tell her aunt about her morning's failure.

As it was, she could break the news almost casually. "Miss Embree was awfully nice," she said as they sat down at the table, "but I won't be good enough for professional work for a while, I'm afraid."

Her aunt nodded understandingly. "Never mind. Fran's opinion is only one. I know a good many people. There'll be other strings to pull. We'll find you a spot yet."

Marel watched her aunt thoughtfully. She was lovely, with soft brown hair swept to the top of her graceful head in a way that made the hats she wore seem exceptionally captivating. She always looked like her apartment—put together in the best and most expensive taste. Earlier that morning, Marel would have listened with the utmost respect to anything she said. But because of an interlude on a park bench, she wondered if she really wanted strings pulled for her.

Unexpectedly she asked a question. "Aunt Peg, did people pull strings for you when you first came to New York?"

Her aunt put her spoon down and made a wry little grimace. "I didn't know anyone who could pull so much as a thread for me. No one could have had a worse time than I did getting started. That's why I'm glad to be in a position to help you."

"But maybe I'd better work a little harder first," Marel said. "Maybe I'm really pretty bad. Miss Embree said I wasn't drawing children the way they are. So I thought I'd like to take some time and do nothing but draw from life. I mean I could go to parks and—anywhere I can find children to draw."

"I like that spirit," her aunt approved. "I do believe you have talent, my dear, but I'm glad you don't want to lean altogether on what I can do for you. There's a branch library not far from here. Why don't you go over there this afternoon and talk to the librarians in the children's room. Perhaps they'd let you draw the children who come there. At least, they'd be quieter models than those in a park."

"That's a wonderful idea!" Marel cried. "I'll go right after lunch."

"Fine. I hope you won't mind having dinner alone. I'm going to the opening night of a play and I'll be dining out."

That meant a date, Marel thought. In the week she had been in New York she had had plenty of opportunity to note and envy her aunt's way of life. She seemed so much younger than her sister, Marel's mother, and she had so much fun. She worked hard at the thing she liked best to do, but she had escaped the scrubbing, cooking, washing routine that was her sister's lot back home. She was never without an escort, and the men she knew seemed very interesting.

That was the sort of life *she* wanted, Marel told herself. To stay young. To do the thing that meant most to her. To have beautiful clothes and a lovely home she had earned herself. All these things were worth working for. But she wanted to have them because she deserved them. Not because someone else pulled strings that made her way easy. She had an idea that Chris Mallory would not approve of too much string-pulling.

When her aunt had gone back to her shop, Marel put on her red-feathered hat again and walked the three blocks to the library building. The children's room was upstairs— a pleasant, bright room, with low round tables and attractive posters on the walls. The librarian behind the desk was helping a mother make a selection, while at the other end of the room a girl about Marel's age was putting books on the shelves.

She was a friendly, cheerful-looking girl with light

brown hair and a nose that went impudently up at the tip. The red sweater she wore strained a little at the seams and she looked like the sort of girl who would be unable to resist a box of chocolates. As Marel came toward her, a stack of books slipped out of her hands and broke the sedate quiet of the room with a series of crashes. The woman at the desk shook her head despairingly, while the girl who had dropped the books struck a melodramatic attitude of chagrin.

"That's the way it always goes," she said, noticing Marel near-by. "Proper librarians never do things like that!"

Marel picked up a book that had landed at her feet and handed it back. As the other girl took it, Marel noticed the ring on her left hand. She was young to be engaged.

"Thanks," the girl said. "Are you looking for something? Can I help you?"

Marel glanced around the nearly empty room. "I was hoping I'd find some children here. You see, I—well, I want to practice drawing children, and I thought——"

"You've picked the right day!" the girl in the red sweater said. "They're having a P.T.A. meeting over at the school this afternoon, and we're running a story hour for the younger children so their mothers won't have to take them to the meeting. There'll be a mob of them in in a little while."

"Do you suppose anyone would mind if I——" Marel began.

"Of course not." She waved a generous hand. "The place is yours. It must be wonderful to draw. Now me— all I can do is tell stories. That's why they put up with me around here. I'm Ginger Williams. What's your name?"

Marel told her just as the first of the children arrived. A small boy in overalls and a yellow sweater, his hair slicked down and his face and hands unreasonably clean. He flashed an oversized dimple the moment he spied Ginger and wriggled out of his mother's grasp.

"Tell me a story!" he demanded. "Tell me the one about the chucklenuts!"

Ginger held him at arm's length. "Whoa, there, young fellow. You've heard that one eleventeen times."

"He's told it himself a lot more times than that," his mother assured Ginger. "Now be good, David, and mind Miss Williams."

She went away, and Ginger tried to seat the little boy at a table and interest him in a book. But David would have none of her scheme. Ginger was apparently his favorite human being and he had no intention of being pried loose from her side.

She raised a comically cocked eyebrow at Marel. "You see what I'm up against?"

"What in the world are chucklenuts?" Marel asked.

"I made 'em up," Ginger said blithely. "And I've been sorry ever since."

The children were arriving by twos and threes now. Ginger took them in charge and began arranging them in a semicircle of small chairs. David got himself under her feet and in her way a dozen times, but even while she scolded him cheerfully, you could tell she loved it.

Marel found herself a table in a corner near a window where afternoon light poured in and quietly took out her sketch pad and pencil. It would be better if she could work unnoticed by her young models. A matter not too difficult to arrange, since they apparently had eyes and hearts only for Ginger.

"Now then," Ginger said, when her small charges had been seated to best advantage, with their wriggling tendencies more or less under control, "what story do you want first?"

"The one about the chucklenuts!" they cried with a single voice, while David, in order to have a special say of his own, added the minute everyone else was still, "The chucklenut story!"

Ginger smiled over their heads at Marel and then put

her finger to her lips. "Ssh! If you'll be very, very quiet, I'll tell you the story of how Sammy Squirrel found the wonderful chucklenuts."

Ginger's voice went sweetly on and the children listened in rapture. Marel listened, too, and watched while her pencil moved on paper. David. David was a honey. If she could only catch that breath-taking expression on paper—— In ten minutes he'd rumpled his hair and smudged his face so that he now looked thoroughly boy, instead of like the small fashion plate his mother had left at the library. There! The way he looked now with his lips parted, his eyes wide and entranced——

There was music in Ginger's voice. She might be overweight, she might drop books and make awkward gestures, but she had a gift for story-telling that was remarkable. Chucklenuts, it seemed, were pretty special. Before you ate a chucklenut, you might look at other people and not like them at all. But chucklenuts got you acquainted with people in a hurry, and when you got to really know someone, you found you had to like him.

Beyond David was a small girl with red curls and the smile of an imp. Marel sketched a few quick lines. There she was on paper holding out a chucklenut to David. Mm, what would chucklenuts look like? she wondered. Like chestnuts, maybe, only they'd have cheerful little faces on their flat sides. Inviting faces that said, "Come and eat me. I won't mind a bit." Because, you see, when you picked a chucklenut, two more grew right away in its place.

The pencil, which had moved so stiffly and awkwardly in the park this morning, seemed now to take an inspired way of its own. Not that she got everything right. Far from it. But she was catching something now—not just stiff exteriors.

The story hour was over before Marel knew where the time had gone, and the mothers began to come for their children. David's mother clucked despairingly over the untidiness he had managed to achieve and carried him, protesting loudly, away from his beloved Ginger.

When the circle had been dispersed and the library had quieted down to a routine state, Ginger came over to Marel's corner.

"You're wonderful at story-telling," Marel told her sincerely. "I don't think I've ever heard anyone better."

Ginger's smile was like her voice, warm and friendly, and nearly as wide as her person. "I love to do it. I'm glad I can. But what about you? I saw your pencil going like anything. Did you get what you came for?"

"Do you want to see how a chucklenut looks?" Marel said, and held out her sketches.

Ginger looked them over carefully and Marel watched her, uncertain for a moment of her reaction, concerned lest she disapprove.

"My goodness!" Ginger cried. "That's *exactly* the way a chucklenut ought to look. I wish David could see those. Look—if you'd do a couple in color, maybe Miss Lambert would like to pin them up in the library. Come along —let's show her."

Marel tried to hold back, to protest. "But they're not finished. And they're not very good really. They're just rough sketches."

But Ginger Williams was not the sort of girl to be thrown off any course she set herself upon. She took the drawings exuberantly out of Marel's hands and carried them across to the girl at the desk.

Miss Lambert took a moment between checking books and glanced at the lot. "These could be worked into something pretty good," she said. "Why don't you two get together?"

"Get together?" Ginger asked.

"Why not? Here you are with a group of stories you've made up yourself that children love. If you can get them down on paper anywhere nearly as well as you tell them, some publisher would probably be willing to bring them out in a book. Of course you'll need illustrations. And here's an artist ready to your hand. I'd say these sketches, rough as they are, show a remarkable understanding of the spirit of your stories. So—why don't you two try to work something out together?"

Ginger and Marel stared at each other blankly for a moment, and then Ginger held out her hand. "Shake, Pardner. We've got us a job. What do you say?"

Marel couldn't say anything. At least not anything sensible. This was a chance more wonderful than anything she had dreamed might happen for some time to come.

"Oh, gracious!" Ginger wailed. "We're going to get busy now. The after-school crowd is coming in. When can we talk?"

Marel collected her scattered wits. "My aunt is going to be out tonight. Why don't you come over and we'll see what we can work out. Here—I'll give you the address."

It was settled in a moment, and Marel hurried home to work up one of her drawings into a more complete form so that she would have something to show Ginger. She ate her dinner in impatient gobbles, waiting restlessly for Ginger's ring.

When the other girl arrived, she had a brown envelope of manuscript under her arm. She stepped across Peggy Pope's threshold and into her graciously lighted living room with eyes as wide with wonder as David's.

"Wow!" she said fervently. "Who lives here? Hedy Lamarr?"

Marel smiled. "I know. I felt like that the first time I walked in too. I guess I still do, really. But nobody handed my aunt all this. She worked for it. She's Peggy Pope."

"Peggy—you mean the hat lady? Mm, no wonder. Bet she designed that hat you were wearing this afternoon."

"She did," Marel admitted. "But you wait. Some day

I'm going to buy hats like that for myself. Did you bring your stories?"

Ginger sank luxuriously onto a sofa and spread her stories out on the mosaic top of a coffee table that had come from Italy. "I've only written down a couple of them," she said. "Mostly they're just in my head. How about looking these over?"

Marel handed her the drawing she had been working on. "You can look at this while I read a story. Then we'll tell each other what we think."

She had been a little afraid of what she might find in Ginger's writing. A story which sounded wonderful told aloud might easily lose its magic and spontaneity on paper. But Ginger's knack with words evidently carried over to the typewriter too, because the life and exuberance and fun were also here in the written form.

"This is good," Marel told her when she had read the last word. "If you can write them all like this, you really have something. But, honestly, I'm afraid your stories are a whole lot better than my pictures will be."

Ginger shook her head. "I've spent some time on those, while you've had to dash something together in a hurry. It's like Miss Lambert said—you've caught the spirit of the stories. Oh, *do* let's work together. I think it would be fun."

"I'd love to if you really want me to try. I'd like to do a scene from this story I've just read. Maybe one of the part where Susan meets the unenthusiastic cow. I'll bet the children love that word—'unenthusiastic.' "

"Do they ever! But look, Marel, this is a sort of gamble, you know. I can't pay an artist anything to do my pictures and—"

"Of course not!" Marel broke in quickly. "But how else would I get a chance? No experienced writer would give me a try."

"Just the way no experienced artist would take a chance working on my stories," Ginger pointed out. "We're in this together, win or lose. And we've *got* to win."

She sounded so in earnest that Marel was a little surprised. "That has a life-or-death sound."

"I need the money," Ginger said. Her plump fingers stacked the manuscript sheets and slipped them into the envelope. Marel glanced at the engagement ring on her left hand, and Ginger nodded. "We want to get married. Of course we can't for another year or so. Mom says I'm too young, and Ken's got to finish radio school first. But I'm trying to save and earn something extra. There'll be so many things we'll need, and we won't have much to start on."

"You *are* plunging early, aren't you?"

"It's what I want to do," Ginger said simply. "Isn't there a big moment in your life?"

Marel shook her head without regret. "Nope! Not for me. I want to be an artist. I want to be successful and famous and earn lots of money so I can have a place of my own like this. Wait till you meet Aunt Peg! She has a wonderful time. I suppose she's quite old—forty at least. But the most fascinating men are ready to jump at the chance to take her out. She has everything she wants and she's done it all herself."

Ginger said "Mmph!" in the sort of tone her unenthusiastic cow might have used. "I suppose it's all right if that's what you want. I suppose I'd even be willing to live in a Hollywood set like this if somebody handed it to me on a platter. But I guess I don't care where I live, just so long as Ken is there. And of course I want heaps and heaps of babies to tell stories to."

Ginger might be an awkward little plump girl, but there was a shine in her eyes that Marel envied. Maybe there was something to having a big moment in your life. Not that she hadn't had plenty of dates back home. And there had been one boy whose pin she'd worn quite faithfully for two whole months. But she'd worn it mostly because that was what other girls did. There hadn't been anything about wearing a pin that was as thrilling as the thought of being a successful illustrator with her name in a book.

After Ginger had gone, Marel went into the guest room that was hers while she stayed with her aunt. It was a dream of a room, with sunny curtains at the window and soft touches of blue and warm peach. It was the sort of room she had always dreamed of having for her own. She did not turn on the lights, but crossed to the wide window.

Outside lights piled up against the New York sky. A sky that was somehow never dark because of the radiance that always beat against it. The great towers were honeycombed with light and very beautiful in a harsh, bright way. Somehow they reminded her of that brassy-looking girl in Fran Embree's studio. Gail Norris—that was her name. That girl fitted these towers. She looked hard and bright too, and lacquered to a glaring finish. Aunt Peg wasn't like that. But Aunt Peg fitted the towers too. Queer the different things a city did to different people.

Anyway, this was what she wanted. The excitement of bright towers. Here you could *be* somebody, have what you wanted of life. Even girls like Ginger, who wanted something very different from what she wanted, could have their wishes here too, if they were willing to work toward their fulfillment.

These towers weren't quite what they looked to be. Not when you knew that little green parks clustered here and there at their feet. Parks where children played and you sat on a bench beside a man you'd just met and laughed over foolish things because it was spring and it was fun to be young.

She wished she could tell Chris Mallory about the book she meant to try with Ginger. Somehow she knew he'd be interested and encouraging. But of course she wouldn't see him again. That was one of the penalties those great towers exacted. They swallowed people up so completely that when you lost someone you weren't likely to find him again.

What about Chris Mallory? What did he want of life? Did he want to be a writer the way Peggy Pope had wanted to be a famous hat designer, and Marel Gordon wanted to be an artist? Oh, well, that was something she'd probably never know. She sighed inexplicably as she turned away from the window and touched a switch that brought the room swiftly to life.

3

Meeting in the Rain

There was no one to bump her through the revolving door
this time. And this time, when she went up in the elevator
and got out at the ninth floor, there were no butterflies
beating against her ribs. She felt determined, if not wholly
confident, and she hadn't a thing to lose.

It wasn't that she expected Fran Embree to tell her
that she'd worked a miracle in a week's time and was
now ready to do professional illustrating for children's
books. That would be silly. She knew how long it would
take to reach the place where she would be given illustrating assignments, but she had worked harder during this
last week than she'd ever worked in her life and she knew
she'd made a little progress. All she wanted now was to
spread her new drawings before Fran and see if she found
in them something of the improvement Marel hoped she
had made.

This time Gail Norris heard her when she entered the
studio and came to the receptionist's window.

"Hello," she said wearily. "Anything I can do for you?"

Before Marel could answer, a phone began to ring in
an inner office and Gail hurried to answer it. While she
was still on the wire, a second phone rang in another part
of the studio.

"Hey, there!" Gail called. "You from art school! How's
about getting that other call for me? I need to be triplets
today. Darn Pearl's offsprings' measles anyway!"

Marel put her folio down and followed the direction
of the ringing phone through the door to a small hall and

across to an artist's workroom—Gail's apparently. Just to smell the odor of paint and to view the disorder of a table strewn with brushes and jars was exciting to Marel. But the phone was insistent and she lifted the receiver to her ear.

"Hello . . . No, it isn't . . , She's on another phone right now . . . Will you wait? . . . Yes, I'll be glad to tell her. Will you give me that number again, please?"

She picked up a charcoal stick as the nearest thing handy and scribbled the number on a scrap of paper fished from a wastebasket, feeling very efficient and secretarial. Gail was still talking when she hung up the phone and she heard the outer door open. Might as well see who that was, too. Apparently Fran was out, Pearl's child, or children, still had measles, and no one else was in but Gail.

She returned to the outer room to find an extremely attractive young woman making herself at home. She was an unusually tall girl, but she carried herself so well that her height seemed just right. Her brown suit and orange ascot had a flair to them, and the auburn hair beneath her smart little hat had been dressed by someone who knew about hairdressing.

Mm, Marel thought. A model. She couldn't be anything else. Maybe one of New York's famous cover girls.

The newcomer looked at her with eyes that were a lovely sea green and smiled in a friendly way. "Hello. You're new here, aren't you? What's happened to Pearl?"

"Some of her family have the measles," Marel said. "I'm not working here. I'm just an innocent bystander. Miss Norris got tied up, so I'm trying to help her out."

The girl glanced at the jewel-studded watch pinned to her lapel. "I suppose Fran isn't here yet? I'm early, so I'll wait."

Marel could hardly take her eyes off the newcomer. She had never seen anyone so stunning off a movie screen. She *had* to be a model.

Gail Norris finished her conversation on the phone and came back to the window. "Thanks!" She nodded in Marel's direction and then spied the other girl. "Hello, Irene. Fran ought to be here any minute. I hope you brought the corrected proofs of Stuart's book. The whole place has been having kittens about that little project. One headache after another."

The tall girl touched the briefcase on her lap. "I practically stood over him with a whip last night. I'm afraid he doesn't understand about deadlines. How are the pictures coming?"

"That's a subject to be discussed only in vivid terms, and there are ladies present." Gail glanced wryly at Marel. "Let's see—you're the girl with the odd name. Marel? Marel what?"

"Gordon," Marel supplied, a little embarrassed. It was Gail's custom, apparently, to say what happened to come to mind, regardless of her victim's reactions.

"That's right, Marel Gordon. This is Irene Allen of Barrett, Brown."

Marel said, "How-do-you-do," wondering what an artist's model had to do with a big publishing house like Barrett, Brown. And who was Stuart who had done something referred to as a truck book?"

Before she could work out the answer to any of her questions, a phone rang again and Gail rushed off to answer it. A moment later Fran Embree breezed into the studio, little and lively and purposeful as ever. She saw Irene Allen and pounced on her delightedly.

"Praise be! Come along and show me what that husband of yours has done this time." Then she spied Marel. "Oh, hello," she said, and her look seemed to imply that this had been a very short year. She and Irene Allen disappeared into her office.

Marel looked at magazines, looked at pictures on the walls, looked at books from the table. Irene Allen had a lovely, low voice that matched the rest of her. The murmur of it drifted out from Fran's office. There was a sort of serenity about Irene Allen that was soothing to watch. The unhurried way she moved, the soft pitch of her voice. More than anyone else she had met in New York, Marel felt she would like to resemble this woman.

After a while Gail came out again and saw her sitting there. "Hi! Still here? Fran's up to her ears. Anything I can do for you?"

"I—I guess not," Marel said. "Perhaps I can come back when Miss Embree isn't so busy. I only wanted to show her—I mean, it isn't very important, and———"

"More drawings?" Gail Norris asked.

"Well—yes. Those I showed her last week weren't very good and I've been working awfully hard to try to clear up some of the mistakes I was making."

Gail looked at her with an oddly speculative eye. "After her for a job, aren't you?"

"Yes," Marel said. "But I know I'm not ready yet. I just want to find out if I'm more nearly on the right track."

"Wait a minute," Gail said.

She went off to interrupt Fran Embree's conference with Irene Allen and was back again in a minute.

"Okay, you're hired. That is, if you'll work for twenty a week to start."

"Hired?" Marel echoed blankly.

"Oh, not to paint masterpieces the way I do. It's not much of a job, Grubby. But not monotonous—I'll guarantee that. We need an extra hand around here to fill in when Pearl has to go domestic. Somebody to run errands and do odd jobs the rest of the time. Of course you'll learn a lot while you're working if you keep your ears and eyes open. Well—what do you say?"

"Why, ah———" Marel gulped. It wasn't the sort of thing she'd had in mind. It wasn't even a living, but . . . "When can I start?" she asked.

Gail nodded her sleek yellow head in approval. "That's

the girl. Suppose you go out and grab a bite to eat. Then you can come back and start in."

"I'll hurry!" Marel cried. Nobody had looked at her drawings, but that didn't matter so much now.

"There's not that much rush," Gail told her. "Hey, wait a minute. It's started to rain. And while rain never hurts the young, you can't go ruining that Peggy Pope affair you're wearing. Here, take the office co-op."

"Thank you." Marel took the little plaid umbrella handed her and then turned back to Gail for a last whispered question. "That girl in there—I've been wondering. Is she an artist's model?"

Gail smiled. "Irene? She looks it, doesn't she? But she's not. She's one of the smartest women editors in this town. She edits mystery novels for Barrett, Brown. Better run along now."

Marel obeyed and ran. She was beginning to see that the Norris bark was worse than the Norris bite. If it hadn't been for Gail, she wouldn't be going to work in as exciting a place as the Embree Studio, where anything at all could happen, and probably would.

The rain was no downpour, but a light spring shower. Marel opened her umbrella and stood looking up and down the street. There was a restaurant a few doors away, but somehow she was drawn again by the park. She'd been coming there every day for a week to sketch for a few hours, and often she had found herself counting up to the fourth window of that building across the park, as if she might see the flutter of a white handkerchief there. Of course she never did, nor did she see the man who had waved the handkerchief. Once she'd even gone over and walked about the main floor of the store, feeling a little foolish as she did so and wondering if she'd look foolish if she happened to run into him while she was there. But she had been safe enough. Not a glimpse of him had she had.

Now, once more, she started across the park to find a

restaurant on the other side, not minding the warm spring rain, enjoying the fresh odor of growing things. And this time it happened. Someone stepped directly in her path, blocking the way.

"Hello, Red Feather," he said. "Don't tell me you're out sketching today?"

She smiled up at him, happy to see him again.

"Now I'm in your class," she said. "I've got a job. I'm going to start to work right after lunch."

"That will bear telling," Chris Mallory said. "How about having lunch with me?"

There was nothing she'd have liked better. He knew an interesting place, he said, if she didn't mind walking a few blocks. She didn't mind anything at all, so they ducked across the park through the rain and down a side street. He tucked her hand into the crook of his arm and held her umbrella carefully over the red feather so it wouldn't get dripped on. It was fun hurrying along together down the wet, shining streets. Somehow rain made everything seem more companionable than it could have been in dry, sunny weather.

The little restaurant was fun too. They found a table on a balcony behind a wrought-iron railing, with a window beside it. Their table boasted a checked cloth and luncheon was served on gay, multicolored plates. Rain tapped at the pane of the window beside them and made the lamplit interior seem doubly cozy and attractive.

"Tell me about your job," she said. "How is it going? I saw your handkerchief the other day."

"Everything's fine," he told her. "But I want to hear about you. How's the drawing coming and what is this job?"

She felt very virtuous in the report she could give him. "I took your advice and came to the park every day. And I've gone to libraries too. I've drawn children until sometimes by evening I've felt I never wanted to see another child. But I think you were right. I think it helped."

"And the job?"

"This time I wasn't even applying for one. I went up to show Fran Embree my new work and everything was at odds and ends there with Gail trying to do six things at once. It was Gail's idea that Fran hire me and I'm to start this afternoon. Gail says it will be doing odd jobs, mostly, but it's exciting just to get into a place like that. There will be lots I can learn that will be useful to me in my work."

The soup was delicious and the rolls crisp. They talked on and on and Marel felt she had never known anyone easier to talk to, or so understanding, so much in agreement with the things she felt and believed and wanted from life. He wanted a lot from life too. For one thing, he was writing a book.

"Oh, not the great American novel," he said, laughing at her exclamation. "As a matter of fact, it's a whodunit. Not literary at all. But that sort of thing has a fascination for me."

"Tell me about it," Marel urged.

"Nothing doing," he said. "When I see a victim coming my way, I see to it that she reads the manuscript. You don't think I'm going to spoil my stuff by telling it, do you?"

"Would you really let me read it?" she asked.

He was laughing at her a little, but he looked pleased too. "Don't think you're going to escape. I seldom find anyone who sounds that willing to read my stuff. Though maybe I'd better wait till it's finished before I give it to you. Then we can see if I've been smart enough, or if you guess all the answers in chapter one."

"How long will I have to wait?"

"Curb your impatience. I've only three more chapters to go."

"Of course you'll have to pay for this," she said. "You'll have to look at all my new drawings. Where are you going to send the book when it's done?" She remembered something, and went on quickly. "Maybe you can get an introduction to Irene Allen through Miss Embree."

"Who is Irene Allen?"

"Gail says she's one of the smartest women editors in town. She runs the mystery department at Barrett, Brown."

"I'll keep that in mind," Chris said. "But right now I'm gunning for big game. If I can get this done in time, I want to enter it in a contest Luna Press is running. The prize is a big one and the publicity will make the winning writer. If I could land that, I'd have enough to keep going for a while so I could take time to write another book. Right now it's tough because I've got to hold down a daytime job and do my writing at night."

"That's the way I'll have to work too," Marel said. "I'll have to fit my own work into spare time because I'll have a job all day. But you'll win the prize. I *know* you will."

He shook his head at her, laughing. "Completely nuts. You've never read a word I've written and you tell me I'll win the prize."

"I just think you're the sort of person who does things well," she told him staunchly. "You wouldn't muddle around and get everything all wrong first the way I always do."

He looked at her gravely for a moment before he answered. "I hope I can earn that kind of belief. I don't think it's very sensible, Margaret Elizabeth, but I like it."

The moment was almost too serious, as if for a second they had slipped into deeper waters than either wanted. Marel glanced quickly away, out the window beside her.

Over dessert Chris said: "Look—before we go back to our respective treadmills, how about arranging to see you again? When I find someone who looks like a prospective reader, I never let 'em go without a struggle. Have you any time on your hands Sunday?"

"Lots of it," she said without hesitation.

"Then how about coming along on an idea-hunting

trip? Maybe you could bring your sketch book and pick up a few ideas of your own along the way."

"An idea-hunting trip?"

"It's this way. Before I can write the climax scene of my book, I need to check a few first-hand details. Some of my action takes place on a ferryboat going over to Staten Island. There's some flying stuff too, and I'm taking the action to the island because there are a lot of small airfields over there. I have a friend who works at one of them. So if you'd care to, we could go across on the ferry Sunday morning and out to the airfield. Then I can get my dope straight and not make a lot of factual mistakes."

"I'd love it," Marel agreed.

"Then it's settled. Tell me where you live and I'll pick you up early."

It was quickly arranged, and then, since time was edging along, they hurried back to the little park and separated. This time Marel went through the revolving door of Fran's building with a burst of speed that showed nearly the exuberance of Chris Mallory's entrance the week before.

What a completely unexpected day this had been! She'd started out innocently enough, not looking for anything in particular, and she had ended up with both a job and a date. Spring in New York wasn't merely fun. It was wonderful. What a story she would have to write home to her mother and dad tonight!

4

First Assignment

A set of pictures was spread over the top of Fran's desk and she studied them through the tilted lenses of her harlequin glasses. The glasses gave her face a pixyish look that made a piquant contrast to her quick, efficient manner.

She glanced up as Marel came to the door. "Hello. Ready for work? What do you think of these?"

They were artist's roughs of truck pictures done in color, and Marel bent over them with interest.

"Little boys ought to go for those in a big way," she said.

"I think they will. And Stuart Allen's done a story that's really funny. The children we've tried it out on have loved it. You wouldn't expect anybody like Stuart to pop up with this sort of thing. He's so very much the professor. There's a coat closet behind you. Take your things off and we'll start breaking you in. Better put on that smock, so you won't go spotting your clothes. You can bring one of your own tomorrow, if you like."

Marel slipped into the indicated green smock and rolled up sleeves that hung too long on her arms.

"I'll show you how to check these color separations," Fran said, "and initiate you in the mystery of registry marks, but first you'd better go see that Gail has fresh paint water and that her brushes are clean. That'll be your first job every morning—to clean Gail's and Eric's brushes."

"Eric?" Marel asked.

"That's right, you haven't met him, have you? Eric

43

Webb. He did these pictures for Stuart's trucks. He's home in Philadelphia right now, but he'll be back here next week." Fran looked up suddenly. "Mm. Eric's going to approve of you. But don't mind him. He's a little crazy, but harmless. Martin says he's the original model for the Eccentric Genius. Martin's my sea-captain husband."

"Oh?" said Marel blankly. "I thought it was *Miss* Embree."

"I had my business launched before I married, so it was easier to go right on being Miss. Run along now and do your chores. And come back here when you're through."

Fran's words about Eric Webb had a faintly ominous ring. Marel wasn't too sure that she was going to enjoy having him "approve" of her. But she could cross that bridge when she came to it.

She went into Gail Norris's littered workroom and looked around. "Miss Embree says I'm to clean your brushes. Where do I start?"

Gail was at work at her drawing board, a child's head emerging under her moving pencil. Even in the rough sketch the little girl's face showed that breath-taking quality that is found only in the faces of the very young, and Marel sighed in admiration.

"You're awfully good. I wonder if I'll ever be able to do things like that."

"Thanks," Gail said curtly, without looking up from her drawing. "I could use some clean brushes and water. You can have the whole mess. There are some rags on the shelf there and a washroom down the hall. Help yourself."

Marel gathered up paint-smeared brushes and a couple of glasses of murky water and bore them away. As she worked, she wondered about Gail Norris. Somehow she looked like the last person in the world who would have a magical touch when it came to drawing pictures of children. To be in character, you'd expect her to do smart fashion drawings which bore very little resemblance to human beings. Gail herself looked as though she were all hard glitter and surface lacquer; as if she couldn't have a heart at all. Sometimes she said hard, rather cutting things and she seemed to sneer at anything young and un-sophisticated. Yet she had gone out of her way to suggest that Fran hire Marel Gordon, and gentleness seemed to be pouring out of her fingertips into the drawing of that child's head.

Marel carried the clean brushes and fresh water back to Gail's studio and then went into the room next to hers. Neatness was in evidence here. Eric Webb apparently had less of a tendency to throw his possessions around the way Gail did. There was a preciseness about the way everything seemed to be in its ordered place. If the occupant of this studio had an eccentric streak, it didn't seem to affect his workroom.

A bookcase in one corner caught Marel's eye and she glanced at the titles. There were a few technical books on art on the top shelf. The second shelf was occupied by a row of picture books. Marel tipped one title into view. It was authored by a well-known children's writer and below the author's name was the phrase: "Illustrated by Eric Webb."

She took a hasty glance through the contents, de-lighting in the bold, gay colors of the drawings. Eric Webb liked the mechanical, certainly, and he possessed a winning sense of humor. A train with a definitely roguish personality puffed across the pages to the delight of young passengers who showed smiling faces at every window. Somehow Marel felt that she'd like the artist who drew pictures like that. But since there was nothing to do here, she'd better get back to Fran Embree, so she could learn about registry marks and checking color separations.

There were two desks in Fran's office and she was

motioned at once to the empty one. Fran dropped the pile of separations before her.

"This is one of the manuscripts we've seen through from the beginning. Irene came in with Stuart's idea about trucks. We liked it and put Eric on the illustration job and sold the completed book to a publisher. The editor has left it in our hands to follow through and see that it gets into print in the best form possible."

She ruffled through the separations.

"You see these little crosses that come up on every picture? They're the printer's registry marks. When you put one transparent sheet on top of another and get those marks matched exactly, all the colors will come out in the right place. Go through the entire set and see that they do. If there are any places where the colors get out of line with the roughs, let me know."

Marel went carefully to work. This was a four-color job, so there were four drawings to each picture. Fran returned to reading galley proofs of another book and Marel busied herself without interruption for twenty minutes. Then she heard Gail's voice summoning her.

"Hey, infant! I want to borrow you for a minute!"

Marel glanced inquiringly at Fran.

"Go ahead," Fran said. "She probably wants you to stand on your head. Anything can happen in this place."

Marel crossed the little hall and looked in Gail's door.

"How on earth do people look kicking their heels in the air?" Gail said. "Be a good child and show me, will you?"

Marel got obligingly down on her stomach and kicked her heels in the air, while Gail sketched. She'd have a lot of things to tell Chris when she saw him Sunday. The fact that she was going to see him made everything that happened seem more interesting, more fun. It was nice to have someone in your life to look forward to telling things to. This was a little different from writing letters home to your family.

"That's it!" Gail cried. "Now I get it. Look—put your head down in the crook of your arms, will you? See if you can look about three years old. That shouldn't be hard."

Marel smiled and did her best to oblige, still thinking of what she would tell Chris. And of one of the things she hadn't told him. She hadn't said a word about the book she was going to attempt with Ginger Williams. That was odd, really, because she had been anxious to tell him about it until the moment when she'd seen him. Then, somehow, it had seemed too ambitious for her modest talents. What if he laughed? What if he thought she was foolish to try? So she'd kept it to herself. There'd be time later on when she began to have some idea of whether she could really do it. She had a feeling she was going to see quite a lot of Chris Mallory. A nice thought that. A satisfying thought.

Gail clicked her tongue against her teeth. "Nope! The head-in-the-arms part is fine, but you'll never get by as a three-year-old. You're not dreaming three-year-old dreams. You're thinking about a man."

Marel opened her eyes and stared, while a slow flush crept into her cheeks. She could feel it warming her skin and hated the give-away glow.

There was a twist to Gail's smile. "Not so far wrong, was I? Boy back home?"

"No," Marel said emphatically, sitting up. She was glad to have a chance to deny the accusation. "There isn't any boy back home."

Gail turned her attention back to her drawing. "That's bad. You've been in New York all of two weeks and you've met somebody you can look like that about. The trouble with women is they haven't any sense."

"I wasn't looking that way—whatever you mean—about anybody," Marel said in some indignation. "I don't know what you're talking about. You're just making things up."

"Am I?" Gail asked maddeningly. "Oh-oh, there's the

outside door. Better go cope with it."

"Coping" with the outside door was not something Marel knew exactly how to go about, but she went to the receptionist's window and said, "May I help you?" to the girl who had just come in. Another artist, apparently, judging by the big folder she carried.

"Will you tell Fran that Erna Lewis is here?" the girl said, and Marel hurried back to Miss Embree's office with the tidings. Apparently they were important because Fran flew up from her desk and rushed into the reception room.

"Erna, I've been practically holding the presses with my bare hands. If you hadn't shown up today, I was going to come over and poison you personally. Have you got 'em?"

The girl pushed her hand wearily against her forehead, thrusting her hat back to a ludicrous angle which seemed to disturb her not at all. "I'm not finished. It's that miserable boat whistle that's got me down. Why anybody had to write about steamship whistles! Eric's an expert on machinery. Let him put in the whistle."

"Eric's in Philly," Fran said. "And if I can't have those drawings today, the printer will never take them on. Is it just the whistle that's holding you up?"

"I've been looking everywhere and I can't find a decent picture of one," Erna said. "I thought I'd get the whistle done and then finish the rest. I've still another hour's work to do."

The phone shrilled in the inner office and Fran nodded at Marel. "Get it, will you, please?"

Marel pulled herself away from the fascinating discussion about steamship whistles and went back to answer the phone on Fran's desk. In reply to her first word, a man's voice began to roar protestingly in her ear. Someone was accusing her of being a slave-driver and a number of other more hair-curling terms. She waited until he stopped for breath and then announced apologetically that she wasn't Miss Embree, but that she'd call Miss Embree right away.

"Who're you?" the voice demanded.

"I—I'm Marel Gordon," Marel said timidly. "I'm new here and——"

"New!" It sounded especially objectionable to be new. "I can't stand another new face! Tell Fran to get rid of you."

Fortunately Fran herself came to her rescue at that moment. Marel held out the chattering telephone with a helpless gesture.

"That's Eric," Fran sighed. "I suppose he's being difficult again."

She made shushing, soothing sounds into the receiver, while Marel tried to reconcile the orderly picture she'd had of Eric Webb's workroom and the sense of humor he showed in his illustrations with the irritable voice she had just heard over the telephone.

"But you'll like *this* new face," Fran was telling him. "It's a great improvement over Gail's or mine. And you will get after that job, won't you, Eric? I can't give you any more time on it. It wasn't my idea that you hop off on a vacation now."

Apparently Fran had some influence with Eric Webb because the sputtering died away and she hung up the phone with a gesture of relief.

"Any resemblance to a madhouse is entirely to be expected," she told Marel ruefully. "Now come on back and help me get this whistle thing started. I think this is where you come in."

Marel followed her dubiously back to the reception room. What she knew about steamship whistles would fit easily into a stamp perforation.

"Suppose you go into Eric's studio and get to work finishing the job," Fran told Erna. "Do try not to muss his things up too much. I think he draws a diagram of everything whenever he leaves his desk, just to make sure nobody touches it. But you can finish up the job there while we track down a whistle."

"I've got a four-thirty appointment," Erna said plaintively, but she took her folio back to Eric's room.

Fran turned to Marel. "You don't by any lucky chance happen to be well enough acquainted with steamship whistles to draw one, do you?"

Marel shook her head. "I've heard them, but I've never met one personally."

"Well, that makes it tough. But you're elected! Take a notebook and a pencil and go out and get me a sketch of a steamship whistle. I don't care how you manage it, but that's your assignment for now."

"But how—I mean where——" Marel stammered in dismay.

"Ingenuity," Fran told her cheerfully. "That's all you need. It's a quality I'm fresh out of, so you'll have to dig up your own. See you later. I've a thousand things to do."

Marel put on her red-feathered hat with less attention to its angle than she'd ever paid before. She felt a little like Hercules must have when he was sent out on his first superhuman task. If she had known New York, she might have known where to go for a whistle, but she wasn't even sure how to find a river.

As she went down in the elevator, she wished she could call Chris and ask him what to do. But that was out. The public library—the logical source—had apparently been tried. Probably by the time she took a trip over to the river and waited for a steamship to go by, it would be too late anyway. Besides, she doubted that she could see one closely enough from the bank to draw a good picture.

Aunt Peg seemed like the next best bet and she hurried to catch a bus for her aunt's shop.

One of the salesgirls recognized her when she came in and waved her toward the workroom in the rear. Marel stepped from the mirrored perfection of the shop to the disorder and confusion of the millinery workroom. She knew from a previous visit that it was neither disordered nor confused, but that her aunt knew where every pin was, every scrap of ribbon or feather.

Peggy Pope looked up from the audacious bit of pink straw in her hands and smiled at her niece. "Through sketching for today?"

"I haven't done much sketching," Marel confessed. "I've got a job. I'm working in Fran Embree's studio. Since this afternoon."

"Sounds good. You'll learn a lot there."

"I know. I'm learning already. But right now I'm stumped."

Her aunt listened to her story of the whistle, working at the pink hat the while. Now and then she nodded thoughtfully. When Marel finished, she looked up.

"I've an idea. It's a slim chance, but you can try it. Wait till I write a number down for you." She scribbled on a scratch pad and handed Marel the slip of paper. "You can use the phone over there. Call Mrs. Carter and tell her you're my niece. She's one of my best customers and she lives in an apartment building overlooking the river. She probably knows all about steamship whistles. Her husband is in the navy."

"Won't she think I'm crazy? I mean——"

"Tell her your story. Tell her about the jam you're in. She's an awfully good scout and she'll help if she can. The point is that she used to be an artist herself, so she'll get your angle."

Mrs. Carter was friendly and easy to talk to. She was also understanding about the problem. But she was no help at all when it came to describing a steamship whistle.

"I suppose I've seen thousands," she said, "but I've never really looked at one. Can't you sort of smudge it in? I'm sure nobody else knows how a steamship whistle looks, either."

"I'm afraid we couldn't get away with that," Marel

said. "It plays an important part in the story. Anyway, it was nice of you to listen. Aunt Peg thought you just might——"

"Wait a minute!" The voice at the other end of the wire took on an excited note. "I've an idea. There's a window right beside me and I can see a boat going by this minute. It's too far away for me to see anything so small as a whistle, but—hold on, will you?"

Marel held on. After a time Mrs. Carter came back to the phone.

"I've got my husband's binoculars and they bring everything practically into my lap. Wait, now—yes, there's the whistle. Have you paper and pencil handy?"

Marel opened the little notebook she'd brought along and picked up a pencil. Mrs. Carter's description was efficient and clear. She was speaking now as one artist to another and Marel had no difficulty in following her directions. When she was done, she had something that might reasonably be considered a steamship whistle.

She thanked the helpful Mrs. Carter, hung up the phone, and took the drawing to her aunt.

Peggy Pope nodded. "Of course. That's just the way they look. I'm sure I've seen lots of them. A good job, I'd say."

Marel hoped so all the way back to the studio. Erna Lewis had gone off to her appointment by the time she arrived, leaving the drawings behind her, finished except for the places that required a whistle.

"I got a description over the telephone," Marel told Fran Embree, "and drew this as nearly as I could make it out."

Fran examined the drawing. "Looks possible. You're a marvel. Get to it right away!"

"Get—to it?"

"Of course. Erna had to leave. Somebody has to draw that whistle in. And it's your baby."

Marel was dismayed. "You mean put whistles right into

those finished drawings? What if they don't come out right? What if I spoil them?"

"You want to be an artist, don't you? Well, here's your chance. Don't you dare muff it." Fran reached out and patted her arm encouragingly. "You won't spoil anything. Sketch them in first and try to imitate Erna's style. She uses a smoother line than you do—you'll have to watch that. And see that the tone of your wash matches. Let me see before you do the final job."

Marel got into her smock again and went earnestly to work at Eric Webb's drawing board. She'd been drawing children studiously for a solid week and her first opportunity to do a bit of professional work turned out to be a steamship whistle! Being an artist certainly led to the unexpected.

When the whistles had been sketched in, Marel began adding water to black watercolor, testing it gingerly on the edge of the paper where it wouldn't matter. It took her a little time, but it finally looked right.

She glanced up to find Fran looking over her shoulder.

"You've got it fine," Fran said. "Nobody'd know those whistles weren't Erna's. And your wash is a good match, too. Go ahead and finish the job."

Marel felt as happy as if she had just completed a whole illustration successfully. Fran moved away and then came back to the door.

"Gail told me you'd been drawing all week," she said, "and that you wanted to show me some pictures. I hope you don't mind that I took them out of your folder and looked at them."

Marel stiffened against the board. She was afraid to glance up at Fran. After a moment the older woman went on casually.

"I was a little worried when you came back here so quickly. I didn't know you'd followed my advice with such determination. I like that. I like the way you didn't give in to discouragement—which is the easy way. You show improvement too. I want to talk to you about those drawings later."

That was all, but Marel felt as if a whole bouquet of orchids had been handed to her. Fran Embree was not given to bestowing light praise. If she said her drawing showed improvement, then it did.

When Fran had gone back to her office, Marel returned to her whistles with renewed enthusiasm. She *would* be an illustrator. She'd be one yet!

5

By Ferry

The weather was perfect on Sunday. A bright, clear, sunny morning, with little puffs of white cloud lazing along in the sky. Marel and Chris stood on deck at the end of the ferry and watched the band of swirling water lengthen between ferry slip and boat. As they moved away from shore the towers of lower Manhattan seemed to group themselves together, rising in slim, straight lines against the blue sky.

"It's beautiful," Marel said softly. "I've looked at pictures of this so many times, but this is the real thing."

Part of her pleasure lay in seeing it with someone like Chris. Even though it was no new scene to him, he felt the magic of it too, and seemed to enjoy it doubly because he was showing it to her for the first time.

They walked around the deck, and Chris told her about his story and about the way the murderer would be sitting on a bench in the main cabin pretending to read a magazine, while those who were with him never dreamed of the danger lurking so near.

"You're giving me creeps," Marel said. "Do I really have to wait till you get the last chapter written before I can relax?"

He had a nice way of laughing. She liked to hear him.

"I brought the manuscript along today," he said. "I decided it was foolish to take a chance on letting such a willing victim escape."

"Then we're even," she told him, "because I brought

my sketch book along too, with the new stuff I've been working on."

They rounded the curve of the deck and Marel tightened her hand on Chris's arm. "Look! Over there. Liberty. I've never seen her before." She knelt on a bench and leaned against the rail, looking out over the water.

Liberty in her green robes, holding her torch aloft in welcome and promise to ships in from other lands. Marel felt her throat tighten. It did something to you, seeing *her* for the first time. No matter how many pictures she'd seen in the movies and in magazines, this was more impressive, more stirring than she had expected.

They watched the statue slip by and recede as the ferry swung around. On ahead the steep hills of Staten Island came into view. They joined the crowd that lined up ahead of time to leave the boat.

Chris's friend was waiting for them near the ferry building—a friendly, easygoing young man in a flyer's jacket and khaki trousers. It was nine miles to the airfield and Marel enjoyed every minute of the ride. The island was like the country, with its hills and fields bright in their spring greenery. It seemed strange to think that this, too, was New York City.

Opposite the airport they drove off the highway and parked near a fence. Marel got out of the car with her sketch book under her arm and walked along at Chris's side, while the friend who had driven them out went back to work. There were planes everywhere. Planes taking off, coming in for a landing, taxiing across the field. Small planes, most of them, painted bright yellow, or red, or silver.

Chris said: "I've got to snoop around and ask some probably foolish questions. I know a little about flying, but my plot needs a special gimmick I never happened to inquire about. Suppose I find a place for you to park and then you can do a bit of sketching if you like while I get the dope I need."

He led her toward a small building which housed the office. A veranda stretched down one side of it. There were two or three people sitting there, watching the planes take off and come in. Chris found her a chair at the far end.

"Think you'll be happy here? I won't be too long."

"I'll be very happy," she said, and she meant it.

She couldn't remember when she had felt so contented in her life. The day was beautiful and there was such a lot to watch out on the field. She had never been this close to so many planes before. And she was here with Chris. Maybe it was silly to feel happy about being out with a man she had seen just three times in her life. But they *did* seem to click perfectly. They enjoyed the same things, they found the same things funny. He was a writer and she wanted to be an artist, and somehow the two lines of work seemed almost parallel.

A yellow plane was skimming in just over the tops of a row of trees at the far end of the field. The people on the veranda were talking about it. They'd watched other planes come in and take off with a casual air, but one of the women showed a special interest in this plane. The breeze was in Marel's direction and words came to her distinctly.

"She's coming in now," one of the women said. "This ought to be good. He used to be around a lot before he went into service. She was teaching him to fly, you know."

The words meant nothing to Marel and she opened her sketch book and looked around for a subject. No children here, certainly, but her whistle experience had taught her that almost anything might come up in illustrating children's books. Planes were interesting to the young —she might as well have a try at sketching one.

She watched the yellow plane drop smoothly down to the field, run straight ahead until its speed slackened, and then turn and come taxiing up toward the fence where planes not in use were lined up. What a funny waddling motion it had as it came up to the field, swinging first right and then left.

Her pencil moved on paper as she tried to draw, not just a plane, but a personality that might interest children. There was really a face on the end of a plane—the eyes, the propeller nose, the mouth, were all perfectly clear. As it came near, she saw the girl in the pilot's seat. One of the airfield boys was motioning her into position, and when the plane came to a stop, the girl opened the door and dropped agilely to the ground. Her bright hair was curly and cropped boyishly short, but in spite of short hair and dungarees she looked feminine and very pretty.

"Wait'll she sees him!" the woman at the end of the veranda whispered.

One of the others said, "Ssh," and glanced Marel's way. Marel bent her head above her sketch book, pretending she had not heard. What the woman had said before connected suddenly in her mind and she recognized uncomfortably that they were talking about Chris. This bright-haired girl in dungarees had been teaching Chris to fly before he went into service!

In spite of her determination to keep her eyes on the paper on her knees, or on the plane she was using for a model, Marel found herself looking across to where Chris stood beside a plane, looking in where a mechanic had opened up the side near the nose. He was apparently showing Chris how something worked.

The blond girl came across the grass, walking with a straight free stride. She was heading for the veranda until the moment when she saw Chris. Then she stopped with her hands on her hips and looked in his direction. His arm came up in a wave of greeting and she changed her course to walk toward him.

"It's a good thing his mother broke it up," the woman on the veranda whispered. "She's an excitement-eater."

"Oh, she's all right," one of the men defended. "Sally's a good kid. She'd quiet down if she got married."

She had reached Chris now and she held out her hand man-fashion. Marel moved her chair on the veranda. Somehow she did not want to watch. She wished she hadn't overheard. There was a hangar across the field. She'd draw that. Once more her pencil went busily to work.

Of course there would have been girls along the way in Chris's life. He was older than she and he was the sort of man that women liked. Besides, she hardly knew him. What did it matter if this girl named Sally . . .

She wouldn't think about it. It wasn't any of her business. Just because he had asked her for a date today didn't mean that she had any place in his life, or he in hers. They both had jobs to do. It was all right to have fun, but they couldn't afford to get serious, either of them. Their work meant too much. Of course she hoped he liked her. She liked him. But that was all. They could spend a pleasant day together, certainly, without either of them getting their feelings involved.

Funny, though, she'd never had to argue to herself about the other boys she'd gone around with. They'd always seemed such kids—even one or two she had liked to the extent of getting mildly romantic. Chris wasn't a kid. That made a difference.

She did not look toward the fence again. She put all sorts of unimportant details into her drawing of the hangar. There was a plane near-by being repaired and she drew that too, with little figures working on it.

What had the woman said? "It's a good thing his mother broke it up." What did that mean? Where was Chris's mother? And did she make a habit of breaking things up? Or was it just that she didn't approve of a girl who flew a plane? What would she think of a girl who was determined to be an artist?

She pressed so hard on her pencil that the point broke and she could not go on until she'd fished around in her purse and found another one. She was thinking the most

idiotic things. If she didn't get her mind off foolish
thoughts, the day would be spoiled.

Not until she heard people coming toward the veranda
did she look up again. The girl in dungarees had walked
across the grass at Chris's side and was coming up the
veranda steps with him. She talked animatedly, waving
her hands, describing some event that seemed to interest
Chris considerably. For the people on the veranda she
had only a casual nod before she looked past them to
Marel. There was an air of "so *you're* what I have to deal
with" in her look. Watching her, Marel began to feel
young and awkward and ill-at-ease. This other girl was
so poised and sure of herself. She knew what she wanted
and went after it. Somehow Marel sensed that no matter
what defeat she had met in the past she still wanted Chris.

He brought her over and introduced her. Marel answered
her greeting and found no words after that. These people
were talking about a world she'd never so much as peeped
into before. A world of planes and flying. They seemed
to shut everything else out of the picture and make their
own interests the center of the world. Probably everyone
did that, but you didn't notice till you got out of your
own little world into someone else's.

Fortunately, it didn't last too long. Chris glanced at his
watch and nodded at Marel. "If we're going to beat the
crowd to Sunday dinner, we'd better be on our way. I
got the dope I wanted, so I'm all set. Ready to go?"

She was ready enough. She wanted to be alone with
Chris and recapture the comradeship of early morning.

They said their good-byes. Sally said, "Be seeing you,"
and Chris didn't deny it. Then they went over to the
highway to catch a bus.

"I think you'll like this place," Chris said when they
were on their way. "I hope we'll be lucky enough to get
a table where I want it."

She was quiet on the ride. She couldn't chatter about
everything and anything the way she had before. She

kept thinking about that blond girl who looked so poised even in dungarees and who had something interesting to say when she talked. How dull Marel Gordon must seem to Chris after a girl like that!

The restaurant was an attractive building, with rambling wings and a peaked roof, set down on the edge of a small lake. Park grounds stretched all about it, with plenty of shrubbery in gay spring dress and trees done in tender green.

Inside was a long room with rough beams arching overhead and a huge stone fireplace at one end. But Chris led her through a second door to a broad stone-flagged veranda where they found a table overlooking the lake. So far they had the veranda almost to themselves, and after the rush of Manhattan this was refreshing. Marel began to perk up a little.

"It's lovely here," she said. "Let's eat for hours and hours and soak it in."

They took their time, and gradually the jarring effect of that meeting at the airfield began to wear off. Once Marel wondered briefly if Chris had come here with Sally too, and how the blond girl looked in something more flattering than dungarees. But she pushed the thought away with determination. Both she and Chris had lived a number of years before they had met. There would be all sorts of closed doors in the life of each that the other couldn't share. It was only from now on that counted.

From now on? No, "from now on" had to do with her drawing, her future, her career. There wasn't time for men just now. Let it be "for now" only. Pleasant moments like this with no serious undertones. That was the way she liked it, and she was sure that was the way Chris would like it too.

But she did want to know more about him, to fill in gaps that had to be filled before they could be really friends.

"On the veranda this morning one of the women said you'd been taking flying lessons before you went into service. Do you really fly? You didn't tell me."

"It doesn't count for much," he said. "Sally Foster wanted to make a flyer of me, but it's too expensive a game. She has her dad's money behind her and she can afford it. It's all right, but I guess I haven't got it in my blood the way she has. I can take it or leave it."

"Tell me about your family," she said. She knew she'd been headed for that question all along. She'd been heading for it ever since that unpleasant woman on the veranda had said that Chris's mother had "broken up" whatever was between him and Sally Foster.

"There's just my mother," he said.

"Do you live with her?"

"No. She has lived out in California since my father died three years ago. She doesn't like our eastern weather. I bach it with a screwball named Mac Conway. You'll have to meet him one of these days. He's quite a guy."

"What does he do?"

"Writes. Only he's good at it. He's got a couple of novels to his credit and goes in for grim reality and raw realism. But he's a good sort. You'll like him."

She wanted to ask more about his mother, but there was no way to manage it and he had offered no further information after his mention of California. Marel felt vaguely troubled. Somehow the sort of man whose life could be arranged by his mother did not sound like the sort of man Chris seemed to be. She must forget that gossip at the airfield. Like most gossip it had probably been distorted clear past the truth.

She shoved her sketch book across the table to get away from her doubtful thoughts. "Want to see what I've been up to?"

He smiled over the drawing of the plane with a face and paused to examine her hangar sketch more carefully.

"Say! This gives me an idea. I can use a hangar scene

in my story. Funny, I never thought of it till I looked at this drawing. Maybe I need an artist in my life."

It was said humorously, casually, but she was pleased. An artist's job and a writer's did seem to go together neatly.

Late that afternoon they went back to the ferry. When they had reached her aunt's apartment, Marel invited Chris up. That morning he had called for her so early that Aunt Peg was still in bed, so he'd had no chance to meet her. A little to Marel's dismay, she found that an impromptu supper party was in swing and that she could arrange no time alone between her aunt and Chris Mallory. Chris would have left at once, but Marel drew him out of the crowd to a door that opened off the hall.

"Wait, I want to show you something," she said. "This is my favorite view."

It was quiet out on the roof, with the noise of the street a distant murmur stories below. The air seemed fresh and clear—clean for city air, and a contrast to the smokiness of the people-filled apartment they had just left.

Marel leaned against the parapet and looked out at the high towers, beginning to light up now in the gathering dusk.

"I like it out here," she said. "It's almost like a different world from the city. Goodness, it's nice to breathe fresh air! Parties can certainly get stuffy."

He leaned on the wall beside her and she could sense that he was studying her with a curious intentness. "So you like it up here in a penthouse garden, do you, Margaret Elizabeth?"

"I love it," she breathed. "Some day *I'm* going to have things like this. I'm going to work hard and become well known and earn a lot of money. Then I'll buy things like this for me."

"I expect you will," he said, but she knew by his tone that he had suddenly drawn away from her and that the magic of this moment above the towers of New York had been spoiled. How she didn't quite know.

"Well, I'll be running along," he said, "and leave you to the party. It's been a grand day. Thanks a lot for coming along. I left my manuscript on the table in the hall. Let me know what you think when you've read it. And you needn't pull your punches. Now I can get busy on those last chapters."

When he had gone, she came back to the parapet, wanting to be alone with her thoughts, loving this moment when the lights winked into sequin trimmings and New York put on her glittering nighttime dress.

Her aunt found her there dreaming. "It's getting cool out here, Marel. Don't you want to come in and meet some of my friends?"

"Of course." Marel turned away from the wall.

"He's nice—that young man of yours," her aunt said. "But remember, dear, you have to decide what you want of life. If you are serious about being an artist, then you need to concentrate on that."

"Of course I'm serious," Marel assured her.

Peggy Pope nodded her graceful head. "Better hold to that, then. New York is full of nice young men. Don't tie yourself down to one. You'll have more fun if you have other dates. And you'll keep your eye on your work better too."

"But I can't have other dates unless I'm asked," Marel protested reasonably. "Chris Mallory is the only man I've met who has asked me to go out with him. I'm not getting serious about him or anything."

"I'm glad of that," Aunt Peg said. "When you're breaking in, you can't split your allegiance two ways. It's either a man or a job. You can't give everything to both."

"I'll take the job," Marel said.

Her aunt murmured approval and led the way back to the party. Marel followed her in silence. Of *course* it was her job. Her drawing. The work she wanted to do more than anything else in the world. It was fun to know a man who appreciated the same things you did, and seemed to like you, but he wasn't all her horizon by any means.

She lifted her chin determinedly as she stepped into the chatter and haze of the apartment. *She* knew what she wanted of life. She wanted to be an Artist. With a capital "A." And she'd *be* one, too.

6

Career Girl

It was hard to know where a month had gone. Into weeks of hard work, mostly, with just enough seasoning of play.

Dates with Chris had furnished the seasoning, and a very pleasant seasoning it was. Not that they'd gone to flashy, expensive places. Chris didn't have that kind of money and Marel was purringly contented wherever he took her. Walks along the river, small movie houses, inexpensive restaurants. Gail told her emphatically that she was a dope. Why not get herself a boy friend who could show her the town? But Marel turned a deaf ear to Gail's scorn and continued to enjoy going out with Chris.

At first when she had come here she had been a little homesick. Nice as Aunt Peg was, she could not take the place of Mother and Dad. But knowing Chris had lessened the aching for home. Besides, it was fun to put him into her letters and try to make him as real to her parents as he was to her. Though of course she was being very casual about the whole thing. She certainly did not want to give them the impression that Chris was coming to be *the* big moment in her life.

As for work—Marel felt she fitted in better now with the pace of the Embree Studio. The idea, as Gail pointed out, was to keep going, but not to get breathless.

Then there had been hours of working on her drawings for Ginger's book. Working when she was already tired and wanted to laze, driving herself to her drawing board. When she was tired, things would not come right, and some of her work had been done over and over. Now she had two drawings finished in color to show.

It was because of the completed drawings that she was excited this morning. All this while she had kept what she was doing a secret from Chris. Today she was taking her drawings in to show Fran Embree along with the stories they illustrated, but first she was going to show them to Chris and tell him about her plans. She was meeting him early for breakfast before they went to work.

Of course, much as she liked Chris and enjoyed his company, she was holding firmly to her goal of training herself to be an artist. That came first. After that, it was all right to have a little fun. Sometimes, however, Chris troubled her. He had moods of being quiet and thoughtful and a little distant. It was hard to understand him then, to guess what was going on in his mind. Mostly she tried to overlook these times and keep on being friendly and cheerful herself.

He was waiting for her in the restaurant near the park when she arrived and they hurried to an empty booth against the wall. When they had ordered, he smiled at her.

"You're a pretty good critic, you know," he said. "I've followed most of the suggestions you made about my story. I've even adopted your title—'Fear on the Ferry.' "

She was very pleased. "I couldn't help much. It's really good. You just *have* to win that prize. Is it nearly ready to send in?"

"Nearly. Now what about you? You've been playing the mystery woman lately. What's up?"

She drew a deep breath, almost afraid to tell him. "I'm illustrating a book."

"Well! I *am* impressed."

"Don't be impressed," she said. "I'm probably crazy for trying. I know I'm not ready yet, but——"

"Never mind the apologies. Tell me about it."

"There's a girl at the library," she began. "Ginger Williams. She makes up wonderful stories to tell the children. Everyone has been urging her to get them down in writing form and try to sell them as a book. But she needs pictures to go with them."

"And you're going to do the pictures? Good for you!"

"Oh, it isn't any sure thing. I'm just having a try." She took her portfolio from the seat beside her. "I've worked over these two drawings until I'm dizzy. I can't tell anything about them any more. Ginger thinks they're good, but I don't know. I'm taking them in to show Fran Embree today and she'll tell me the awful truth."

"Let's see," he said, and she put the two pictures into his hands.

He studied them gravely for several minutes before he handed them back to her.

"I think you're going to get there, Margaret Elizabeth. You've a lot of talent to start with and you can make yourself work—which is even more important. Just hew to that line and don't let anything stop you."

Her chin came up determinedly. "I won't. But do you think these are good enough to show Fran?"

"As a layman who doesn't know much about it, I'd say they are. They look good to me. Much better than the stuff you took her that first day."

The waitress brought their breakfast and after that they were both oddly quiet. Marel made several stabs at conversation, but Chris had dropped into one of his moods of silence. Not that he wasn't friendly, and almost overly kind. But he had that withdrawn feeling about him again —as if he'd gone off somewhere by himself; somewhere she couldn't follow.

In spite of the encouraging things he had said about her drawings, her spirits felt a little dampened, and the morning which had started out so bravely lost some of its flavor. What was he thinking when he got like this? Was it something she had said or done that displeased him?

She finished her wheat cakes in silence, giving up the

effort to talk. If he wanted to withdraw and think about distant matters, she could do the same thing. She felt both resentful and hurt at the same time.

When breakfast was over, they walked across the park again and to the door of her building.

"Good luck, Margaret Elizabeth," he said. "I hope you get all the things you want most in life."

Somehow that had a queerly final ring. As if he were saying good-bye to her for good. And he had not mentioned seeing her again as he usually did. She *couldn't* leave him like this. She had to find out what was the matter.

"Chris," she began, "have I———"

But he would not let her continue. "Better run," he told her, "or you'll be late. And so will I. I hope your book sells a million copies. Good-bye now."

He did not wait for her to go through the door, but hurried off to the short cut across the park. She stood where she was for a stunned moment watching till he disappeared. Then the early morning crowd jostled her through the door and into the building.

All the way up in the elevator the limpness of disappointment stayed with her. Somehow she had hoped for a special send-off from Chris, so that she could take her drawings up to Fran with hope and courage. It wasn't that he had not approved of them, or of her trying the book. She was sure he had been sincere in his praise and in urging her on to do what she wanted to do in her art work. What he had taken away was the feeling that if she had any small success he would be there for her to run to with the news. But there wasn't a thing she could do about it. Just wait to see if he called her again.

Of course he'd call her. Of course he'd want to know what Fran said. She mustn't read more into a mood than really existed. He'd been like this several times before. It didn't mean anything.

She braced her shoulders and mentally gave herself encouraging pats all the way down the corridor to the studio. No matter how Chris Mallory behaved, she still had her work to do. And what Fran Embree said counted more than anything else. She went directly to Fran's office and laid her folio on her desk.

Fran was already deep in a manuscript, but she looked up with a cheerful "Hello."

"I think you must sleep here," Marel said. "If you ever do sleep. Would you have time to look at these somewhere along the line today?"

"Of course," Fran said. "What are you up to now?"

"Something I oughtn't to be trying, I expect," Marel confessed. "But I wish you'd give me your opinion anyway. A girl I know at the public library is doing some stories, and I'm having a try at illustrating them."

She laid the pictures face down on Fran's desk. Fran was occupied with the manuscript of the moment and left the drawings where they were.

"I'll have a look later, Marel. And tread softly this morning—our wandering genius has returned."

"Wandering genius?" Marel glanced up from buttoning her smock.

"Ssh. Eric's come home to the fold. Tiptoe in and see if you can do anything for him. And smile sweetly. He's in a mood."

Marel did not feel too much like smiling sweetly at anyone, and for the moment she was a little tired of men with moods. But she went quietly to the door of Eric Webb's studio and looked in.

He was wiry and dark and younger than she had expected. Rather good-looking in a somber sort of way. At the moment he was at work at his drawing board and his heavy black eyebrows were drawn into an alarming scowl.

Marel coughed gently and he looked up to scowl at

her instead of his work. "Who're you?" he snapped.

"I'm Marel Gordon," she said. "I work here. I think I talked to you on the phone once."

He unfolded the frown so that he did not appear quite so ferocious and looked her over carefully. As if she were a bug on a microscope slide.

"Hmph," he grunted finally. "Well, it's something to have a fresh young face around this morgue. The only trouble with fresh young faces is that there's seldom any brains behind them."

Marel felt herself flushing indignantly. This Eric Webb person was impossible. He was even worse than he had sounded on the telephone. It didn't make sense that he should paint wonderful pictures that showed an understanding of children and a real sense of humor. Where would *he* get a sense of humor?

"Miss Embree said I should see if there was anything you wanted," Marel told him coolly.

"Yes," he said. "To be let alone. Now go away and don't bother me."

She went willingly and quickly. As far as she was concerned, it would be too soon if she did not see Eric Webb again for forty years.

Gail was just coming into her studio when Marel reached her door. She had dressed her brassy hair in the fifth new style Marel had seen since she'd come to work for Fran Embree. This effect was a pompadour with dozens of tight curls towering above her forehead.

"Goodness, but you look mad," she said after one glance at Marel's face. "Somebody bite you?"

"Practically," Marel confessed. "It's Mr. Webb."

"Don't tell me our little chum's back! Pay no attention. He has complexes. They're not contagious, so don't worry. Look—how's about helping me clean house today, if Fran doesn't want you for something else? Now that Pearl's on deck again—for the moment—you don't have to bother about the door or the phones."

Gail's possessions certainly looked as if they needed tidying and Marel went to work willingly enough. Whatever else happened on this most discouraging of days, she wanted to keep busy. Then she wouldn't get to brooding about Chris, or the impossible Eric Webb, or her doubtful future as an illustrator. She began screwing caps on jars of paint, throwing out scraps of charcoal and crayon, separating pencils with broken points from those ready to use and making a general attack on the disorder of Gail's worktable.

After a time Gail looked up from her drawing board. "The domestic type, aren't you? Look out some man doesn't come along and scoop you up."

"No danger," Marel said.

"What about Chris Mallory? He's been around here an awful lot since you started to work here."

Marel lifted her shoulders in what she hoped was a gesture of complete indifference.

"You're not fooling me," Gail told her. "I've seen your face light up a couple of times. I must say it's not very light now. This is a big town, and you can have a lot of fun in it if you don't get your heart involved. Once you make that mistake—zingo—you're off scrubbing floors and changing diapers before you know it. And there goes your chance at a career."

Probably it was the way the day had got off to such a wrong start that made her feel contrary, Marel thought. But she was as tired of older women who handed out free advice as she was of men with moods.

"You sound like Aunt Peg," Marel said. "All these warnings and stop signs."

"Well, you'd better stop, look, and comprehend. Not that kids like you ever do."

"But my heart isn't involved in anything," Marel protested. "You've been going to too many movies. I want to be an artist. I'm going to be one. And I'm certainly not going to get myself married for years and years. But I want to some day. And I don't see why it can't be worked out. I mean if two people whose interests are similar and sympathetic——"

"You mean like a writer and an artist?"

"I *don't* mean that. But since you've handed me the example, we can use it. Why wouldn't it work out? I mean if the girl was terribly interested in the man's job and he was interested in hers——"

Gail smudged in a shading of charcoal with a gray duffer. "Don't be funny. No man's that interested in his wife's job. When he gets married, he wants to marry a wife, not a job."

"But why can't a girl have both? I mean——"

"I know what you mean. And it can't be done. You have to want one thing enough to go after it with all you've got. Nothing comes free. You have to pay the price of hard work and make everything else take second place. Look at me! I'm beginning to click now so that editors are coming after my stuff. Life's getting to be just one deadline after another. Where do you think I'd fit in a husband and a house and kids?"

"You do work awfully hard," Marel admitted. "I've thought about that. I've even wondered if I'd be willing to work that hard on a job of my own. Do you like it?"

"I love it!" There was no hesitation about Gail's reply.

"Don't you care about having a home?" Marel asked.

"I have a home. Three nice little rooms that suit me fine right down near the middle of things."

"I don't mean that kind of home. I was thinking about the kind that would have a husband in it and maybe——" She broke off because of the way Gail was looking at her. It was a queer look, half amused, half angry.

"I have what I want," the other girl said shortly. "I'm my own boss. Nobody's telling me when to come and go, or fussing when I burn the chops. And my heart's all in one piece, which is a very nice feeling. That doesn't mean I don't date when I feel like it. But I don't always go with the same man, and I don't waste time on men who can't take me where I'd like to go."

Marel worked on, wiping up dust and smears of paint, putting everything in order. Gail's hard philosophy was not for her. She could not accept it. Of course she wanted to get married—some day. And she wouldn't want to go out with one man just because he made a lot of money, and turn another one down because he didn't. As far as she was concerned, a ride on a ferryboat could be just as much fun as going to a swank night club. A lot *more* fun— if you were with the right person. Gail wouldn't understand that. Her idea of fun was different.

But Gail was not to be silenced. A note of exasperation crept into her tone. "I know I'm wasting my breath, but you *could* have a career ahead of you. You've got the spark of talent that's necessary and you've got a lot of drive and ambition. But if you go out and get yourself tied up in a marriage knot, that will be the end of it."

"But the right kind of man——"

"There isn't any such. Oh, sure, a man likes his wife to have a cute little hobby or two, so long as it doesn't take her attention away from him. But let it really begin to take up her time and the first thing you know she has to give it up—or else it's the rocks. There's no other choice."

"I don't believe that. What about the girl who edits mystery novels for Barrett, Brown? Irene Allen?" Marel asked. "She's holding down a job and doing all right, isn't she? How is her marriage turning out?"

"You're asking me! Ask her. You can't tell by looking at those things from the outside. Stuart's the bookish, retiring kind. If Irene didn't earn good money, where would they be? If you get married, pick a man with money. Then maybe—*maybe,* mind you—he won't mind your going on with your drawing as a sort of hobby."

Again Marel had nothing to say. Gail's next question came abruptly.

"I know you've got a lot of pretty dreams," she said. "Every kid has. What's yours? What's your idea of a real home?"

Marel was startled into an answer. It seemed to pop out without requiring any thought, as if it had been waiting there all the time.

"The right man," she said, "and a house on a hilltop. A house with a fireplace and a view."

Gail waved the stick of charcoal at her. "How do you think you'll get that if you run around with somebody like Chris Mallory and become serious about him?"

"I'm *not* serious about him. That's silly. Besides, he'll be going places one of these days. You wait and see."

"Sorry." Gail turned back to her drawing. "*You* can wait. I haven't time."

Marel might have made a heated retort, but Fran came into the room just then with the drawings and Ginger's stories in her hands. She put the two pictures down on Gail's worktable.

"This one's good, Marel. You've really caught it. There's good action, good feeling in the other one too, but parts of it are out of drawing. You'll have to do it over. I've scanned one of the stories. I didn't mean to take the time till later, but I got interested. If this Williams girl and you will work hard enough and get this done up right, I'll see if I can place it with a publisher for you."

Marel could only stare. This was more than she had hoped for in her wildest dreams. She knew Fran Embree didn't take on the job of selling anything she didn't believe in. She must see possibilities in this or she wouldn't make such an offer.

"Mind you," Fran said, "you'll have to work. Bring

your friend Ginger up to see me and we'll hash over a few points together. And you'll have to put that little nose of yours, freckles and all, right to the grindstone. Understand?"

"Oh, I will!" Marel promised fervently. "If you really think I can do it——"

"I don't know whether you can or not. But I'd like to see you try." She went to the door of Gail's studio and put her head into the hall. "Eric! Come here a minute, will you? I want you to look at something."

Marel waited in dismay. The last person she wanted to have see her work was the unpleasant Eric Webb. There were sounds of complaint and protest from the far studio, but after a moment or two Eric appeared at the door.

"This is why I leave town," he said. "Never a moment's peace! No sooner do I get going than there are interruptions. Always interruptions."

"Yes, my lamb," Fran said calmly, ignoring his sputtering. "You've met the new member of our establishment, haven't you? Well, take a look at these. What do you think?"

He came over to the table and looked down at the drawings, his dark brows drawn into a scowl again. Marel braced herself. Only what Fran said mattered. She mustn't let this man's insults get under her skin.

"What am I supposed to do?" he demanded. "Murmur sweet nothings? There are too many artists in the world already. Why should I take bread out of my own mouth?"

Gail cocked an amused eyebrow at Marel. "I'll translate. You've just been handed a terrific compliment. He's regarding you as future competition."

Eric picked up one of the pictures—the one Fran liked—and carried it over to the light. In spite of bracing herself, in spite of telling herself that what this man said didn't really matter, Marel waited anxiously. Somehow she sensed that he knew more about drawing than anyone else in this room. No matter how much she disliked him as a personality, she had admired his work before she'd ever met him, and she could not help but await his opinion anxiously.

As he looked at the drawing, a slow change came over his face. The darkness seemed to lift away from it as a surprising smile flashed on.

"It's for a book," Fran explained. "Another youngster is writing the stories, and this one is tackling the illustrations. I don't know if either of them can make good, but I think they both have something."

"About stories I don't care," Eric said. "But about a fresh touch like this—that's something to find! Look, you two!" He glared abruptly at Fran and Gail. "You keep your commercial hands off this little girl. Leave her to me."

He came over to Marel, still glaring. "You—what's your name?"

"Marel Gordon," she told him faintly, lacking the courage to remind him that he'd already been told twice before.

"Marel!" he said. "That's the way you'll sign your stuff. Just Marel. Distinctive. Easy to remember."

"Wait till she has something to sign," Gail said dryly.

Eric paid no attention. "Come along with me, you— Marel. This other drawing—this is bad. Horrible. But even here there's a something. Come along!"

Marel glanced inquiringly at Fran, who nodded assent. Eric Webb went out the door and back to his own studio, with no effect of frantic hurrying, but with more speed than Marel had ever seen anyone display before. She followed him breathlessly.

"Sit over there," he said, and she took the one extra chair in the room.

He pinned a sheet of drawing paper to a board with thumb and tacks and brought it over to her, handed her a pencil.

"You're pretty bad, you know," he told her in his sharp, quick voice. "You've got a long way to go. But you have something to start with. That's more than most of 'em have. Now then—get busy and do this one over. See this? See that line? Wire. Wood. And what have you got inside? Wet macaroni. Not flesh and blood and bones. Well—what're you waiting for? Go ahead!"

"I—I can't with you watching me," Marel said. "I don't know how to begin. I mean——"

"Oh, so you're the chattering kind? That's the trouble. Women always think they can draw with their tongues."

"But I do have a job," Marel said uncomfortably. "I mean Fran isn't paying me to come here and work on my own stuff."

"Why isn't she? When she gets somebody like you—young and green and fresh——"

"And without any brains?" Marel added.

"Who says you haven't any brains? Do you think you could turn out work like that at your age without brains?"

"Eric Webb says so," Marel told him, wondering if the sky would fall on her head.

He made a wry face. "That Webb fellow! Never quote him to me. I have a very low opinion of his intelligence and I seldom agree with anything he says. But you and I—we're going to understand each other. I can teach you a lot, Marel, if you'll listen. If you want to learn."

"I *do* want to learn," she said.

He was like a different person now, not all sputter and sparks, but almost gentle and very much in earnest. With quick, magical strokes on paper he showed her where her drawing was wrong, and how to remedy the fault. She could understand now what he meant by wet macaroni.

"It means work," he told her. "It means giving up a lot of other things in order to do this one thing well. It means courage and patience and not very much money."

"But artists do earn a good living," she protested. "Some of them do."

"Sure," he said. "But the picture's all wrong. You get into commercial advertising and you make a pile of dough. But your name doesn't mean much and there's something inside you that goes hungry. You know what I mean? You know what I'm talking about?"

She wasn't sure that she did. She glanced toward the row of books in his case. The books which bore Eric Webb's name as illustrator.

"Maybe I understand," she said. "I mean I'd like to do books as good as the ones you've done. I'd like to have the feeling that there were children everywhere enjoying them, really getting something out of work I'd turned out."

"That's it." He patted her shoulder. "That's why I'm crazy enough to work at this game. That's why we all are. That hardboiled Norris female and Fran Embree, who's no artist, but knows plenty about art. They're commercial, sure. They're making money by working like slaves. But they're doing it mainly because they're crazy about it. That's what I want to know. Can you be as crazy about it as that?"

"I think so," Marel said. "I think I can."

She proved it by working straight through her lunch hour, so she wouldn't be doing this on Fran's time. Somehow the things Eric Webb said had caught fire in her imagination. They'd given her a courage and confidence that glowed more brightly than anything she'd ever known before. She was still afraid of him, but she respected him now. Maybe he was a little crazy—or maybe that was an act he put on for some reason of his own—but he certainly knew more about drawing than anyone she had ever known in her life and she felt he had the gift of teaching too.

Gail came grumbling in after a while with a chocolate bar and a carton containing a malted milk. "Don't starve yourself for art," she said. "It isn't worth it. And don't let our genius here crack the whip too hard."

Eric said: "You're jealous, my pet. You wish Eric Webb would sit down and teach you how to draw."

Gail threw a pastel crayon at him with an excellent and deliberate aim and went off, dusting her hands.

"You're coming to my class," Eric said. "Thursday nights from seven-thirty to nine-thirty. I'll expect you this week."

He kept surprising her more and more. "Class? Oh, I'd love to! But I'm afraid—I mean how much do you——"

He looked insulted. "You don't think I do it for money? I take only three or four. Hand-picked. You pay me by showing me my judgment was right. That's good for the ego. This Webb fellow gives me a pain, but I have to live with him. Such an ego I have to keep feeding! You'll come to my class. It's settled. Now then—beat it. You've taken up enough of my time."

He looked as annoyed as if it had all been her idea instead of his, but she was getting more used to him now. She gathered up her work and went back to her job with Fran.

What an exciting day this had been! What events she would have to tell Chris about! More and more she thought of telling Chris first and of letters home second. Which did not mean that she loved her family any less, but only that—well, Chris was Chris. He'd laugh over her account of Eric Webb, but perhaps he'd be pleased too because Eric thought she had talent. And pleased that Fran wanted her to go ahead with her drawings and had offered to place the book with a publisher. Surely he'd call her to find how she had come out on that. His odd mood of this morning would lift. Probably by tonight she'd hear from him again.

She began to long for the day to be over so she could get back to her aunt's apartment and within reach of the phone. Somehow she felt that no achievement could be really fun if she couldn't share it with Chris. Tell him about it. Have him proud of her.

7

I-Love-Him, I-Love-Him-Not!

Marel frowned at the chubby leg and knee of the little boy in her drawing. Had she caught it this time? Or would Eric tell her it looked like wet macaroni?

"Ginger," she said, "take a look."

The two girls were working at Ginger's that evening. Ginger lived in an old apartment building with her mother and father and an assortment of brothers and sisters, married and unmarried. They occupied two apartments on one floor and a good part of the hallway between.

Ginger had a small room of her own. In it was a battered desk that had lived through the ownership of a succession of brothers before being inherited by Ginger. Her secondhand portable typewriter sat on the desk and at the moment she was copying the rough draft of a story into its final typewritten form.

She came over to stand behind Marel. "It's sweet," she said. "You've caught that little-boy expression of David's perfectly."

"It's the legs I'm worried about, not the face," Marel told her.

"What's the matter with them? They look like legs to me."

"I hope they'll look like legs to Eric too." Marel sighed. "Sometimes I think I'm getting worse instead of better since he's been working with me. He scares me so."

"Don't you let him bully you," Ginger said staunchly. "I'd like to meet that guy one of these days. I told Ken about him and he says he sounds like a lot of pose and hot air."

Marel shook her head and went back to work on the drawing. "He's good, Ginger. He really is. He's so good that it's worth putting up with his tantrums just to learn from him."

"But you said you felt you were worse off than before you started with him."

"That's because it makes me self-conscious to think about all the things he wants me to think about. When I get so used to them that I do them automatically, I'll stop feeling as if I were all thumbs."

"Well," Ginger said dubiously, "I don't know. Ken says——"

Sentences that began "Ken says" were apt to go on for hours, so Marel cut in quickly. "Eric's class really is wonderful. There are two girls besides me and one man. And they all think Eric is tops. One of the girls was ready to cry the night I was there because he said such nasty things about her work. But even she knew the scolding was good for her."

Ginger went back to her place at the typewriter. "Ken thinks it's wonderful that your Fran Embree is interested in our book. Goodness, Marel, if this sells and we get an advance, Ken and I can get some of the furniture we need."

"I do believe," Marel said ruefully, "that all publication means to you is armchairs and kitchen tables. Ginger, what about your writing? If this book clicks, won't you want to write after you're married?"

Ginger shrugged. "I guess it isn't too important. Writing is all right, but I wouldn't put it ahead of a husband and kids. Would *you* put your drawing ahead of a husband if you were getting married?"

"I'm not getting married," Marel said in a firm and final tone.

Not only was she not getting married, but at the moment she wasn't even having any dates. Two weeks had gone by without a word from Chris. At first she had expected to hear from him any day, but the telephone never brought his voice, the mail brought her no letter. It was just as if she had never known him at all, so completely had he faded out of the picture. She had felt a little angry at first. There wasn't any sense to such behavior. They had been good friends one day—nothing at all the next. How it had happened she didn't know, and she was still wondering if there was any connection between her ambition to be an artist and Chris's sudden withdrawal of his friendship. Anyway, such treatment wasn't fair.

But Ginger's question kept tugging at her, even though she shrugged it aside. *Would* she put her drawing ahead of a husband if she were getting married? How could she know the answer to that?

The desire to draw was so much a part of her that she could not imagine living without it. It was almost like breathing. In the hurt that had set in after her annoyance had faded, she knew how much Chris meant to her. How dangerously close she had been to falling in love with him. And yet if he were to say to her, "I love you, but you'll have to give up this drawing nonsense and just be a wife"—could she do it? Could she ever be contented if she could not draw?

Probably not. Ginger was lucky to have a flair for writing, yet not have it rule her the way the urge to draw ruled Marel. Just the same, if it were possible to find a man who wanted her to have the drawing too, and whom she could help and urge ahead when it came to his own work, then why couldn't they have a marriage, a *partnership* much richer than either could have alone?

But Chris, apparently, wasn't that man.

Oh, dear, her drawing was going all wrong again. Eric would think she was hopeless when he saw this. And she'd never finish the pictures for the book at the rate she was going—having to do each one over and over before Eric would give it his okay. Sometimes he made her feel that she should have taken up dishwashing instead of drawing pictures. And then, just when she was so discouraged she was ready to throw her drawing things out the nearest window, he'd smile that angelic smile of his and tell her she had "something." A "spark," a "touch." And for that praise she would redouble her efforts and work like two slaves, hugging her chains.

The thing that seemed so unfair about Chris was that everything should just end—without a word. "Hello" and "good-bye"—and that was that. Why didn't she have a right to know why? Even if the reason hurt, it would be better than wondering all her life what had happened. She was beginning to think it would be better to toss her pride out the window and give him a ring on the phone. Then she could tell by the way he greeted her whether he'd missed her at all as she had missed him. No—that didn't make sense. Men had the best of it at a time like this. If they missed you, they could call you up. If they wanted to know something, they could ask you. They could arrange to see you when they pleased. But all a girl could do—according to convention—was sit around and wait. Men, so everyone told her, didn't like women who ran after them.

She put down her pen full of India ink with a hopeless gesture. "Guess I'm tired tonight, Ginger. Nothing seems to come right. Maybe I'd better go home."

Ginger swung away from her typewriter. "If you ask me, that Eric person is bad for you. All you do is moon around in a discouraged way lately."

Marel concentrated on fastening the cap on her ink bottle as if the action were the most important thing in the world. She could sense Ginger's lively gaze upon her, speculating.

"Look," Ginger said, "you haven't fallen in love with this Webb creature, have you?"

That was so funny that Marel began to laugh. She

laughed until her sides hurt and the tears were ready to come, but all the while she didn't feel a bit amused.

"All right," Ginger said, in relief, "but if you ask me you're acting just exactly like a lady in love."

"*You're* a lady in love," Marel pointed out, "and you're not acting like me—so what makes you say that?"

"I'm past the painful stage," Ginger said cheerfully. "At least for now. I have everything settled. Marel, what's the trouble?"

She hesitated for a moment, wondering if she dared confide in Ginger.

"I'm not admitting there is any trouble," she said at last. "At least not anything serious. But there's a man I've had a few dates with, whom I like awfully well. I thought he liked me too, and we really had lots of fun together. Then all of a sudden, without giving any reason, without even saying good-bye, he stopped seeing me, stopped calling me. If he doesn't want to see me any more, that's all right with me." She put her chin up at the angle Chris had called her "red-feather chin." "But it seems to me I have a right to know the reason."

Ginger uncurled from the chair before her typewriter again and bounced herself on her bed with a thud that set the springs creaking. Marel saw to her relief that the other girl wasn't going to laugh or utter any "I-told-you-so's." Ginger might be a bit light-headed sometimes, a bit chattery and overexuberant, but she had a good warm heart and in some ways she was very wise.

"You know, don't you," Ginger said calmly, "that the reason might hurt you to find out. That could be why he just went off without saying anything. He wouldn't *want* to hurt you, even if he had to. He might think it was kinder this way. I mean if he just decided he'd rather not take you out any more, or if he's met somebody new."

That girl at the airport on Staten Island, Marel thought. What if it wasn't somebody new, but somebody old? That Sally Foster who could be attractive even in dungarees and was probably a knockout when she dressed up. He had gone around with her once and Marel hadn't needed to have any pictures drawn to know that Sally still wanted him. If that was the answer——

"Even if it hurts," she said, "I'd rather know. I hate feeling so in the dark, so helpless."

"Nobody's helpless," Ginger told her. "Do you really want this man?"

"I—I don't know." Marel made a gesture of uncertainty.

"That's silly," Ginger said. "You either want him, or you don't want him. If it's just your pride that's hurt, then you don't want him much and you'd better find somebody new and patch up the pride. But if it's your heart that's hurt, that's different."

"But I don't know—I really don't know. I want so much to be an artist. And everybody says I won't have time to pay attention to just one man."

"Everybody says!" Ginger's scorn was open. "Anybody who says a girl won't have time to settle for one man is nuts! How about not sidestepping any more? How about not ducking the question because you're afraid of it? Do you want him, or don't you? Be honest."

Marel turned away from Ginger's straight gaze and examined the picture she was working on. What was important in her life? What mattered most? The drawing looked stiff and forced. She had been working on it while she thought about something else, while her main interest was on Chris. And that wouldn't do. That was bad for her drawing, bad for her. Maybe Ginger was right. Maybe she had better face the thing she didn't want to face. Maybe she *had* better be honest.

"I think I want him," she said.

Ginger bounced happily on the bed. "That's more like it. I'd hate to believe you were just an old paintbrush. In that case, go after him. Stop being helpless."

"But men don't like girls who chase. They don't like——"

" 'Everybody says,' I suppose?" Ginger's scorn was evident again.

"But if he really doesn't want to see me——"

"If he really doesn't want to see you, then it's true that you'd only be a nuisance if you ran after him. You can't make him like you if he really doesn't. But you don't know that for sure yet. Do you?"

"No. No, I don't," Marel said. "I feel as if there was something here I don't understand."

"In that case, get after it and clear it up. You won't be happy till you know one way or the other."

"You mean get in touch with him—call him up?"

"Sure," Ginger said. "Why not? For all the attention you've paid him, maybe he has a broken leg, or he's caught cholera, or something. The least you can do is find out."

Marel began to gather up her drawing things. "Then I will. You're wonderful, Ginger. I *did* need to talk to somebody. You know what I'm going to do? I'm going to take care of it right away."

"That's the stuff," Ginger applauded as she went with Marel to the door. "You don't get what you aren't willing to fight for, you know. And if you're smart, you'll fight for something besides the chance to push a brush full of paint across a sheet of paper."

She could hardly wait till she could get to a drugstore where she could telephone. She'd be likely to catch him in because he'd probably be home working on his book. That contest deadline was coming up just ahead. She decided to phone from a drugstore and avoid any questions her aunt might ask.

She dialed his number and waited anxiously as the phone began to ring. It was hot in the little booth and perspiration started out on her forehead and in the palms of her hands. Why didn't he answer? Oh he *had* to be home!

Then someone took the receiver off its hook and a

man's voice said, "Hello." But it wasn't Chris's voice. It was someone strange.

"Is Chris Mallory there?" she asked breathlessly.

"Yeah, he's here," the voice said, "but do you *have* to talk to him?"

"Well, I—that is——" Marel floundered for words. "If he's very busy——"

"He's plenty busy," the voice said curtly. "The trouble with you females is you don't know anything about dead-lines and how a writer works."

"I'm sorry," Marel said weakly. "I don't want to——"

The voice never gave her time to finish a sentence. "You *ought* to be sorry. Chris works all day on a job. Then he comes home and tries to get some time in on his book. And what happens? The telephone begins to ring and it's neglected maidens calling up to know why they haven't heard from a guy. Will you for gosh sakes let him finish his book in peace?"

"I'm sorry," Marel said hurriedly. "I really am. I—I wouldn't think of interrupting him now."

"You can leave your name if you want to," the voice told her grudgingly, "and I'll tell him you called. I'll tell him later."

"Thank you. I—I won't bother," Marel said and hung the receiver shakily on its hook.

When she was outside again, walking along through the summer evening, the funny side of it began to strike her. Chris was certainly lucky in having a dragon like this Mac Conway to play interference for him. Probably Chris himself didn't know what Mac was doing. But if his friend helped him get that book done, then he was doing him a favor, and even if Marel Gordon's nose was a little out of joint, she had to admit that she was no help to Chris if she interfered with his work.

Somehow she felt much better now. This was the answer, of course. Chris was spending every minute he could spare working on the book. When that was off his

hands, he'd have time for dates again. Of *course* that was
it. A contrary voice tried to whisper that he might have
found time to phone her, and that his lunch hours were
still open, but she silenced the voice without listening to
it very closely. Tomorrow she'd phone Chris again. But
she'd call him at work where there wouldn't be any dragon
like Mac Conway, or any book to interfere with. And
when she got him, she'd go right to the point.

Her determination to take some decisive action made
the hours easier to get through. It was not knowing what
to do, not being able to make up her mind, that had kept
her in an unhappy, unsettled state. Now that she had
decided to find out just what was the matter with Chris,
she felt much better. In spite of wondering who the other
"neglected maidens" were who'd been calling him up.
Sally Foster, maybe?

The next day she waited until early afternoon, found a
moment when Fran was out of the office so that she could
have reasonable privacy, and then called the advertising
department of the store where Chris worked.

She had no trouble getting him this time and the familiar
sound of his voice coming over the wire made her know
how much she had missed hearing it.

"Hello, Chris," she said. "This is Marel."

"Why, hello!" Was there a lift to his voice, as if he
was glad to hear from her, or was that something she
imagined because she wanted so much to have it so?

"How is the book coming?" she asked.

"I finished typing it last night," he said. "It's ready to
go and I feel as if I'd just come out of prison."

There was a pause, and she wondered if he would ask
to see her, now that his prison term was over. But he
waited as if he were wondering why she had called. She
had a weak moment of wanting to hang up and run away
without forcing the issue. Just say lightly that she'd wondered about him, tell him "so long," and hang up. But

that wasn't why she had called him and she would not give in to the impulse.

"Chris," she said, "I'd like to talk to you. Could I see you for a few minutes tonight after work?"

The long hesitation before he answered frightened her. If he had wanted to see her, he'd have said "yes" quickly.

"I'm sorry, Marel," he said finally, "but I'm planning to go over to the airport on Staten Island tonight. They're expecting me."

He didn't say who "they" were, but she knew. Knew without further question. It was Sally Foster he was going to see. And there was nothing in the world Marel Gordon could do about it.

"I'm sorry too," she said lightly. "Well, back to the mines. Good luck on your book. 'Bye now," and she hung up quickly so she would not have to listen to any forced apologies he might give.

Disappointment was like an illness, she thought, as she put the phone aside. He *had* sounded glad to hear from her at first. She was sure he had. So what was the matter? Even if he could not manage to see her tonight, he might have asked if some other time would do.

Everything had hung on her phone call and it had netted her exactly nothing. She still had a dozen questions in her mind and the answers to none of them. Should she rest on her pride now and give up? You couldn't fight when there was nothing to catch hold of, nothing to fight for. And you couldn't go flinging yourself at a man when he had shown not the slightest interest in holding out his hands to catch you. She'd better get to work—that's what she'd better do.

On Fran's desk was a stack of samples of artists' work with a rough sketch clipped to the top drawing. In spite of herself, Marel smiled. The sketch showed a filing cabinet with a furiously busy figure standing before it. The figure was of a girl with a perky red feather stuck in her hat.

Gail's pictorial shorthand. Gail never wrote anybody a note. She drew pictures and left them all over the place. This one evidently meant that the girl who owned the red-feathered hat was to get busy and file the pile of samples.

Marel took them up and went listlessly to the cabinet behind Fran's desk. In that file were kept samples of original work, as well as tear sheets of printed copy of all the artists for whom Fran Embree acted as agent. Most of the artists had some particular specialty. If an editor called up and wanted someone who was good at drawing animals, or farm scenes, or city scenes, or was good at machines and engines like Eric, or cuddly babies like Erna Lewis, that file held all the answers.

As she slipped the folders into their alphabetical niches, Marel wondered not too happily if pictures of hers would ever grace that file. Would editors ever come to know her work so that they would call up and ask if she was free to take a new book assignment, the way they asked for Gail? At the moment she felt she'd never be successful in anything. Not in love or in a career.

"Hold it!" cried Gail's voice from the doorway. "Don't move a muscle!"

Marel was used to this sort of thing by now and she obligingly "held it," though she wasn't sure what portion of her anatomy Gail was trying to catch. The other girl had snatched up a pencil and was busily working with the paper held flat against a convenient wall.

"Okay," she said, "relax. It's perfect. I'll remember you in my Aunt Minnie's will."

Marel returned her attention to the file without interest in what Gail had sketched. Filing was something she could bury her sorrows in to some extent, or at least hide them.

"I know you're perfectly fascinated," Gail went on, "so I'll tell you. I've been absolutely stuck on that teen-ager's face Fran wanted for chapter three of the career book opus we're taking on. The girl in the story is supposed to be suffering from a broken heart. Temporary, of course, like all broken hearts. And I simply couldn't get it till I saw your face. Thanks completely."

Marel pulled out a lower drawer of the file and bent over it, the better to conceal the expression Gail had been so pleased about. A guinea pig—that's all she was in this place! Not even a human being. You could be dying right before somebody's eyes and all they'd do would be to grab for a pencil and sketch pad so they could catch your death agonies. Artists!

Gail had gone off for a moment, but she was back again posthaste, her high-heeled sandals clicking across the floor of the little hall.

"Hey, wait a minute!" she cried. "I just thought of something. How come you're making like a teen-ager with a broken heart? Don't you know you're a career girl?"

Marel dropped to her knees beside the drawer and turned her back on Gail as if putting folders in the right section of a file was the most absorbing interest in her life. She could feel the intensity of Gail's interest and it annoyed her even more than her indifference of the moment before.

"So?" Gail mused. "You *don't* know you're a career girl. Instead of keeping your eye on your job—which is the only safe, comfortable place for an eye—you've gone and let it wander toward some man. And now you've got what you always get from men—sore places in the ego."

"Oh, go away!" Marel mumbled from her stooped-over position.

"Maybe you need glasses if you have to file with your nose like that," Gail suggested helpfully. "Well, all I've got to say is don't let Eric hear about this. He hasn't any patience with broken hearts."

"Will you please let me alone!" Marel cried.

She could feel herself getting angrier by the minute. Ragingly angry. Angry at Gail for poking her with pins as if she were a bug on a slide. Angry with Chris for just going off and dropping her without the faintest warning or explanation. Angry with all these people who tried to pull her one way and then another. People like Ginger, who said, "Never mind the job, land your man." Like Gail, who said, "Forget about men and look to your job." Like Eric, who bullied you and criticized you and pushed you up with one hand while he thrust you down with the other. But more than anything else she was angry with Chris.

She twisted her head around and looked at the clock on Fran's desk. It showed ten minutes to five. Well, this was one time when she was going to leave ten minutes early. She'd make it up tomorrow, but nobody was going to stop her now. Gail was still watching interestedly from the doorway. Marel thrust the last folder into a place where it didn't belong and scrambled to her feet.

"I'm going home," she said. "I'm leaving right this minute!"

Gail's low whistle was expressive. "Whoever he is I feel sorry for him."

Paying no attention to her, Marel got her handbag out of a lower drawer and gave her hair a quick fluffing before the closet mirror. It was too warm now for hats, except for dress-up occasions, so the red feather was resting safely at home. She'd have to powder her nose on the subway—no time now.

There was time for only one thing. To get out of the building and onto a downtown train before Chris left. So he was going to Staten Island on the ferry, was he? Well, she was going to Staten Island on the ferry too. And let him do what he might about that!

Men were unreasonable and impossible and altogether too complicated. Instead of acting in a simple, direct way that let a girl know where she stood, they did inexplicable, unkind, illogical things. Well, she'd had enough. She was

going to see Chris whether he liked it or not. She was
going to be down at the ferry building waiting for him
to come aboard.

8

Lady in Pursuit

Marel dropped her fare in the slot and went through the turnstile into the ferry building. At one side a lighted sign bore the legend, "Next Boat." Maybe she'd be on the next boat and maybe she wouldn't. That depended on Chris.

She found herself a place against the wall where she could watch the line of turnstiles and check everyone who came through. She *hoped* she could check everyone. The rush-hour crowds were on their way and the rate at which people were pouring into the building appalled her a little. But she couldn't miss Chris. She couldn't possibly! Even if her eyes didn't see him the minute he came in sight, her heart would surely tell her he was there.

On the way down in the subway, her anger had faded out. That was the trouble with the way she got angry. Some people could get indignant and stormy and stay that way until they had really blown up. But no matter how mad she got, it never seemed possible to stay mad for more than ten minutes straight, and then all the storminess faded out, and even if she still felt unhappy about her hurt, she could not be resentful or indignant.

So she was not resentful or indignant now. She was a little bit frightened at her own audacity, but quietly determined to carry out her plan. She almost wished she could have seen Chris during those few minutes when she was ready to make sparks fly, but perhaps it was just as well that she felt quieter now, so she could talk to him calmly and just ask him for a reasonable answer to the question which troubled her so much.

The crowds rushed by, jostling her even in her place against the wall. How could there be this many people in the world? How could there be so many tall young men who carried themselves almost like Chris? She'd always thought him quite distinctive-looking—not a bit like anyone else. She'd liked the way he held himself, the way he walked—so much more springy and erect than other men. Yet here she was fancying that he'd come in sight with about every fourth man she saw.

Then he was there, pausing at a newstand, buying a paper, and she wondered how she could for a moment have thought that anyone else looked like Chris.

Her heart began to thump harder than ever. What if he were annoyed with her? He'd have every right to be, certainly. She wasn't being wise, or sensible, or any of the things she ought to be. She was just following her heart foolishly, and hearts, as Gail kept telling her, only got you into trouble.

He came through the turnstile, walking briskly, not looking left or right. She had to take quick little running steps to keep a few paces behind him. The incoming ferry had unloaded and the gates were sliding open to let the homeward-bound crowd through.

Apparently Chris was not heading for the upper deck this time, where the view was best. He followed the crowd to the left and Marel had to use her elbows a little and shove her way after him. Two or three people looked at her indignantly, but she didn't care. When an ordinarily considerate and mild-mannered young lady decided to go after what she wanted, even people twice her size recognized determination and let her by.

There! He'd found a place in a corner near a window and had settled down to reading his paper. Marel squirmed past a girl who was heading for the place next to him and dropped into the seat in the nick of time. The girl gave her a dagger-filled look and went on to another place.

He could probably hear her heart thumping, Marel

thought. It was really much louder than the throbbing of the boat engines as the ferry pulled away from the slip. All the breath had gone out of her and her courage had gone with it. She was just plain scared and wished she were any place on earth but sitting next to Chris Mallory. Maybe if she got up quietly and walked away to another part of the boat, he'd never know what she'd done. Not ever to see him again seemed suddenly preferable to having him look around, discover her here, and perhaps show the distaste he might very likely feel.

Then, just as she was trying to convince her knees that they were not made of wet macaroni like the knees in her drawings, but of flesh and blood and sinew that was perfectly capable of carrying her wherever she wanted to go, he looked up in turning a page of his paper and saw her.

There was no distaste in his look, no dismay behind the warmth of his smile. He looked very much like a small boy who had suddenly been given a Christmas package he had never expected to receive.

"Hello, Margaret Elizabeth," he said.

She relaxed a little. The worst was over now. Whatever followed couldn't be as hard to get through as what she had already forced herself to do.

"I've missed you," she told him quite simply.

Maybe it wasn't in the rules to say that. Maybe it wasn't the sort of thing a girl ought to say to a man who had been deliberately avoiding her. But it happened to be the truth.

He pulled her hand through the crook of his arm and gave it a little pat and all her courage came back. It didn't matter that he'd behaved so queerly. It didn't even matter if he was going over to Staten Island to see Sally Foster. All that mattered was that she was here and that she knew he was glad to have her here.

"Let's get out of this," he said. "Let's get up on deck where we can breathe and talk."

They went up the stairs side by side and around the

deck to the rear of the ferry. The sky above the city was a drab gray this evening and smoke and fog swirled about its towers, cutting them off from the ground, dimming their outlines, so that lower Manhattan looked like a fairy city—a mirage floating in space. Gulls dipped and glided in the wake of the boat, alert for anything edible which might come to the surface.

Marel stood with her hand still tucked through Chris's arm, feeling very close to him, sensing a contentment and peace in the moment that she had never known before. She was almost sorry when he began to talk. Words might send them apart again.

"What about your drawings?" he asked. "What did Fran think of them?"

So he *was* interested. Even though he'd never bothered to call and ask how she had come out.

"I thought you didn't care," she said. "You never even phoned to ask." That sounded reproachful, and she wished she had not said it, wished she had not let her hurt over his behavior creep into her words and into her voice.

"The trouble is that I care a lot," he said quietly. He wasn't looking down at her now, but out across the boat's swirling wake toward the floating towers of Manhattan. "Even an outsider like me can recognize talent when I see it. I think you've a big future ahead of you, Marel, if you play your cards right."

"What do you mean—play my cards right?"

"Just that you'd better keep your eye on that job and not go running around with guys like me."

"What's wrong with guys like you?"

"Oh—just that my main asset at the moment is a lot of ambition and not very much else."

"Check," she said. "That seems to be my main asset too. Maybe you ought not to go running around with girls like me, if that's a handicap."

"It's not any joking matter," he told her. "The last thing I'd want to do would be to stop you from going places with your drawing. Or even to slow you up."

She gave his arm a squeeze of impatience. "But how could you possibly stop me? You've always been as encouraging as anybody could be. Why, it was you who helped me by telling me I ought to make Fran change her mind by getting out and drawing children."

He withdrew his interest from the misty towers and looked down at her. It was a look that left her a little breathless—a look that was solemn and tender and almost stern, all at the same time.

"That isn't exactly what I mean," he said. "Encouraging you is one thing. Interfering with your work is another."

"But how could you interfere with my work? You're talking such nonsense."

"Am I? What if you begin to mean too much to me? What if I begin to mean too much to you?"

She could not help leaning her cheek against his arm for a second. "I think that would be awfully nice. And not at all interfering."

For just a second he covered her hand with his own again, and then took it away, drew his arm from the touch of her cheek. She looked up, surprised and a little hurt, to find that the look in his eyes was all sternness now.

"When you care quite a lot about a person, Marel, you have to *try* to be sensible, even if you'd much rather not be. Don't you see where we're heading if we keep on seeing each other, keep on liking each other more and more?"

"I think it would be wonderful," Marel said. "I don't see why two people can't go places much better together in their work than they could alone. It would be such fun to help each other, to believe in each other, to—to work for something *together*."

"You're sweet," he said. "But you're not making sense at all."

She moved away from him crossly. "Who wants to be sensible all the time? You sound like Aunt Peg, or that

Gail Norris at Fran's. Or like Eric Webb. He thinks I ought to turn into some sort of work machine with crayons for fingers and watercolor in my veins. I don't want to! I think Ginger's right, and there are a lot of things more important in life than being successful at a career."

She felt very eager to convince him, very earnest about what she was saying. Her words might have gone on fervently for quite a while longer if he hadn't bent suddenly to kiss her on the mouth. She gasped and looked up at him, all desire to talk fading out of her.

He was smiling now—that warm smile that had penetrated her annoyance the very first time she'd met him.

"There!" he said. "See what happens when I get near you? That's what I mean. I figure everything out sensibly and decide to stay away from you for your own good and mine—and look what happens!"

"But staying away isn't for my good at all," she protested, "and I hope it's not for yours either. Only being together is for *our* good."

"You *are* sweet. And even though I know we're both crazy if we try it with things as they are now, I want to marry you. I've been staying away because I didn't think I ought to say it. Now it's out."

There was no need to give him an answer. She knew her answer was in her eyes for him to read. His arm was tight around her and she had a feeling that this was one of the most perfect moments in her life; that she ought to hold it close and not let it get away. This moment with the mist blowing in from the sea, the gulls swooping above gray water, and the now distant towers of Manhattan Island a mirage across the bay.

But no moment, however lovely, could be held forever. There were always new moments crowding in, claiming their own right to be lived. Together they returned to some awareness of where they were and Marel looked hastily about at other inhabitants of a world that had seemed for a little while to belong to two alone. But the evening commuters were busy with their papers and their own conversations and none of them appeared to be taking the slightest interest in a girl and boy who had just got themselves engaged. Not even the kiss Chris had given Marel seemed to have caused more than a passing glance.

"We might as well face it," Chris said. "We're picking ourselves a rough road to climb."

"Others like us are climbing it every day," Marel pointed out.

"That doesn't make it any easier, or in our case any more sensible," he said. "But, honey, if we work things out ahead of time, plan carefully and with a lot of give-and-take in what we do, maybe we *can* work it out."

Marel nodded blissfully. Whatever practical matters were troubling Chris, she could not bother about them now. Only a little while ago she had been feeling alone and unhappy, and now she wasn't alone any more. Being alone was something for girls less lucky than she—girls who weren't engaged to be married. Why, she would never have to be alone again as long as she lived.

She tucked her hand through Chris's arm again. "Chris, do you have to go out to the airport tonight?"

He shook his head. "No. I'll make a phone call when the boat gets in. This evening I want to be with you."

"That's nice," she said happily. "I hoped it was something you could get out of." She could feel almost kindly toward poor unfortunate Sally Foster who could not have the man she wanted. "Chris, let's celebrate. Let's go back to that little restaurant on the lake again for dinner. It must be beautiful there in the evening."

"Whoa, there, young lady." Chris's tone was cheerful, but firm. "I thought you weren't paying a bit of attention to me a few minutes ago. You'll have to come down out of the clouds and face that grim reality I was trying to get you to look at."

She smiled up at him happily. "What grim reality? I don't see any."

"Right here under your nose," he said. "If we're going to be married in the not-too-far-away future, then the first thing we have to consider is saving every penny we can. That means no more splurges. Maybe you won't like the place where I'll take you to dinner tonight."

"Wrong again!" she said. "I'll like any place where I can have dinner with you"—and was rewarded by the warm touch of his hand over hers again.

The throbbing engines of the ferry stopped and they left the end of the boat to walk forward with the crowd. People pressed about them on all sides, but somehow Marel felt that she and Chris were quite alone. No one else mattered but just the two of them, and so long as they were together, she knew they could solve any problem that confronted them.

They left the boat and walked down Bay Street arm in arm. There was a diner on the edge of the sidewalk and through the windows they could see people sitting at booths eating, and on stools along a counter. All the booths were taken, but two stools at the end were vacant.

"Are you game?" Chris asked.

She presented him with her "red-feather" look. "You'll have to do better with your grim reality if you're trying to frighten me. I think eating at counters is fun."

So they went into the diner and sat at the counter, and everything *was* fun, from the sound of hamburgers sizzling in a pan to a noisy juke box wailing, "Just give me the moon over Brooklyn——" She hardly knew what she was eating because she was so happy. It was such a relief to have her whole life settled way ahead. Even though there were details to be worked out still, they could wait for now.

She was coming to the ending of all her childish story-books: "And they lived happily ever after." That's the way it was going to be when they were married. She bit a little absently into her hamburger and became aware of an aroma drifting her way. Not from her own hamburger, but from the one right next door—Chris's hamburger. Could it be possible, or was she mistaken? Was he actually eating raw onions? At a time like this? When they had just got engaged and the whole romantic evening stretched ahead of them!

She turned her head cautiously and looked.

"Hi!" he said cheerily, and bit into the aromatic affair he held in his hands.

Yes, she was right. He was eating raw onions. And apparently doing it without a care in the world, or a thought for the effect upon the young lady of his dreams.

Marel sighed. So this was the grim reality he had been talking about? Well, she might as well begin getting used to it.

And then the sigh turned into a quiet chuckle, without Chris being aware of either. It was funny, really. Men—even men as wholly admirable and satisfactory as Chris —just weren't romantic by nature. Never mind that. *She* was going to make a success of her marriage, no matter what. Even if it meant learning to put up with raw onions, she was going to succeed at it.

9

The World Comes In

Her aunt had guests this evening, but Marel had shut herself into her own room to work. These days she fully understood Ginger's desire for the book to be a financal success. She, too, was building for the future. She, too, wanted nice things for the place where she and Chris were going to live. If they ever found a place to live. She had heard talk about the housing shortage before, of course, but it had meant nothing personal to her until now when it began to concern her own life.

Two weeks had gone by since that evening on the ferry, and while everyone assured her two weeks were nothing beside the futile efforts of people who had looked months for a place to live, it seemed an agonizing length of time to Marel. Now that everything was settled, she and Chris were both anxious to set a day for the wedding. But you could not set a day when the possibility of finding a roof to put over your head was apparently a very remote one.

Marel ripped the sheet of paper from her drawing board and stuffed it into a wastebasket. She was all thumbs tonight. If she had a good drawing table to work at! A board that had to be propped against a chair back was awkward. She pinned a clean sheet of paper and started over. The picture in her mind seemed clear enough, but what came out beneath her wayward pencil resembled it very little.

She hummed to herself as she worked. Scraps of popular tunes over and over again. Not because she felt particularly gay or happy, but because humming sometimes seemed to help her pencil. It was a silly habit, probably, but one she often indulged. Back home it had become a standing joke that Marel guided a paintbrush with her vocal cords. But now not even humming seemed to help.

Perhaps the difficulty in working grew out of her own mental and emotional stress, she thought. It wasn't just the difficulty of finding a place to live which would not be too expensive for their modest combined incomes. There were other things, too.

Getting married, as she was discovering, meant a lot more than valiantly conditioning oneself to raw onions. It meant a number of quite appalling problems.

She had supposed—naïvely enough, as she now realized —that getting married was something which concerned Chris and herself alone. Now she was beginning to understand that, on the contrary, it seemed to concern dozens of other people too, and that these others had no hesitation about making her business theirs. None of them waited for advice to be asked, but were only too ready to present it to her in large quantities, quite free of charge, whether she wanted it or not.

She had hoped that those close to her would be happy, pleased, glad for her happiness. The reality was disappointing. Dad and Mother had written her a warmly affectionate letter, which, nevertheless, was entirely set against her marriage. She was so young, they pointed out. Could she not wait a year at least? They were in sympathy with the way she felt about Chris, but how, they demanded, could she be sure of her feelings so quickly? Sure they would last? You could not really know a person in so short a time. There was always the danger of crediting the loved one with qualities you wanted him to have, rather than those he really possessed.

Marel recognized the truth in their words and yet she felt she *did* know Chris. She knew him with her heart, and every new thing she learned about him only served to support her staunch belief in his fineness. But to others that sort of reasoning seemed futile and foolish. You had only to look at divorce records to recognize the logic behind the warnings.

Then her parents had gone on to other points in their letter. It was too difficult to manage a marriage when you had to work all day. Wouldn't it be better to wait till Chris could afford the kind of marriage where his wife could give home-making the time it deserved?

Marel wrinkled her nose over that. What an old-fashioned idea! Most young wives worked at first these days. Waiting was unthinkable.

Next they inquired about her art work. Why not stay with her new opportunity until she was experienced enough to work alone at home? Did she mean to give that up so quickly when she was just getting started? Apparently it hadn't occurred to them that marriage need not end everything else she wanted to do. Probably they felt that way because it was the way her mother had chosen. As a girl she had had a talent for drawing too, but she had neglected it and put other things first when she married. Of course *she*, Marel, would never give up her art work. Chris wouldn't want her to. There was no question of that.

Her parents closed the letter with a plea that they meet her young man before she married him. It had been hard for her to answer and explain that Chris could not afford a trip to Chicago just now and that they did not want to wait. As soon as they could find a place to live, they would be married.

She had not shown her parents' letter to Chris. She was beginning to be a little fearful of his rather grim intention to do what was right for her, regardless of whether she felt it was for her own good or not.

There had been no letter as yet from Chris's mother, and what Chris had told her had not served to set her mind entirely at rest in that direction.

"Mother's fun," he'd said. "You'll like her. But don't expect her to come over to our side in one jump."

Nevertheless, he assured her, his mother's attitude would make no difference. Sooner or later she would get around to seeing things their way. She was an awfully good sport, really. And in the meantime they would go ahead.

In spite of Chris's reassurances, all this had a slightly frightening ring. It made her see quite sharply that, in marrying a man, you married not only him, but his family and even his friends. It occurred to her to wonder if Chris's friends would like her and if she would like them. She had not fitted in too well with the people she had met out at the airport. And Mac Conway had terrified her the time he had played dragon over the telephone. She was even a little fearful about producing her own friends for Chris to meet.

Ginger, for instance. Her liking and admiration for Ginger increased the longer she knew her. But what if Chris thought her silly and empty-headed and did not look beneath the surface for the kindly qualities that were there?

Everything had been perfect that night on the ferry and she had so wanted to keep it that way. Keep the closeness that had existed between them and not let it be spoiled by outsiders. But you couldn't live like that. The world came in whether you wanted it to or not.

Her interview with her aunt had been surprising. Peggy Pope had taken the news in a resigned but unenthusiastic fashion at first. Her expression said plainly that she had been afraid of this from the first moment she had seen Chris.

"We all have to decide what we want most from life," she told Marel. "I've decided for myself and you have the right to decide for yourself."

"But I'm not giving up my work," Marel protested.

Her aunt shook her head pityingly. "I know you think you're not, but I'm afraid you aren't facing facts realistically. It's hard enough now to work all day and come home and do your drawing at night. But at least you have no housekeeping here. No meals to get or floors to scrub. Your evenings are your own."

Marel had started to protest, but her aunt shrugged her aside. "I know. There's no use talking to a girl with stardust in her eyes. I know just how it feels."

"Do you?" Marel said. She had not meant the words as a challenge. It was difficult to imagine Peggy Pope's clear, steady gaze blurred by anything so impractical as stardust. Her aunt's quick response surprised her a little.

"You young people!" she said. "You always think no one but you has ever been in love."

"Of course I don't," Marel denied. "Anyone as attractive as you are——"

Her aunt went on as if she had not heard. "I came so close to marrying when I was twenty that I still gasp sometimes when I think of it. I suppose I felt about him the way you do about Chris. But there were other things I wanted more. He didn't fit into my plans just then."

"Have you always been glad you made the choice you did?" Marel asked softly.

Her aunt looked about her beautiful living room and there was an odd twist to her smile. "Not always. Sometimes it's very lonely. I suppose that's why I'm always filling it with dozens of people. Sometimes I wonder if dozens can ever be a substitute for one."

Marel was silent, a little embarrassed. This was a side of her aunt she had never seen before, had never suspected existed. Peggy Pope broke the awkwardness of the moment by going over to her writing desk and pulling out the chair.

"I'm going to write to your mother," she said. "I'm going to tell her what a fine young man Chris is. Don't worry about your parents—we'll talk them around to seeing it your way."

And so she had found a strong and unexpected ally in her aunt.

Ginger, of course, had been the one person heartily on Marel's side from the beginning. She had been satisfyingly surprised, delighted, and encouraging. And Marel loved her for it.

"Now you're doing the sensible thing!" said Ginger. "And don't you let anybody talk you out of it. I'm dying to meet him. Maybe we could arrange a double date."

So far Marel had avoided that. She had a feeling that Chris ought to get used to Ginger a little at a time. As she, perhaps, would have to get used to his friend Mac.

Fran Embree had been comfortably encouraging. "You can do what you set out to do if you're determined enough," had been her verdict. A remark which had brought a Bronx cheer from Gail. Gail had been the worst one of all—open in her derision, pointed in her comments about Marel's lack of intelligence.

"Here you are in the city of New York where there are plenty of men who make real money. And do you give yourself a chance to meet any of them? No! You go off and get moonstruck over the first boy who looks at you. And like all the other idiots before you, you think a diet of moonbeams is going to make you happy. What's more, you're crazy if you think this won't finish you as an artist. The world isn't made so a woman can swing marriage and a career at the same time."

Marel wished she could avoid Gail. It was difficult to have to work with her every day and listen to her scoffing until she was ready to scream. It wasn't that she had anything in particular against Chris, but just that she apparently resented the entire male sex and had no good word for any one of them. Enough money, she seemed to feel, might make a man worth putting up with, but no other quality counted.

There was one person who still had not heard the news. Eric Webb. Eric was out of town again, and for Marel that was a momentary relief. There was no telling how he would receive the news.

"You'd think I was marrying half the town," Marel told the pictured little girl who was reluctantly emerging on the paper beneath her pencil. "If people would just let you work out your own life——"

"Marel." Her aunt's voice called her away from her work. "Chris is here. He says to get on your things and come running."

That sounded exciting and she put the drawing board aside without regret. Her work would probably never come right if she sat there all night when she was in a mood like this. Ordinarily Chris was all too considerate about not interrupting her work. He made dates with her ahead of time and avoided calling her on evenings when he knew she would be working. That he would break in like this meant something unexpected had happened.

"Don't get too hopeful," he told her on the way down in the elevator, "but I've got a lead on an apartment. Some people are moving out and want to sublease. It's down in the Village and the rent wouldn't be too much. I've got the tip from a friend who lives in the same building, and there's just a chance that if we move fast enough we might land it."

They moved as fast as a subway and their own feet would carry them and arrived breathlessly before a building of "walk-ups." The possibility wasn't very high up— just the third floor, and they both rang the bell at the same time. For luck.

The man who came to the door was friendly and seemed to like them on sight. He excused the disorder the little apartment was in, due to the unexpected move they were making which necessitated hurried packing.

"My wife isn't in right now," he said, "but you can have a look."

So they looked, and Marel's yearning to have the cheery little place for her very own began to grow. The living room was comfortable in size and so was the kitchen. The bedroom was small, but papered attractively. There was no dearth of windows, and the apartment would be bright and cheerful during the day.

"We've got to have it," Marel whispered to Chris, and he nodded in agreement.

She could see how it would work out. A corner of the bedroom could be fixed up with a desk and Chris's typewriter, and she could have her drawing things in the kitchen. When they both came home from work evenings, they wouldn't have to be apart as they were now. They would be working together—and what a wonderful feeling of comradeship that would be! Just to know that she could cross a small hall and look in a door to see Chris at his typewriter. Or if he got lonesome for her, he could come out in the kitchen and see how her work was going. Maybe he'd have a snack out of that shining little refrigerator and talk to her awhile before he went back to his typewriter.

Her mental pictures were so real she could hardly wait.

"I'd like you folks to get it," the occupant said when they'd finished their tour of inspection. "But I'll have to wait till Ann comes in. I expect her any minute. Why don't you sit down and I'll go on wrestling with these books I'm packing."

So they sat down on the little davenport that might very soon be theirs, since the place was rented furnished. Already in her mind's eye Marel could see changes she'd want to make. These people weren't setting their things off to the best advantage. A switching about of chairs and lamps would help. And of course pictures of their own, little things, possessions that would make the place theirs for as long as they were in it.

It seemed almost too good to be true. Were Mr. and Mrs. Christopher Mallory really going to live here? Were they going to be as lucky as this, when thousands of people out there in Manhattan were unable to find homes?

"Ann" came in before long and seemed a little startled to see them. Her husband introduced them as prospective tenants and his wife shook her head wearily.

"I'm terribly sorry. I suppose I should have left a note, but I didn't think anybody else knew about the place. I rented it this morning to some people a friend sent over."

So that was that. Marel pushed the furniture mentally back into its awkward set-up and went quietly down the two flights of stairs at Chris's side. The disappointment was bitterly hard to take. To get that close and then be turned down!

Chris tucked her hand through his arm as they walked along and gave it a little squeeze. "That was tough, honey. But there'll be other places. Next time we'll be luckier. At least this was a nibble. That's something. It shows there are places."

But Marel's gloom only deepened. It wasn't fair! When two people loved each other and wanted to get at the important matter of working out their lives together, it was all wrong to be stopped by such a silly thing as not being able to find a place to live! Being married ought to be all burnished gold. So many little tarnishing things seemed to be dulling the shine.

"Let's take a bus," Chris said. "There's no need for a subway rush now. Unless you're anxious to get back to work."

Marel shook her head. "I can't work tonight. Things won't come right."

"I know," Chris said. "It's like that with me, too, sometimes when the words won't come."

It was nice having someone whose work was like enough to hers so that he understood. Everything seemed to augur well—if only they could solve this one tough problem. She looked up at lighted windows—row upon row above their heads. All those lucky couples who had homes. The lamplight seemed so warm and friendly that it emphasized the loneliness of the night outside.

They turned a corner and came to a stop because their

path was blocked. Blocked by—of all things—a wedding party. The church doors stood open and a crowd had gathered to watch the bride come down the steps to a waiting limousine.

Chris and Marel stood where they were, watching. She was a very young bride, Marel saw, as the girl came down the church aisle and out to the head of the steps. She walked proudly, with her hand on her husband's arm, and her eyes were shining with happiness. Bridesmaids flocked out after her, gay in flowery pink dresses.

Marel's heart got into her eyes as she watched. This was a wedding with trimmings. The sort of wedding little girls dreamed about when they were still in doll-playing days. The sort of wedding Marel Gordon could not have because it would cost a lot of money, and neither Chris's family nor hers could afford to spend money like that. But it was the sort of wedding she'd dreamed about long before she met Chris.

The bride vanished into a big car and her husband got in after her. The bridesmaids ducked into other cars and the party set off down the avenue—to a reception somewhere else. The crowd broke up and wandered off. The sidewalk was only a sidewalk now—not a magic carpet to another girl's happiness.

Chris and Marel walked past the church door in silence and Marel did not turn her head to glance in.

"I suppose they even have a home to go to after the honeymoon," she said.

Chris's silence made her look up, and she was sorry at once for her words. He looked stern again, the way he did when he was going to do something for her own good. And she had begun to dread having things done for her own good.

"I'm making you miss a lot of things a girl prizes," Chris said. "I don't blame you for feeling that bride is a lot luckier than you are."

Marel would not let him go on. "Luckier than I? How silly! I'm sorry for her, really."

"Sorry for her?"

"Of course. She doesn't have you, does she?"

They laughed together, and all the hurt and disappointment was eased. Chris's eyes were warm with affection as he looked down at her.

"I'm afraid you haven't much sense, Red Feather," he said, "but I do love you."

10

A Row of Twigs

They sat on a rocky ledge and swung their legs over the side of a deep canyon that was a highway with cars speeding along at the bottom. The bushes and trees of Central Park shut out the tall buildings and here they could be almost alone. It was midsummer now and the evenings were long and light.

"But *we're* going to be different," Marel said. "We're not going to make all those silly mistakes people keep warning us about." She broke off, and watched the flying cars for a moment before she went on. "Do you suppose everyone who gets married thinks the same thing? So many marriages do seem to go on the rocks these days. I wonder if those couples were sure they could make a success too?"

Chris considered soberly. "We might as well face it that we're trying something extra hard. You want to keep on as an artist, which makes things that much tougher."

"You sound like all the others!" Marel protested. "I've been hearing that on every side—from Mother and Dad, from Aunt Peg, and of course from Gail. Even from Fran. Do *you* think I ought to give up the thing I want to do?"

"Of course not." His answer came reassuringly and without hesitation. "There are lots of women today who are proving they can have successful marriages and do an outside job too. Let's make you one of them. At least we're willing to think ahead." Chris broke a long twig into even pieces and laid one of them down on the rock between them. "Let's make a check list. Take a memo, Miss Gordon."

Marel turned to a fresh page in her ever-present sketch book. "Yes, sir," she said, pencil poised.

"Let's begin with the things we know are going to be tough at first. Like coming home at night tired and having to get meals, do dishes, keep house."

"That's my worry," Marel said. "But I don't think it will be so bad. I think I'll love it in *our* place."

"Novelty wears off," Chris pointed out. "After a while it will be just a chore. There had better be a fair division of labor at home."

Marel wrote down *Fair division of labor* and smiled to herself. Chris *was* different. Gail had said, "Wait till you have to work all day and then come home to the lion's share of housework—because your husband doesn't think that's a man's job."

"Maybe we can take turns at different chores," Chris went on. "I'm not such a bad cook. While one of us is getting dinner, the other fellow can be straightening up the apartment."

Marel refrained from saying, "What apartment?" and asked instead, "Who washes dishes?"

"Mm," Chris frowned judicially. "Now there's something I don't like, but——"

"Then I'll do it," Marel offered eagerly. "I won't have you doing things you don't want to do."

He patted her hand. "Don't be reckless with your offers, my good woman. You'll be doing a lot of things you won't be crazy about either."

"Okay, then. Let's say the fellow who gets dinner doesn't have to do dishes. We'll divide up the week, so nobody does dishes every night."

"Agreed," said Chris, and Marel scribbled industriously on her pad.

"One of our biggest problems," Chris went on, "will be arranging time to get in our own work. I mean my writing and your drawing."

"We'll put ourselves on schedule," Marel said promptly.

"So much time for dinner and dishes, and then to work. We'll have separate offices and keep out of each other's hair that way. I'll take a corner of the kitchen and you can have the bedroom or the living room. At the same time every night we get to our jobs."

"Not every night. You know—all work and no play. One night a week we take off and do the town."

"Spending all of fifty cents, I suppose," Marel said. "I'm afraid we aren't going to have much money left over for having fun."

"Not on our salaries, maybe, but that's the advantage we have over lots of couples. Either my book or yours will start bringing in royalties and that will make things easier."

"You said you needed a new overcoat," Marel reminded him. "If there's anything extra, it will have to go for clothes."

Chris dropped another bit of twig in the row, tabulating in his own way. "The park's free. Buses don't cost much."

"And there's always the Staten Island ferry," Marel added, writing down, *Recreation once a week.* "Just the same, I *would* like to have dinner at the Blue Peacock just once before I'm ninety-eight."

Chris chuckled, and dropped another marker in the row. "Women! Achievement always gets measured by going some place and eating an expensive meal. Never mind. We'll go to the Blue Peacock when I win that prize. I promise!"

Marel clasped her hands about her knees and pulled them up so she could rest her chin against them. "I know it seems silly to you. It's just that—that I've never been to a place like this Blue Peacock. I suppose it is silly to spend money that way, but——" She gave up trying to explain. The Blue Peacock was near Fran's studio, and she passed the place every day on her way to work. Her aunt dined there fairly often, thought it was nothing special in her life. Somehow the swank little restaurant had come to be a symbol in Marel's mind. A symbol of the sort of thing she was cut off from now. Some day she and Chris would be successful and well known and they'd dine in places like that with their friends. Mr. and Mrs. Christopher Mallory entertained——

"Daydreaming?" Chris asked. "Come on back. We haven't finished our list of pitfalls yet. What's the next dragon we have to watch out for?"

"This isn't a marriage-career problem," Marel said, "but I think husbands and wives could be a lot more polite to each other. I mean they do snap sometimes. They can be courteous to strangers and outsiders and then not bother about being polite to each other. Chris, let's not quarrel! Let's not hurt each other's feelings."

"I hope we won't," Chris said. "But I doubt if any two human beings ever lived together in complete amicability. But maybe it is a marriage-career problem in a way, because, with each of us holding outside jobs, we may get extra tired sometimes. And tiredness makes for raw nerves."

"Then let's allow for that and be extra patient and considerate. If we try to get the other fellow's viewpoint instead of just our own——"

"Looks like I've picked myself the right kind of wife." There was affection in his eyes again. "Understanding is a pretty good foundation to build a marriage on. Did you write down *Dinner at the Blue Peacock?* Whoever gets the first break treats the other."

"Agreed!" Marel cried, and scribbled another line on her pad. "Now let's talk about expenses. Chris, I want to take on my share. I'm working, and it isn't right for you always to pay my way and yours too."

He looked a little unhappy over that. "Maybe that's only a convention, but a man does like to be able to take care of his wife."

"That would be all right if I was just going to be a housewife. But I'm going to be an earner, Chris. Some day I'm going to earn a lot. I don't want to wait for that.

though. The convention's already old-fashioned. It belongs to the days when girls never worked. I'd like to start splitting expenses right now, even before we're married. That's the fair way, and I think fairness between us is the most important thing of all."

There was a way he had of looking at her sometimes. He did it now. First he looked up at the sky as if he was interested only in how late it was getting to be. Then he looked down at the cars speeding by in the canyon below as if their movement fascinated him. After that he looked all around at everything else in sight as if he had forgotten she was there. Then the circle of his interest narrowed down until suddenly he was looking only at her, and for that small moment she knew she was the center of his world. When he looked at her that way, it was as if he had kissed her very tenderly. It was the sort of moment that made her happy clear through. It made happiness something she could feel, as she could feel hot and cold. Then the moment was gone. It could not be held, ever. But it would come again. It always did.

He had run out of twigs, and he picked up another to break into markers, quite matter-of-fact again.

"There's another problem we have to work out," he said. "Right now we're content enough to be alone and leave other people out of the picture. But do you realize we don't even know whether you'll like my friends or if I'll like yours?"

"I've thought of that," Marel said. "I'm not a bit sure you'll like Ginger, and I'm not sure I'm going to like your Mac."

"Mac's okay. You couldn't dislike him. And everything you say about Ginger sounds swell. Anyway, we do have to get together some mutual friends and see how we click. I've known married couples who couldn't stand each other's friends. That means going separate ways, and we don't want that."

Marel put down, *Make mutual friends,* on her list.

"There's another thing too, Chris. Our families. What if your mother doesn't like me? That letter you had from her wasn't very encouraging, was it?"

His mother had written, finally, but he had not shown her the letter. He had seemed a little dispirited for a day or two after it came, but then he'd shrugged the effects of it aside and had not mentioned it again. But she knew his mother must have set herself against his marriage to Marel Gordon. As she had set herself against that girl at the airport—Sally Foster? Had Chris wanted to marry Sally? He had never told her about that and she had not dared to ask. In fact, she wasn't sure she wanted to know. Anyway, he seemed to be holding out against his mother's disapproval this time.

"Don't worry about Mother," he said. "She's out in California and she probably won't be coming this way very soon. Once we're married, she'll get used to the idea. But that is a point, Marel. It's got to be you for me, and me for you, from now on. We can't allow anybody to cut between us. Not even our own families. We stand by each other, see?"

That made her feel a great deal better, and she wrote, *Stand by each other—no matter what.*

"We'd better be getting back," he said and started to sweep away the little row of twigs he had laid out.

Marel caught his hand in time. "Wait!" she said. Bit by bit she picked them up, laughing a little as she did so. "I want these." Into her coin purse they went, and she did not mind how foolish or sentimental he thought her. Somehow those twigs stood for a pact between them. They represented the separate items of the partnership they'd entered into that evening. Perhaps some day she might want to take those twigs out and look at them for a reminder. They would bring back this evening when they'd worked out the plan for a sort of marriage agreement—a promise to hold the future safe.

As she picked up the last twig, Chris reached for the

list she had written and tore it from the book. "You can have the markers. I'll keep this," he said.

They walked back across the park, hand in hand, and caught an open-topped bus where they could ride down the avenue with the summer breeze cooling their faces.

Chris came up with her in the elevator, to be met in Aunt Peg's apartment by a bombshell which exploded practically in his face the minute he stepped through the door. It was Ginger, and Marel, dismayed, had no time to introduce him. Ginger took care of that herself.

"You're Chris Mallory, aren't you? Oh, Marel, he *is* nice! Why didn't you tell me how good-looking he is? Heavens, I've been having kittens all over the place. I thought you'd never get here. Where on earth have you been? And me with an apartment for you and practically fighting off all New York so you could get to see it first."

Marel forgave her everything on the spot. Chris could straighten out the jumble, manage any embarrassment he might feel, and get used to Ginger as best he could. If she had found an apartment for them, nothing else mattered.

"Where?" Marel demanded. "Ginger, stop chattering and talk sense. Do you mean you really know about an apartment?"

"Of course! What do you think I'm talking about? I've been camped here for an hour and a half. You ought to let people know where you're going. It's in my building, and I've been taking care of the janitor's kids when he had to go out, so his wife's indebted to me and she's going to make him make the building manager let you have the apartment because you're my friends and I talked her into it. That is, if you want it."

"Do we want it!" Marel echoed. "Come on, Chris, what are we waiting for?"

On the way over, Ginger got her tongue straightened out a bit and her excitement under control. It was not, she explained, a very good apartment. But maybe it would do till they could find something better. If her own family would stand for it, she would marry Ken and take it herself. But she still had to wait out a whole loathsome year.

If it was an igloo, a shack, a tent, they'd take it, Marel decided. If they could just be together, anything would be all right. But in spite of her willingness to put up with anything that had a roof and a door, the apartment was a little dispiriting to view.

It was nothing like the Greenwich Village place which had so won her heart. There wasn't even a separate kitchen to this. Some doors at one end of the room opened upon various contraptions that pulled down and opened out to reveal a sink and stove and a row of cabinets. This was definitely a one-room apartment. There was a bathroom and a fair-sized closet that was partly occupied by a bed that would roll out into the room at night.

There was a window in the bathroom and two in the living room, all opening upon an alley two floors below. The previous occupants had not been fussy about cleanliness and the place was dingy and grubby. As Marel looked into the "kitchen," a cockroach ran across the sink.

Chris was already shaking his head. "This won't do. We wouldn't have space to breathe. It was swell of you, Ginger, but I'm afraid——"

Marel shut the sliding door upon the fleeing cockroach and faced staunchly about. Never mind if some of her dreams were getting a bit raveled about the edges.

"Chris," she said, "it would be a way to make a start. It isn't much, but we needn't be here all our lives. It's dirty, but it can be cleaned. It won't take much furniture, so we can get fairly decent things."

"There's stuff that will polish off cockroaches," Ginger offered, eager to help the course of romance. "And goodness knows when you'll get another place if you pass this one up."

That was the main selling point, even with Chris. But he made one last protest.

"What about those separate offices we were going to

have? How are we going to get our work done in one room?"

"We can manage somehow," Marel insisted. "I'm not doing so well, now, just for worrying about how things are going to turn out. There won't be as many interruptions, once we're married."

So it was settled. They went down to see the janitor and from there to call on the building manager. A lease would be ready for them in a day or so.

Marel had an uncontrollable skipping tendency in her toes all the way back to her aunt's apartment. Now she could really believe she was going to be married. Now they could set the date for the wedding.

11

Present from Eric

The date was set for early September and the intervening weeks were filled with a bustle of preparation. Second-hand furniture stores were haunted for necessary items. Decorative and useful bargains were pounced upon with glee and gloating by the bride-to-be. One of her finds was a really graceful pottery lamp with only a bit of chip where it wouldn't show (with its back to the wall) and a faded parchment shade which her paint box soon had looking better than new. Aunt Peg had come generously across with the gift of a really good sofa and some spending money besides, and Marel's parents had sent enough linens to give them a start. There had even been a gift of kitchen utensils from Chris's mother.

The little apartment was scrubbed to shining brightness and Chris and Marel both turned to and added liberal doses of paint where it was most needed. The wallpaper, even when cleaned, was on the depressing side, but there would be enough gay touches to relieve its dull, faded hues. Though there were a few small disagreements about furnishings.

Chris, Marel discovered, had an unexpectedly ascetic streak. He liked things stripped practically to a battleship order of utility. "Cluttery" was the word he had for Marel's squirrel-like fondness for possessions, for splashes of color and general frivolity.

"But we've got to make it look as if somebody lived here!" she wailed when he turned thumbs-down on her choice of flowered curtains.

"Don't worry," Chris assured her; "in that amount of space it's going to look as if an army lived there without our helping it along. Honey, let's try something a bit more tailored and simple. It will make the room seem bigger, instead of pulling it together the way that ballet-skirt stuff will do."

Marel gave in without further protest. The thing to do with a husband was keep him happy, and when the curtains of his choice were up, she had to admit that they gave the room a touch of gracious dignity it badly needed. True, they were more expensive than those she had wanted, but they would probably wear a lot longer, and it gave her a special feeling of satisfaction to please him. In turn, he was willing to compromise and let her have the slightly giddy dishes on which her heart was set.

"It's probably the children's-book influence coming out in you," he told her, laughing a little over her enthusiasm for the bright pattern. "I take it the young like their color slapped around with a lavish brush."

Even he had to admit, though, that when the cabinet doors were opened at the end of the room, the row of gay dishes made a sort of exclamation point that brightened an otherwise drab set of shelves.

The wonderful part was that it seemed to be give-and-take with them all the way down the line, with each going a lot more than halfway when it came to giving. That was the way it should be. That was the way to build. And most of the time their tastes, their likes and dislikes, fitted practically into the same pattern, and the more one discovered about the other, the better satisfied they both were.

The wedding had been set for a Friday afternoon. One day was all either could very well take away from work. The honeymoon would last all of one weekend and they would both have to be back on their jobs by Monday morning. Chris's friend, Mac Conway, had proved himself a friend indeed. Marel was still a bit doubtful about and a little dismayed by his outspoken manner. The first time he had met her he'd told her just what a writer's wife ought to be and he seemed to overlook entirely the fact that she wanted to be an artist as well as a wife.

However, he had a cabin up in Connecticut, where he ran away sometimes to finish a book when the town began to crowd in on him too much. The place was hardly more than a shack, he warned them, but the country thereabouts would be pleasant in September and it would at least give them a chance to get away from New York. What was more, he had offered them the use of his roadster to make the trip. Marel had rearranged some of her views about Mac Conway and thanked him warmly. It would be wonderful to go up to Connecticut for a honeymoon weekend away from everyone in the world but Chris.

The minister who would marry them was a friend of Chris's too, and Marel liked him at once. Chris took her over for a call one evening a couple of weeks before the wedding. He was young, and he had just gone into his own small church in an outlying neighborhood. They would be married there, and Marel liked the idea of a church wedding, even if the phrase did not mean an elaborate affair. Aunt Peg would come, of course, and Fran Embree. Mac Conway had agreed, protesting violently at first, to be best man. Marel had invited Gail, but the Norris female, as Eric called her, had flatly refused to be seen anywhere near a wedding so foolish as she considered this match to be. Nevertheless, she had gone out and spent a sizable sum on a dream of a negligee for Marel.

"You're so busy spending everything on pots and pans that you're forgetting about being beautiful for your man," she told Marel crossly. "That's important too. No after-marriage slump when it comes to how you look around the house! And don't you forget it. You don't have to cook in your best clothes, but no uncombed locks and no face like an unmade bed. Understand?"

Marel had said meekly that she understood, but she felt that she needed no tips of that kind. Personal neatness came first on her list of "musts," and she did not mean to have Chris faced by an untidy wife, even at breakfast.

Eric Webb was the odd one when it came to figuring out his reactions. Marel had broken the news to him somewhat timidly when he had come back to town and he had taken it with complete indifference. She had added hastily that getting married wasn't going to interfere with her work and that Chris wanted her to keep on with her class.

Eric looked as interested as if she had announced that she was going to have boiled potatoes for supper.

"Of course you'll keep on with your class," he told her. "You want to be an artist, don't you?"

She had said that she did—and that was that. The wedding preparation flurry, that affected even the activity of the Embree Studio, touched him not at all. The female chatter, the consultations, the accounts of bargains discovered, were all so many lapping little waves that moved not a grain of sand on the Gibraltar rock of Eric's consciousness. He scolded Marel about not working as hard at her drawings as she should, and seemed willing to allow her not a moment off because of so unimportant a matter as getting married.

Then, the day before the wedding, he sprang a surprise. He asked her to have lunch with him. She was leaning over a drawer of the filing cabinet when he stopped beside her and proffered the invitation. Marel looked up in surprise and he smiled his unexpectedly kindly smile.

"After all, it's my last chance before you're a married woman," he said. "And I do want to talk to you."

She was a little embarrassed and completely at a loss. It wasn't that Chris would mind her lunching with him. One of the things Chris and she had talked about was freedom of action for each of them. No possessiveness, no jealousy. If it so happened that Marel wanted to lunch with some man of her acquaintance, or if Chris wanted to take a woman friend of his out for luncheon—each was to feel perfectly free. Mutual trust was terribly important, they had both agreed. But the way Marel felt she didn't want to lunch with any man but Chris just now. Other men did not really exist for her. Chris, being a man, seemed perfectly aware of any pretty girl who went by, but for her it wasn't like that. She had a blind spot where all other men were concerned. She would much rather not accept Eric's invitation, yet she did not know how to refuse gracefully. Never before in the weeks of their student-teacher association had Eric ever seemed to see her as anything but an animated paintbrush.

"That's awfully nice of you," she told him. "But I— that is, I'd meant to do some last-minute shopping on my lunch hour and——"

"No excuses," he said cheerfully. "Fran will give you extra time off later this afternoon if you need it. But today you're having lunch with me. How about going over to the Blue Peacock?"

She shook her head with a determination that must have surprised him. "Oh, no! I couldn't! I mean—well, it would take so long to eat there. Couldn't we go some place where it would be quick and——"

"An automat, maybe?" he asked dryly.

He looked as if his feelings were a little hurt and she felt unhappy over that. He had been awfully good to her and had shown her much more patience than she probably deserved. It had not been kind almost to snap at him like that. Now she didn't know what to say.

But he settled the matter himself. "All right. If you have a special aversion to the Blue Peacock, we'll go some place else. Go put on your red feather and we'll be on our way."

She could not explain that the Blue Peacock was a place she was saving to go to with Chris when one of them had earned a real check. Eric wouldn't understand senti- mentality like that. So she let the whole thing go and went meekly to put on her hat. Probably there was a reason behind this unexpected invitation, but being Eric, he'd get around to it in his own way.

In the end he took her to a nicer place than those where Chris and she usually dined, but she had no special interest in her surroundings, no particular taste for the delicious food and excellent service, because the man across the table wasn't Chris. After all, tomorrow she was being married, and to focus any attention at all just now on another man was beyond her power.

Eric was in a conversational mood and seemed to be enjoying the sound of his own voice, and she was relieved to find that she wasn't expected to hold up her own end of the talk. An occasional nod at what she hoped was an appropriate place seemed to serve well enough.

Her mind was miles away running over a thousand details. The new hat that was another present from Aunt Peg would be ready by tomorrow morning, her aunt had assured her. She herself would put on the finishing touches and it was going to become Marel as no other hat ever had.

"Tomorrow! Tomorrow!" her heart kept singing all through a meal she scarcely knew she was eating. Mrs. Christopher Mallory. There couldn't be a name in the world more satisfying to own than that. Marel Mallory. That was nice too. It went together. That would be the name she would use in Ginger's book—if ever she and Ginger got it done. Right now Ginger was way ahead of her and the drawings were just poking along. It was a good thing Ginger understood perfectly and did not mind the delay.

"Marel Mallory, the well-known children's artist, you know." That was the way people would refer to her. She wouldn't be one of those women who clung persistently to her own name. The thought of taking Chris's name from now on and making herself known under it filled her with bliss.

"So you see," Eric Webb was saying over his serving of apple pie, while Marel nibbled uninterestedly at a dish of vanilla ice cream, "if you're really willing to buckle down, it looks as if you may see publication by spring of next year."

She came out of her dreams with a jerk and stared at him. "Publication by spring?" she echoed feebly.

"I didn't think you'd heard a word I'd said for the last half hour," Eric told her testily. "And after all the trouble I've gone to find you a publisher!"

"Find me a publisher? Eric! I'm sorry. I—I was thinking about something else. Tell me and I'll listen."

"I've got a good mind to call the whole thing off," Eric went on, scowling at the wedge of apple pie. "This, my ungrateful wench, was supposed to be your wedding present from that slave-driver of an Eric Webb. I was even naïve enough to think you might like it dressed up in the wrappings of a special luncheon celebration."

"Oh, Eric!" Marel wailed. "I *am* sorry. And I'm the worst drip ever. It's just that—well——"

He forgave her with his nice smile. "I know. A girl doesn't get married every day. A good thing, too. Okay. I'll tell you all over again. I got as much of the manuscript from Peg as your friend Ginger turned in, and I took the set of pictures you left at the studio for me, and I showed the whole thing to one of my publishers last week. Fran said to go ahead, and if I didn't land anything for you, she'd take over where I left off.

"Anyway, Anita Johnson, children's book editor of James MacLane Company, took it home with her. And she phoned me the next day to say she liked what I'd shown her and wanted to see the rest. If it holds up, she'll have a contract for you. They've done three of my books and they do a good job."

Marel was too excited to thank him properly. She could only sigh, "Oh, Eric!" again and beam at him happily across the table. Unexpectedly he reached out and squeezed her hand.

"You're a good kid, Marel. And you're a hard worker. If anybody can swing the trick of balancing marriage and a career at the same time, I think you can. And don't pay any attention to what that Norris female tells you. But it won't be easy. I've gone softy today, but the minute you get back to the job next week, I'm going to crack a whip that will sting if you don't get on at a faster pace with the rest of the pictures. Anita says she can't give you more than a month to finish the job if she's to get the book out by late spring."

"A month!" Marel echoed in dismay.

"It's not a chance you can afford to pass up. MacLane is too big a house. Most beginners don't get an opportunity like that."

"I know, Eric. And I'm so grateful I don't know what to say."

"Never mind the words. Thank me with some work."

She nodded resolutely. "I will, Eric, I've just *got* to do it. It will mean such a lot to Chris and me. I'm glad he has his own work too. He'll understand if I have to be a neglectful wife for a few weeks."

She could hardly wait to get back to the office and telephone Ginger at the library. Ginger's squeals made the receiver ring and must have brought shushes from the other librarians. Before hanging up, Marel swore her to secrecy. She had no intention of having Ginger spill out the wonderful news to Chris before she did.

It would be all she could do to keep it to herself for another twenty-four hours, but she wanted it to be the very first present she would give Chris as his wife. With a contract would come a money advance and they could certainly use that. Chris would be proud of her too. He was as ambitious for her as he was for himself. Really, he was a much better writer than she was artist, and it would never do for him to succeed while she lagged behind. She would have to keep pace with him, be worthy of his success when it came, by matching it with success of her own.

Courage and determination were like bright flames within her all that day.

12

"And So They Were Married . . ."

You expected a wedding ceremony to be the high moment of your life. You thought ahead of time of how exalted you'd feel, how filled with love for the man you were going to marry. The solemn words the minister spoke would carry a ring of deep meaning, and when you said the words, "I do," you'd be uttering a promise you meant to keep sacred.

That's the way you thought it was going to be. But when it really happened, you were too frightened and jittery to savor it the way you'd expected to. Instead of moving slowly and solemnly toward the moment when the minister uttered his final pronouncement that would make her Chris's wife, everything seemed to flash by for Marel like a speeded-up movie, so that she could not digest it as it happened. And afterward she couldn't remember any of it very clearly.

She could remember the way her voice squeaked into a high note when she didn't mean it to and the way Chris's hand shook when he slipped on the ring. Then it was over, and Ginger was hugging her, while Aunt Peg looked misty-eyed, and Mac Conway pumped Chris's hand and told him for gosh sakes now to get back to his typewriter.

She could hardly recall leaving the church and getting into Chris's borrowed car, everything seemed to happen in such a breathless rush. Once she had a crazy impulse to reach out as if she could stop time with her two hands and say, "Wait! I want to know what my own wedding is like. If you go so fast I won't be able to remember."

Days later, she asked Ginger if everything had gone at an unusual rate of speed and Ginger said, "No." So probably it was simply her own jittery and confused state that kept what was happening from seeming clear-cut.

Not until she and Chris were in Mac's car together and they pulled out into the stream of New York traffic did the world stop flying by and settle down to a more ordinary pace. Not until then could she really believe that it was over and she was married to Chris.

When they stopped for a light, Chris looked around at her. "You're very beautiful this afternoon, Mrs. Mallory. I like the hats you wear."

She knew then that her new beige and brown outfit was a success and she leaned her cheek against his shoulder for an instant to thank him for that "Mrs. Mallory."

"Happy?" he asked.

She just said "Mm-mm" lingeringly, but she knew it was enough answer and that he was happy too.

Aunt Peg had wanted them to come back to her apartment after the wedding, but they'd both vetoed that ahead of time. The drive to Mac's place in Connecticut was a long one, and neither had any desire to stand around making conversation with a lot of friends, however nice they might be. Their honeymoon time was all too short as it was.

At sundown they stopped for dinner at an attractive roadside inn. A waitress led them to a small corner table where the lamplight was soft and music from a radio drifted down the room. A girl was singing "Night and Day," and Marel knew that always when she heard the song she would remember this lovely moment here with Chris when being Mrs. Mallory was a very new and wonderful thing.

Now she could make the promises she could not think of when the minister was speaking the words of the wedding ceremony. She could make them to him with her eyes as she met his gaze across the table, and she knew he was promising her too. Promising that moments like this would come again and again, when they were not two people, but one. Not with separate interests and ambitions and desires, but one for the other from now on.

This was the time to tell him what Eric had done for her. This was the time to share her first possibility of success and make it—not her success, but *theirs*.

"Chris," she said, "I've been waiting for the right moment to tell you. Eric Webb has found a publisher who wants Ginger's stories and my pictures. If we have them both ready in a month, I think the book will be published next spring."

His happiness for her, his pride was warm in his eyes. "I'm glad, Margaret Elizabeth. You deserve it too—you've worked plenty hard."

"I'll have to work harder than ever this month," she warned him. "Maybe I'll even have to neglect you to get this job done. Maybe I'm going to be a very unsatisfactory wife."

"I'd be a very unsatisfactory husband if I couldn't stand by and help out when you have a job as important as this to do. When that book comes out, I'll get such a swell head there'll be no living with me. I'll bet I'll act as if I drew every picture."

"You practically did," Marel told him. "If it hadn't been for you I might have given up in discouragement right at the beginning."

There was nothing quite so nice as having a husband to be proud of you, she thought happily. When his turn came and he sold his book, she'd be equally proud of him. She'd make him feel that having a wife to share his happiness with was something pretty nice too.

She said as much to him, eagerly, wanting him to understand her feeling in the matter, and was puzzled by the silence that fell upon him.

"What's the matter, Chris?" she asked. "Have I said the wrong thing?"

"Of course not." He shook his head to reassure her, but his attention seemed to have wandered away from her to the music of the radio and she was troubled by the way they seemed for a moment to lose the sense of closeness and understanding between them.

Then the disturbing instant passed and Chris was himself again. But she noticed that he did not return to the subject of her nearly accepted book.

When the pleasant meal was over and they were in the car again, driving through little towns that alternated with long stretches of rolling countryside, Marel made a further attempt. She did not want him to think her happiness over her book was completely selfish. She was just as eager for his success as she was for her own.

"Wait till you win the prize!" she told him. "My turn came first, but that's only an accident. My splash will be a very small one compared to the one you're going to make. And that's the way I want it to be, Chris."

He glanced at her quickly and then back at the road ahead. "What do you mean by that?"

She was a little surprised at his question. "Why—only that I want you to be tremendously successful. I want the very best for you. I think a husband *ought* to be—oh, I don't know how to say it."

"You mean you wouldn't want to be married to anyone who was a failure?"

That was a queer way to put it and seemed to have nothing to do with the case.

"I mean I want to be married to you," she said simply.

He squeezed her hand, but his attention was focused on the road. "We're coming to the turn any minute now. I've been up here with Mac and I know just about where it is. There's a white picket fence along the highway and then a side road——"

"There's a fence!" Marel cried.

"That's it." Chris swung the car into a dirt road that wound uphill between tall pines. It was getting dark now and they needed the headlights.

Below the road Marel could hear the rush of water from a shadowy ravine. The climb was bumpy, the road narrow, and every turn sharp. All Chris's attention was on his driving. It was a little breathless mounting the steep dark road that would take them to Mac's cabin. *Their* cabin for two heavenly days.

The car came out in a small clearing and Marel could see a small house ahead.

"Here we are," Chris said.

They got out of the car and Chris, loaded with bags, led the way to the rustic veranda that circled the cabin. But he would not let her go in at once. He put the bags down at the door without unlocking it, and led her around to the back of the house.

"I want you to have a glimpse of the view before the last light's gone. Do you see the little lake down there through the trees?"

She nodded happily. It was very beautiful. Pines all around, slanting downhill to the shine of water. The moon had come up above one tall pine and already the water's darkness was lightened by a touch of gold.

"If you're not too cold," Chris said, "I wish you'd wait here for me a few minutes. Do you mind?"

She did not mind. There was a chill September touch to the night, but her coat was warm, and there was a lovely feeling of anticipation just standing here looking down at the lake, savoring the beauty of the moment.

She smiled softly to herself, remembering what she had told Gail. A house on a hilltop, she'd said, with a fireplace and a view. That was what she wanted. Well, here it was. Maybe it was only borrowed for a couple of days—but it was something to keep forever through the years ahead. Later, when she and Chris had both made their mark, perhaps they'd own something like this together. Tonight, however, she had no wish to quarrel with Fate over the fact that it was only a loan.

She could hear Chris moving about in the house behind her and she wondered contentedly what he was doing. It was nice to have a husband to look after you, to get things ready for your comfort. She'd do her share of that too as soon as she could.

Then he came back and slipped an arm around her. "Come along now, Margaret Elizabeth. I wanted everything to look right before you came in."

It looked not only right—it was the final perfect touch. The cabin was small, but it boasted a stone fireplace at one end. Chris had set a fire of logs merrily blazing and he'd drawn Mac Conway's shabby but comfortable couch up before the hearth.

"Sit down and toast your toes, Mrs. Mallory," Chris said.

There was one little shadow between them that had to be erased before she could settle down wholeheartedly to watching the lively crackle of the fire, with her head on Chris's shoulder. There was still the strange thing he had said in the car.

"Chris, you're not going to be any failure," she told him. "Even if your book shouldn't win a prize in the contest, the publishers will probably want to print it anyway and——"

"They don't," Chris said shortly. "They don't want it at all."

She curled around on the couch to face him in dismay. "Chris! It didn't come back!"

"It did," he said. "Yesterday. Not only no prize, but no sale."

"What perfectly stupid idiots!" Marel cried, pounding her fists indignantly against the cushions of the sofa. "If their editors aren't smart enough to know a good book when they see one, they don't deserve to publish Christopher Mallory. Oh, Chris, I've read heaps of detective stories and yours is a thousand times better."

"I guess not," he said.

"You'll send it out again right away, won't you?"

"I don't know. Maybe it's no use."

She wanted to shake him. "Now you listen to me, Chris Mallory. I won't have a husband who gives up like that, any more than you'd have a wife who gave up because somebody told her she couldn't draw children."

A reluctant smile came back to his mouth. "Maybe you're going to be the successful one after all."

She wanted to cry she was so disappointed for him. And he had been such a good sport. He'd been properly happy about the chance her book was going to have, without intruding his own disappointment.

"Look, Chris," she went on, more quietly, "I believe in that book, if you don't. I'm going right after Fran and get you an introduction to Irene Allen. She's the woman I told you about who edits mysteries for Barrett, Brown. That manuscript's going to get published if I have to take it around to every office personally myself."

He pulled her close to him, so that her head found the hollow of his shoulder. "You know something, honey? It's good to have a wife. Especially when she's the kind of wife who won't let her husband give up. I'm ashamed of that fellow, Chris Mallory. Of course the book's going out again. I can't let you be the only success in this family."

It was lovely to watch the fire for a while in silence, just being together. As a log fell and sparks showered upward, a quiet realization came to Marel.

This was the moment she had been looking forward to. This was the place where all the storybooks ended: "And they lived happily ever after." Ever since she'd been a little girl she had read stories like that. "And so they were married——" That was the ending. That was all.

How foolish the storybooks were! No ending this, but the very beginning. The beginning of Mr. and Mrs. Christopher Mallory. Everything that had gone before was just the opening to the story. It was from now on that mattered. The hero and heroine didn't live happily ever after just by accident; they had to work and try with all their might.

Just because she had won the Prince did not mean that all the rest of Cinderella's days were spent wearing glass slippers to a ball. Probably there were times when the Prince got grumpy and things went wrong in the kingdom and he took it out on his family. Or times when Cinderella's children misbehaved, or got sick and things went wrong for her. It wasn't how you got along during the good times that mattered so much. It was how you behaved when everything went wrong. Winning the Prince was a small matter. It was *keeping* him that counted.

"Penny for your thoughts," Chris said.

But she would not tell him. There was no point in promising out loud to make him a good wife. That was something she meant to show him in deeds, not words. So she just snuggled her head more comfortably on his shoulder and smiled a little private smile to herself.

13

Home Girl

Marel had been Mrs. Christopher Mallory for two whole weeks. Tonight Chris was working late at a job that had to be finished at the office, so she had the tiny apartment to herself. She had not bothered about a proper dinner—just a few bites of this and that to keep going on. Maybe she'd have a late snack when Chris got home. Right now she would not even bother washing the few dishes she'd used. The whole evening stretched ahead of her, and tired though she was after a frantic day at the studio, she was eager to get to her drawings.

They were coming along beautifully. Even Eric had taken to beaming over them, instead of scowling, and Fran Embree had remarked that marriage certainly agreed with her. Gail sniffed and muttered, "You wait," under her breath, but Marel only laughed at her. Gail was a natural-born sourpuss—a Calamity Jane of the worst type, and Marel told her so.

She knew how happy she and Chris were, how perfectly everything was going. Now life had a meaning and aim it had never had before. They were working together. So what if they came home tired at night with jobs still to be done? They did them together and laughed. Or rather, Chris had been doing most of them. He was tops. He was all the things Gail had tried to tell her a husband wouldn't be.

"Look, honey," he had said when she had tried at first to take over her share of the domestic duties, "you have an important assignment on your hands right now. You

142

need to make every minute count. I'd be a heck of a husband if I didn't see that and pitch in and help. So you get to your drawing board and start setting the world on fire, and I'll cope with the dishes. Besides, I think I'm very fetching in your ruffly apron."

He looked so silly clowning around in blue gingham and organdy ruffles_that she laughed herself weak. But she loved him doubly for understanding and for wanting a big future for her as much as she wanted it for herself. While she worked at her drawings, she promised herself that she would make it up to him as soon as this job was done. Then it would be her turn to do dishes and dusting, and he could get more time for his writing.

She had been able to do nothing as yet about fixing up an introduction to Irene Allen. The editor was in Chicago visiting some authors with promising manuscripts. But Fran had promised an introduction as soon as she came home. Stuart Allen's book would be out in a couple of weeks and a big party was to be given for him. Marel and Chris would be invited—Fran had promised that— and there would be an opportunity for Chris to meet Irene informally and set the stage for a visit to her office with the manuscript of *Fear on the Ferry* under his arm.

She hummed happily to herself as she worked, wishing Chris would come home and get to his typewriter. They'd had three or four happy nights of working together and it had been wonderful to look up from her drawing board any time at all and see Chris across the room at his desk, his eyebrows quirked into peaks of concentration while he pecked at the keys. It had been fun to run over to him when her picture was going nicely and have him approve of what she'd done. Sometimes she didn't wait for the excuse of showing him her work, but stole up behind him, to lean her cheek against his and read what he had written over his shoulder. Then back she'd go to her own work, humming contentedly the while.

"Like a cat purring a tune," Chris said once as he

ripped a sheet of paper from the machine and wadded it into a ball to feed the yawning mouth of the wastebasket. Sometimes it seemed as though the wastebasket got more words than the story, but when she protested, he gave her a queer cross look she didn't understand and pushed away from the desk.

She would change all that as soon as she got these drawings done and her deadline out of the way. Then she could take over the housework and Chris could hurry to his typewriter the minute dinner was over. It would be fun to do dishes to the clatter of typewriter keys. Anything was fun with Chris right there in the same room.

Marel jumped as the doorbell shrilled. That bell always sounded like a fire alarm in their small apartment. It was Ginger, probably, and Marel was just as glad that Chris was not home. Not that he was ever anything but nice to her. He teased her and made her laugh, but Marel felt, nevertheless, that Ginger was turning into something of a problem.

Living in the same building made it too easy for her to drop in whenever the spirit moved her. She had finished her stories and seemed to think that the pleasantest way possible for her to spend an evening was to drop in and watch Marel draw. Marel did not want to be unkind, but she wished she could find some tactful way to hint that Chris might not be enthusiastic about his wife's friends around every single evening.

Marel went to the door determinedly. This would be a good chance to drop a few gentle hints to Ginger. Perhaps she could put it that she worked better without someone hanging over her shoulder—which was certainly true enough.

She pulled the door open with a "Hello, Ginger," on her lips, only to find Mac Conway grinning at her from the hall.

"Hi, Mrs. Rembrandt," he said.

He had nicknamed her that before the wedding, and

sometimes she felt the joke was wearing a bit thin.

"Hello, Mac," she said. "Chris isn't home yet. But come on in. He ought to be along in a half hour or so."

As a matter of fact, the last thing she wanted just then was to ask Mac in. Her work had been going swimmingly, and Mac was such a scorner. He gibed at everything. Chris said to pay no attention—that was just his way, but sometimes he got under her skin. However, if Chris could put up with Ginger, she could certainly put up with Mac. After all, if it had not been for him they would never have had a real honeymoon. She must remember that and be grateful.

He came ambling in and sent his disreputable gray felt whirling across to the sofa where it teetered on the back for a moment and slid off on the floor. Marel picked it up in silence, knowing from experience that if she did not it would remain where it fell until Mac was ready to leave. It was a mystery to her that Chris, who was himself as neat as a pin, had been able to share an apartment with Mac, who had no more sense of order than a magpie. But at least they had more than one room for the two of them.

Mac was what Chris termed a "big guy." He wasn't fat—just big. He went up and out, long and wide. When he sat down in their secondhand chairs, Marel always shuddered a little inside, half expecting the outraged legs to spread themselves in all directions and let him to the floor with a crash. But once more the chair he selected merely creaked a pained protest and held him up.

"Do you mind if I get back to work?" Marel asked, wondering if she could with Mac sitting there taking in every line she drew. What he knew about illustrating for children could be collected in a teardrop, but Mac never admitted his ignorance about anything. In fact, he took it calmly for granted that he knew more than the experts without even trying. And the maddening part of it was that he had a streak of brilliance that led him to shrewd and telling criticism, even on subjects about which he was completely uninformed.

"Chris had to stay at the office," Marel went on, picking her pencil again. "He's had a lot of late work the last few days. I hope it lets up pretty soon. He gets home all tired out."

Mac was looking at her in a disconcertingly fixed way and she began to wonder if she had pencil smudges on her nose, or if her hair was going in all directions. But she knew he liked to do that to people. He couldn't work it with Chris, because Chris never paid any attention. Once Marel had mentioned mildly to her husband that it was an annoying habit and Chris had said, "Ignore it. He only does it if he thinks it will get your goat. Mac's okay. And he's plenty smart. Wait till you really get to know him."

She went back to her humming habit while she attempted to concentrate on the picture that had been going so well until this interruption. But Mac's fixed stare made her feel all thumbs and she knew Mac knew it.

"Do you always do that?" he asked after a while.

"Always do what?" she asked blankly.

"Da-da-te-dum—that burbling-brook stuff."

"Burbling brook? Oh, that!" She dismissed it airily. "Of course I do. It helps me draw."

"I'm beginning to understand," he said. "Don't kid yourself, little girl."

She looked up startled. "Don't kid myself about what?"

"About Chris's working tonight. I knew he wouldn't be home. That's why I came over. To talk to you."

Dismay was like something that ruffled the skin of her arms. She was goose-pimply with it.

"What do you mean?" she asked. "How did you know he wouldn't be home?"

"How do you think? Because he's over at my place."

"At your place? Mac! What is it? Is anything wrong?"

Mac's grin had a laconic twist. "Not for you, Mrs.

Rembrandt. Yours is the career that's going to count in this family. Anyway, that's the way it looks. A red velvet carpet for you, with Chris running a sweeper up and down it so you won't trip over a mote of dust."

She tossed her pencil down helplessly. Work was impossible now. "I don't know what you're talking about, Mac. I don't know why Chris would say he was working and then go to your place. But if he sent you here, perhaps you'd better tell me what it's all about."

"Of course he didn't send me here. If you tell him I came, he'll probably knock my block off. Ever see Chris get mad? He doesn't do it often, but when it happens—look out!"

"Mac, please! If something's wrong, I want to know. Why *are* you here?"

"Okay," Mac said, "I'll tell you. I'm here because I happen to think Chris has a writing future. Not just as a detective-story scribbler, but in the novel field. This whodunit is finger exercises. Chris has a good book in him. A lot of good books. But under this present set-up he'll never get any of them down on paper."

"You mean because he isn't getting enough time for his work?"

"How much writing has he managed since he got married?"

That wasn't fair. She had done everything she could do to help him get to work. She had seen to it that his battered desk had been set up in the best possible place to get what light there would when he was home in the daytime. She had brushed his objections firmly aside when he had pointed out that it certainly didn't add much of an esthetic touch to the room. That desk was important to him and she had felt that it was part of her job to make everything as right for his work as possible.

She waved her hand at the desk now, but before she could speak, Mac cut in.

"Sure. You can bring the trough to the horse, but you

can't force him to drink. Writing is something you can't do in a public square. Not unless you were born in a newspaper office, and Chris wasn't. He's been standing on his ear to make everything right for you. But he can't work in the same room with you. So he clears out every chance he gets."

"I didn't know," Marel said. "I didn't dream——"

Mac snorted his scorn. "Women! A selfish lot—all of 'em. Out for their own ends, and never mind——"

But this time she would not let him finish. "That's not true. It's not fair. Chris wouldn't agree with you for a minute. This is an emergency job. I've got a deadline to make. Surely you can understand that. As soon as the pressure lets up, everything will be different."

"As soon as the pressure lets up, you'll look around for a job that will put it on again. It's the same for both of you. So maybe you'd better do something right away so Chris will have his chance too."

She almost hated him for the things he was saying, for cutting into her light-hearted happiness. Everything had been going along so beautifully. For her. But what he said was true. Chris had written practically nothing since they'd been married.

She made a limp gesture of discouragement with her hands. "If only we could find an apartment with even two rooms. But I don't think there's one in the entire city of New York. The worst of it is that apartment hunting takes time, too. And I can't stop to do that until this job is done."

"Maybe you can carry your drawing board some place else easier than Chris can lug a desk and typewriter around," Mac said. "What about going back to your aunt's evenings?"

"No," Marel said. "I won't do that."

He mimicked her maddeningly. "No indeedy! I won't do that," and she wondered how Chris could stand having him for a friend.

She could not explain to him that her aunt might take an arrangement like that as evidence that marriage and a career would never fit together satisfactorily. But she did not have to go to Aunt Peg's. There'd be some other way.

"I'll work it out, Mac," she assured him. "I don't like you much for telling me, but I guess I had to be told. I'll do something. Right away."

He picked up his bedraggled hat and started for the door. In the hallway he turned and gave her one of his long stares.

"Okay, Mrs. Rembrandt. I guess you've surprised me a little. I expected to get thrown out on my ear. Maybe you'll do, after all."

"I'm overcome by your praise, Mr. De Maupassant," she said, managing what she hoped resembled a gay smile. She kept it fixed on her lips until he was out of sight down the corridor. Then she closed the door and went back to hurl herself full length on the sofa.

The possibility of working was gone for good. She was too upset now. Too worried.

She would have to make a change immediately. She would have to get out of Chris's way so he could work. Suddenly she felt achingly tired. She felt hopeless and discouraged. Part of her energy had been coming from her happy eagerness, her confidence that she and Chris were going to get off on the right foot because he was being so understanding a husband. But if she was not being equally understanding as a wife, then she was failing in the very first weeks of her marriage. It did not matter that Chris pretended he didn't mind. That would wear thin in a hurry if his own desire to write was being turned aside because of her. She knew how she would feel if her instinct to draw had to be frustrated, defeated, postponed. There would be no living happily ever after in that.

Chris found her there on the sofa when he came in.

After one quick look at the empty place before the drawing board, he crossed the room and sat down beside her.

"What's the matter, honey? Been working too hard?"

She sat up and put her arms tight about his neck. She wasn't too good an actress and this *had* to be good. Maybe she could do a better job if he couldn't see her face.

"I don't know, Chris. The picture wouldn't come right tonight. I—I've been wondering——"

"Yes?" he prompted. "What is it? Tell Papa."

"Chris, would you mind very much if I tried to make some arrangement with Fran to go back to the studio every evening for a while until this job is done? I think I could work better there. You know—there's more of a— a drawing atmosphere."

"Why, of course I wouldn't mind," he said. "I can understand that a room can have a depressing effect. And this place is pretty much of a dump."

He sounded discouraged himself for the first time, and she could not have that.

"It is *not* a dump, Mr. Mallory. You're speaking of the home I love."

"You ought to have a studio to work in," he said.

"That would be very nice," she agreed. "And you ought to have a study. Is that what writers call their workrooms? But I don't think either of us can have what we want until we earn it. Maybe if I put in a stint at Embree's and you put in a stint here, we can both be working. What do you think?"

He took her arms from about his neck and held her away where he could look at her. "I think you're swell. I'll admit I've been getting a bit restless lately because I've wanted to get back to work. And it's true it isn't too easy to work with another person in the same room. In fact, I'll make a confession."

"Yes?" she said, though she knew perfectly well what was coming.

"I didn't stay at the office tonight. I went over to Mac's

and had a try pecking at his typewriter. But I can't do that often because he needs it to peck on himself. And besides, it doesn't feel like my old wreck. It works so well it scares off the ideas."

"We won't let that happen again," Marel said in a small voice. She wanted terribly to tell him the truth. To make her own confession and let him know that she had not seen the spot she was putting him in until Mac had pointed it out. There was a dishonesty about taking credit that wasn't due her. But if she told him the truth—then he'd probably be reluctant to shove her out of the apartment. And he would undoubtedly be annoyed with Mac besides. The important thing was to get him writing again, no matter how it was accomplished. At least her eyes were open now and she would see to it that they stayed open. He must never be given the feeling that because her book had an interested editor waiting for it, and his had been turned down, that his work was less important than hers.

She slipped matter-of-factly off the couch and stood up. "Now that our futures are settled, I'm hungry. How about a snack?"

Husbands, she had discovered, were always enthusiastic about snacks. Together they raided the tiny icebox, sliced rye bread and dipped into jams and cheese spread. They got in each other's way and dropped things and bumped into corners. And it was wonderful fun.

Let Gail have her nightclubs and expensive shows; let her sniff at other people for being simple-minded! Marel wouldn't trade a single cracker crumb shared with Chris for all those sequin trimmings Gail called life.

14

Time for Fun

This was her last picture!

Marel yawned widely and stretched her arms above her head, trying to pull the kinks out of her back. Gail's drawing table was an improvement over her own board and chair arrangement, but she got tired anyway.

The studio seemed so lonely at night. The building corridors were hushed and quiet and all along them doors, that stood open and alight in the daytime, were closed and dark. The advent of the scrubwomen was the only interruption in the entire evening, and in spite of the clatter and noise they made, Marel was glad to have the ghostly quiet broken.

Fran had been willing enough to let her come back for a couple of hours every evening and Gail, of her own accord, had offered the use of her workroom. She had had the quiet she needed to work, and yet these last drawings had not gone too well.

"Wooden!" Eric had snapped over the last three she had shown him. "The test of a good workman is whether he can stay with a job and finish it with the same enthusiasm he got into it at the start. You're fed up with this and it shows."

She was fed up with it. But there were reasons Eric did not know about. Coming back to the studio every night was wearying. She saw too much of it during the day. The little apartment she shared with Chris was "home" now, even if he did have various less flattering names for it. She was happy and contented working there.

But now she saw very little of it.

She hurried home at night, took her turn at getting dinner, or doing dishes (she refused to let him take on more than his share any more), and then rushed right back here to get to work on her drawings. Then there was a walk home again afterward because they could not afford extra carfare every day, and she tumbled into bed weary to her very toes.

Tonight she had attached the drawing she was working on to its place on Gail's drawing table, tired before she began. How could she get life into a picture when she seemed to have so little energy left in her own body? It was all very well for a busybody like Mac Conway to step in and tell her about Chris's needs, but what about *her* needs?

Tears stung her eyelids and she blinked them back in annoyance. Feeling sorry for herself wouldn't help. Chris had started work on a new story. That was the main thing. That made any sacrifice of hers worth while. Even if she spoiled her own chances, it was important to give Chris his.

But the picture on her board was going so completely wrong that she might as well start over. She took out the thumb tacks and attached a fresh sheet of paper to the board. She *must* work. She must not give in to her weariness and discouragement.

An hour slipped by and the picture began to grow on paper again. She sensed that it was wooden, lifeless, but she could not tell why. The scrubwomen had gone to another floor now and the building corridors were still. She wondered if she dared give up for tonight. There were still a few days left in which to do over the other three, but every minute was valuable—she could not waste any of her remaining time.

Her concentration was so complete that the sound of footsteps in the corridor did not penetrate her consciousness right away. Then gradually she became aware of the fact that someone was walking slowly up and down outside the Embree Studio door.

A prickle of dismay went down her spine and she listened intently for a moment. Yes, she could hear the sound quite plainly. Not the ringing footsteps of someone who walked boldly and openly with a purpose in mind, but a soft hush-hush of sound that was secretive and undefined, like the steps of a person who bided his time, waiting.

Alarming thoughts tumbled through her mind as the quiet loneliness of the building seemed to pile up about her. Had she locked the door? She wasn't sure. There was the telephone—but if she needed help quickly, could it bring it in time?

She tiptoed into the little reception room and listened to the sound in the corridor. The steps went past the door and paused. There was a long moment of silence, but she knew the walker had not gone away. He was waiting outside the door. Then, softly, under his breath, the man in the corridor began to whistle.

Relief went through Marel like a wave, washing fear away with it. Laughter left her weak. She would know that tuneless whistle anywhere. She ran to the door and pulled it open.

"Chris! You frightened me practically into chills and fever. I've been listening to you walk up and down, wondering if I should call the police, or just start shrieking out the window."

He grinned at her shamefacedly. "Sorry, honey. I didn't mean to scare you. I've been trying to decide whether I dared interrupt your work."

"Come in," she said. "I'm ready to quit anyway. But what are you doing here? Why aren't you back at your typewriter?"

He followed her into the studio. "The end of the story wouldn't come right and after a few tries I gave up for tonight. Besides, I've been struggling with a guilty conscience. I mean about chasing you out every night, when you must get awfully sick of this place during the day. I don't think you've been doing so well on your last drawings, so I came up to see for myself."

She wished she could hide tonight's stumbling effort from his eyes, but he walked over to Gail's drawing table and looked down at it.

Then he shook his head. "Not so good, is it?"

"What's the matter with us?" Marel asked unhappily. "Why won't our work come right?"

"Maybe we're trying too hard. Remember that day in Central Park when we checked over the pitfalls we might tumble into in this matter of juggling marriage and our work at the same time? Well, I think we've fallen right into one because we forgot to look where we were going."

Marel recalled the little twigs she had wrapped up and put away in her purse. Not once since that day had she gone over the items they'd listed. It had seemed as though by listing them they had solved them and she had not thought about them any more.

"Which one?" she asked.

He pointed a finger at her. "Go put your bonnet on, Mrs. Mallory, and come with me."

"But my drawing—there's so little time left!"

"You're not getting it right this way. No arguments now. Come along."

So she got into her things and they went downstairs together and out of the building. Oddly enough, she felt her spirits lift a little just to put work behind her and let responsibilities slip from her shoulders.

Out on the street, Chris tucked her hand cozily through his arm and hurried her to the nearest subway station. While they waited for an uptown train, he turned out the contents of his pockets.

"I believe I will be able to contribute seventy-five cents to this festive evening," he said. "How about you?"

She smiled and opened her purse. "Maybe fifty, but

I'll have to eat cheaper lunches or I can't spare that."

"Then I'm afraid it's cheaper lunches for you," he said. "Do you realize that we haven't done one thing just for the fun of it since we were married? We've been so concerned about getting on with our work that we've forgotten to have fun as we go along. So tonight we play."

"How?" she said. "What do we do? I mean it's too late to go to a movie and——"

"Movies!" He snapped his fingers. "An unimaginative solution. Suitable for some other occasion, but not for tonight when we need to do something a little crazy and break the routine. How do you feel, Mrs. Mallory? Dignified and sophisticated and New Yorkish? Or do you think you could be young and silly just for tonight?"

"Easily," she admitted. "I'm beginning to feel practically tenish. Maybe even nineish. So what are we going to do?"

"It's a surprise," he shouted as their subway train roared into the station, silencing any further effort at conversation.

They got out at Times Square and walked up into the glare and bustle that was Broadway. Colored signs winked and flashed above the heads of a kaleidoscope of people. There could be no striding briskly along the sidewalk for the crowd shuffled at a snail's pace, but nobody seemed to mind.

"This is fun," Marel said as they fitted into the moving stream. "I feel better already. It's as good as a play and it won't cost us any more than subway fare."

"Piker!" he chided. "You'll change your mind in a little while when you see where we're going. Whoops! Hold it! Never follow the crowd when you come to a curb. You'll get run over for sure."

Taxicabs zigzagged past as they balanced on the curb, waiting for the light to change. When they reached the opposite sidewalk, Chris pulled her toward a building.

"Here we are. Are you sure you're feeling nineish?"

"I'm getting younger every minute," Marel said. "Is this where we spend our money?"

They'd stepped into a crowded, garishly lighted arcade lined with penny and nickel games of every variety.

"Your fortune told for three cents!" Chris cried. "Here's where we start."

A gypsy mask looked down upon them from the front of the machine. Chris crossed the gypsy's palm by feeding three pennies into a slot and Marel turned the necessary dials. A slip of paper slid out to inform her that this was her lucky week. She must watch for a tall dark stranger with great wealth because she was going to fall in love with him."

"That lets me out," Chris said sadly. "Guess I'd better keep an eye on you from now on"—and they laughed together as if they'd really been ten years old.

After that they stopped at a shooting gallery where painted ducks moved placidly before a gaudy backdrop. Marel had no luck at all as a marksman because she jumped nervously just before every crack of the gun. Chris, it developed, was an expert. Duck after duck went down and he looked as pleased and proud as a small boy over his achievement. He was awarded a remarkable glass dish that must have been worth all of a penny. Marel suggested that they leave it in the nearest trash can, but Chris was as proud of the atrocity as if it had been cut glass. In fact, Marel thought, she had not seen him look so carefree and happy since their marriage. Fun, it seemed, was a necessary part of living. They mustn't forget about it again.

At the next game, where a spot of light could be aimed at tiny airplanes that floated across a glass screen, Marel proved herself a champion, while Chris's score was a mere 80. She suspected that he was missing on purpose to make up for her failure with the ducks and they got into a laughing argument over who was giving whom a handicap.

When their pennies began to run out, they stopped for

hot dogs with mustard (and one with onions), saving the last dimes to get them home on the subway.

"Next week," Chris said, "we'll go highbrow and take in a free art show. I think I've had enough of penny arcades for a year."

"Never mind!" Marel told him. "It was fun. And I know it was good for us. It's queer, but that drawing board doesn't scare me any more. I feel sort of tired in my feet, but rested in my head, if you know what I mean. Besides, just think of the exciting time I'm going to have watching for that tall, dark, wealthy stranger. Do you think I'll meet him at an art show?"

"If you do, I'll pick up a blonde," Chris threatened, and their step was light-hearted as they walked back to the apartment.

15

Quarrel

The girl in the mirror had a sparkle of excitement in her eyes and Marel smiled back at her happily. Dates with your husband were fun. And this party for Stuart Allen was extra special. Usually their dates had to be inexpensive movies and walks in the park. Or just window-shopping and talking about where they would go when they were rich and famous. Places like the Blue Peacock that were out of reach now.

Stuart Allen's publisher was giving a party in honor of the book he'd done, and Fran Embree, who had been in charge of the production of the book from the beginning, had a finger in the pie at the party. It was to be a five-to-seven affair, but Fran had said that did not mean that you got there at five, or that you left at seven. That was just something the party throwers always put hopefully on their invitations, but never expected to have followed.

Of course the party was important in Marel's eyes because it meant an opportunity for Chris to meet Irene Allen informally and find out whether she would care to read his manuscript. But it was a date too. A dress-up date, and not many of those came Marel's way these days. Fran, leaving early herself, had let Marel go too, so that she could hurry home and change into another dress. Chris would have to leave directly from work, but she was going to his office to meet him at five-thirty.

She'd used her best bath salts, she'd set her hair the night before, and she had taken extra special trouble

with her make-up. Gail, looking at the scarf tied around
her pin curls that day, had snorted scornfully.

"This is just another publisher's party. They're all alike
and they're dull as dull."

"But I've never been to a publisher's party," Marel had
protested. "It won't be dull for me. I'll love every minute
of it."

Gail had shrugged in a manner that indicated she felt
she was dealing with a sub-normal mentality and had
let the matter go. But no douses of cold water could
dampen Marel's enthusiasm, her gay anticipation of a
happy, interesting evening.

Near the end of the afternoon Gail had come unexpectedly up behind her and had started pulling out the
pins that held dozens of flat little curls in place.

"Relax!" she ordered as Marel gasped her dismay.
"Among my many useless accomplishments is a knack for
doing hair. I can't stand the way you let your hair fly in
the breeze. How about a new hair-do? You can go right
on checking those proofs while I operate."

"Well—I suppose so," Marel said doubtfully.

Gail took the comb Marel handed her and began
running it through the curls, loosening them into soft
waves.

"Mm. Let's see now. How'd you like to look like Irene
Allen?"

"If you can make me look like Irene Allen—!" Marel
breathed fervently.

So Gail had gone ahead, skillfully copying the older
woman's upswept hair style.

Now, looking at the result in the mirror, Marel was in-
creasingly pleased. She looked older this way, not like a
kid out of school. It *did* something for her. Even her
Peggy Pope wedding hat took on an air when she tilted it
at a most fetching angle over the pompadour of curls in
front. Too bad to hide them, but at least the smooth,
diagonal sweep across the back of her head was set off to

best possible advantage beneath the saucily tilted brim. She daubed a drop of her best perfume behind each ear and stepped back to view the sum total with complete satisfaction. Chris Mallory was going to have his eye knocked out and no doubt about it.

The rush-hour jam ruffled her a bit on the way to his office, but it had no effect on the jauntiness of her spirit. Maybe it was silly to let this date seem so important, but she did not mind being silly. It was fun to have a husband to dress your prettiest for and to go out with.

Chris was finishing up some work at his desk in the big offices of the advertising department when she came in. He nodded at her a bit absently and she found a chair where she could wait till he was through. The girls in the department were picking up their things, leaving in groups of two and three. Some of them looked her over curiously as they went by and she found herself wondering what they thought of Chris's wife.

Then Chris shoved his last batch of copy aside, tidied his desk, and came over to her.

"All set?" he asked. "Do we eat first, I certainly hope?"

Of course an office wasn't the right place for a man to make compliments about his wife's appearance, but she did feel a little dampened. To knock a man's eye out, you ought to be able to manage it at the very first glimpse he had of you. Most of the time Chris saw her in the dark, sensible clothes she wore to work, or else in the slacks that were comfortable to wear at home. Gail's handsome negligee occupied a hanger in the closet because spare time lounging wasn't something which had much place in her life just now. So this was *special* and he should have noticed.

But Chris's interest in the party was not as great as his interest in food, apparently, and he seemed not to have observed that his wife was looking her prettiest and had a new hair-do.

"We can't eat first," she explained patiently as they

went down in the elevator. "Everybody eats afterward. Gail said so. Besides, there'll be nibbles going around on trays and you can sustain life with those."

Chris said, "Ugh! Nibbles! I'm hungry."

"But, Chris, this is important. You're going to meet Irene Allen. I've been planning it for ages. It's all on account of your book."

Chris hurried her across a street in time to catch a light, and then they stopped to wait for the bus that would take them to the uptown hotel where the party was being held.

"Don't count on it too much," he told her. "Meeting your Irene Allen at a shindig like this won't make her like my book any better if it's a lousy book—as I vaguely suspect."

"It is *not* a lousy book," Marel said indignantly. "And Fran Embree says personal contacts count for a lot. If there are two good manuscripts on an editor's desk and she knows and likes one of the writers, then he's likely to be the one who gets the contract."

Chris looked unimpressed. "If you think I'm going to talk pretty to some female editor just so she'll publish my book, you're off the beam, honey. It's got to sell on its own merits, not because I have pretty blue hair and two heads."

"Oh, Chris!" Marel began a reproach, but their bus came along just then and they managed to crowd aboard. After a couple of blocks a seat emptied and they slid into it quickly.

Marel glanced at her husband more critically than she usually looked at him. Why did he have to get into an obstinate mood tonight of all nights?

"Of course your book will sell on its own merits," she went on quietly. "I'm sure Irene Allen wouldn't be impressed by even six heads of blue hair. But I still think a personal introduction might help."

"Okay," Chris agreed. "Let's get to the party and get it over with. Then we can eat."

Oh, well, Marel thought, I do look nice, even if he hasn't looked at me twice. And I need a party sometimes. I need to dress up and have fun, even if he doesn't.

They did not talk much the rest of the way. Chris stared gloomily out the bus window, probably envying all the lucky people who were going home to hot dinners, and Marel thought unhappily about how husbands, who *ought* to be the ones to appreciate how their wives looked, never seemed to notice what they wore or whether they took any pains to look nice. As far as this particular husband went, she might as well be wearing the latest in tasty gunny sacks and be completely bald.

But he did notice her hat when they reached the hotel and were checking their things.

"New bonnet, Mrs. Mallory?" he asked.

She shook her head. "No, darling. I wore it at my wedding. Remember? But I do have a new hair-do."

"Yes," he said, "I noticed. It's sort of flat in the back, isn't it?"

Marel turned away quickly to powder her nose before a mirror. Quickly enough to hide the tears that sprang up in her eyes. "It isn't really tragic," she told her reflection. "It's only funny. This is the way men *are*. Even the nicest of them. You might as well accept it, my girl, and laugh it off. You love him like the dickens, and sometimes—most of the time—he's pretty swell."

The tears had been blinked swiftly out of sight by the time she turned back to him. They followed the chatter of voices across the hall and found themselves in the middle of the party.

Fran saw them and hurried over. "Hi, kids. Come on in and have fun. I'll get you over to meet Stuart and Irene as soon as the mob thins out a bit."

So this was a publisher's party, Marel thought, looking about her as Fran went dashing off to greet other newcomers. Some of her early excitement began to return and she glanced eagerly at Chris to see if he was feeling happier.

He wasn't. He looked as if he hated crowds and wanted nothing in the world more than to get away. So he could eat.

"Here comes Eric Webb," Marel whispered. "Do be nice to him, Chris."

She knew Chris disliked Eric and in this sort of mood there was no telling what he might say that would irk the artist.

Eric at least was in a pleasant mood and had apparently left his snappish alter ego in the check room for the moment.

He gave Chris a nod of greeting, but his main attention was for Marel. "So!" he said. "You're not only a hard worker, but you're pretty, too. Funny, I never noticed before. That shade of blue suits you. And the new hair-do is very chic."

She hoped Chris had heard every word, and that he was feeling properly ashamed of himself. But she could tell at a glance that he wasn't. When Eric went away, he said, "That guy!" disgustedly.

"We don't have to wait for Fran to introduce you to Irene," Marel said in a low voice. "I can do it. Let's go over. Then we can go home."

She couldn't care much about the party any more. All her bright anticipation had crumbled. She walked determinedly across the room, leaving Chris to follow her or not as he chose. He followed, for he was at her elbow when she reached the group around Irene.

The editor looked more like a cover girl than ever. She wore black with a dash that emphasized her good looks and graceful figure. And somehow the hair-do was more effective on her red hair than it could ever be on Marel, even though Gail's clever fingers had attempted an imitation of it. She looked like the sort of woman no circumstances would ever find at a loss. Irene Allen had everything—brains and beauty and wit, graciousness, charm.

She smiled at Marel in her most friendly fashion and remembered her name without having to ask. And she greeted Chris when Marel introduced him, as if he were someone she had been waiting to meet.

"Fran told me about your book," she said. "If you haven't found a publisher yet, I wish you'd let me see it."

So that was that, Marel thought. The purpose of coming here had been accomplished without either Chris or herself having to say two words. Now they could leave and get that dinner Chris was perishing for.

But Irene's interest in Chris and his book was drawing him out of his gloomy mood. Before he knew it he was answering her questions, thawing as the warmth of her personality made itself felt.

Marel breathed a sigh of relief. Now all she needed to do was get away. Chris could manage this better alone. She would only be a fifth wheel if she stayed around and kept them politely including her in the conversation.

"There's Gail," she said when a pause came in the talk. "Do you mind if I run over to see her?"

Neither of them minded and she slipped away, leaving Chris to do his stuff with Irene. Whether he thought it was important or not, a good impression on an editor would not hurt. He wouldn't have to work at it consciously. All he needed was to be his usual attractive, cheerful self.

Gail had found an empty couch and was sitting there munching bits of toast and anchovy, watching the scene around her with a bored and cynical eye.

"Hello," she said as Marel dropped down beside her. "Kind of reckless, aren't you?"

"Reckless?" Marel was puzzled.

"Sure. Turning your man over to a glamour gal like Irene."

"But she's an editor. Maybe she'll like his book. It's business, that's all."

"Oh, sure, sure. But if I were you I'd find a nice homely editor to sic him onto if it has to be a female."

Marel hoped she looked her exasperation. "Gail! You can think of more unpleasant ideas per minute than anybody I ever knew. And that one is nonsense. She must be years older than Chris. Ten at least."

"The fascinating sort improve with age," Gail said, apparently taking Marel's remark as a compliment. "And I wouldn't say that at thirty-five Irene Allen exactly has a foot in the grave."

A waiter went by with a tray and Marel helped herself to a couple of intriguing-looking snacks that only taste would identify and settled back against the couch. She meant to let nothing Gail said ruffle her.

"I'm sure Irene is perfectly satisfied with her own husband."

"You hope," said Gail. "That's a matter I wouldn't be knowing about. Of course you don't have to take my advice, but I wouldn't want a man of mine enjoying himself so completely with as appealing a dish as our little mystery editor."

Marel glanced quickly across the room in spite of herself. Chris did appear to be having a wonderful time. And he had apparently forgotten about being in such a hurry to go home.

"Never mind, kid," Gail said sympathetically. "You're looking pretty snappy yourself tonight. How did Chris like the new hair-do?"

"He said it looked kind of flat in back," Marel admitted lamely. She did not want to confess to Gail that he hadn't noticed her appearance at all, except for that one criticism.

"Men!" Gail put all the disgust she could muster into the word.

"Chris isn't 'men,' " Marel told her loyally. "Not the

way women mean it when they say it that way. And I'd be a horrid sort of wife if I couldn't bear to have him talk to an attractive woman without wondering if I was losing him. My goodness, Gail! Marriage has to be based on mutual trust, doesn't it? If I had a husband I could lose as easily as that, he wouldn't be worth keeping. After all, Chris saw something in me or he wouldn't have wanted me for his wife. I've got to have confidence in him and in myself too."

Gail yawned widely. "Guess I'll go home. Every party gets worse than the one before."

Marel was so indignant that she did not want the subject casually changed. "Don't you see, Gail, we've got to trust each other."

"Very pretty," Gail said. "That's what I used to think too."

The other woman was studying the base of the ring finger on her own left hand, rubbing it with the fingers of the right.

Marel looked at her sharply. "What do you mean?"

"Didn't you know? I was married once. About a thousand years ago. It didn't take. I had a lot of ducky little notions about mutual trust and respect and other idiocies of the kind."

"You mean—?"

"I stuck it out for four years. I'd never want to live like that again. I divorced him."

"But I know Chris—I mean Chris wouldn't——" Marel had begun to stammer in her earnestness, but Gail would not let her finish.

"Well, I've had enough of one party. Sure, kid. All wives think like that. At first. I hope you're the one who's right about it."

She got up and wove her way through the crowd to the door without speaking to anyone. Marel watched her go, glad that she was leaving. There was something almost vicious about Gail when it came to her attitude toward men. She could be downright kindly in other ways. She could make the most generous and friendly of gestures, even while she accompanied them with biting words. But her bitterness toward men was upsetting to see.

"I wouldn't be like that for anything," Marel thought to herself. "It only hurts her and makes her unattractive and hard. Besides, there are always two sides. Maybe her husband had his side too."

Once more she looked across the room at Chris. She didn't mean to watch him. Each time she meant not to look again, but something drew her eyes in his direction. He seemed to have forgotten he had a wife, he was so enjoying himself with Irene. She saw that Stuart Allen had joined them, but he seemed to be a fifth wheel too. He didn't look as if he were having a very good time at his own party. Odd that Irene had married a man so different from herself. Stuart had none of her sparkle and confidence. Mostly he seemed quiet and ill-at-ease. When she saw Eric Webb coming toward her, Marel smiled at him eagerly.

"Here, here, we can't have the young and beautiful sitting by themselves." Eric's rare good humor was still upon him. The way he talked at the studio gave the impression that he hated the sight of people and parties, but evidently that was just part of the curious act he seemed so often impelled to put on. Now that he was here he appeared to be enjoying himself well enough. He took her hand and pulled her up from the couch. "This is no way to meet people. Come along with Papa Eric."

She went with him willingly enough. She even made an effort to be much gayer than she felt, and she was sure she was talking nonsense a good part of the time to the people he introduced her to. But at least she was giving the impression that she was enjoying herself—in case anybody across the room happened to glance her way.

The party seemed endless. Fran had been right in saying that people wouldn't go home by seven. Marel's face was growing stiff with the effort she made to smile and she had a horrid suspicion that it might freeze into an artificial grimace she would wear forever after. Then, just when she felt she could not laugh at one more feeble witticism—either her own or anyone else's—there was Chris at her elbow.

"Hi there, kitten," he whispered. "Having fun?"

"Wonderful fun!" Marel lied fervently.

"Good. I had fun, too. The Allens are swell. And what do you know! I'm going to take my book over to her office tomorrow."

"That's grand," Marel said, and she meant it clear through.

"Well, let's get going," Chris suggested. "I'm hungry enough by now to eat that wedding hat of yours, Mrs. Mallory. And I didn't think a hat was something I could ever look at with anything but loathing again."

"Why can't you stand hats?" she asked him on the way to the check room.

He shuddered in an exaggerated fashion. "There was another crisis at work today. The gal who writes the female fashion ads got sick and had to go home. Right when a new batch of hats had arrived in the millinery department to go on sale tomorrow. So it was up to yours truly to write the ad. Wait till you see tomorrow's paper and read the ravishing raves your only husband has written about the most gosh-awful array of freakish inventions you ever saw. But now I'm hungry. I could *eat* a hat. In fact, I guess that's the only thing that should be done with some of 'em."

Marel felt a thousand times better on the way home. So that was it! He had not been unappreciative of the way she looked. It was just that he had been writing little fantasies about women's hats and general appearance and he had become so sick of the subject of feminine fripperies that Cleopatra herself wouldn't have been able to knock his eye out.

She was glad now that she had not let him see how hurt she had been by his indifference to her appearance, or that she'd minded his crack about her new hair style. By hanging onto her temper and her feelings she was ahead of the game on all scores. And now she could understand why he'd behaved as he had.

Once home, it didn't take long to get a warmed-up dinner on the table and she watched Chris eat with growing satisfaction. It wasn't so hard to be a good little wife. It took some patience and understanding and generosity, maybe, but it was certainly worth it. And if he liked Irene and Stuart Allen, that was all to the good. It certainly did not mean that he liked Marel Mallory any the less. That! for Gail and her ugly suspicions! Marel snapped her fingers mentally and filled Chris's plate up again.

As the food took its mellowing effect, the erstwhile invalid began to sit up and take notice. Of his wife, for one thing.

"You know, honey," he said, "if you don't mind my saying so—I don't much like that hair business you've fixed for yourself. It—it doesn't do anything for you, as the girls say."

She was disappointed, but not heart-broken. If he liked her hair better some other way, then she was perfectly willing to experiment.

"Now you take the way Irene Allen wears her hair," he went on. "That looks pretty terrific, don't you think?"

Marel had been carrying a load of dishes to the sink. She paused, went back to the card table they used to dine on, and set them down carefully.

"What about Irene Allen's hair-do?"

"Oh, nothing special," he said. "But maybe you could try fixing your hair like that sometimes and——"

It was a good thing, she felt, that she'd got those dishes out of her hands. They couldn't afford a new set just now. This was the end. This was the last straw. The camel's back had snapped right through and she was completely sick and tired of being a sweet and dutiful wife.

Irene Allen's hair-do! The exact hair-do she herself was wearing at this minute!

She said just one word and she put into it as much feeling as Gail Norris had ever managed. *"Men!"* she said, and then she ran over to the beautiful couch that had been Aunt Peg's wedding present, threw herself flat on her stomach, and burst stormily into tears.

Chris came over and sat down beside her. He sounded a little annoyed and not too sympathetic, so she blew her nose loudly on the handkerchief he offered and wept harder than ever.

"But what's the matter, honey?" he asked in bewilderment. "What have I said? If you have to take on like this just because I admire the way another woman wears her hair—if you're going to be jealous of praise of other women——"

This was injustice piled upon injustice. "I'm n-n-not jealous!" she wailed. "I think you're impossible! I wish you'd go away!"

She didn't want him to go away. She wanted to cling to him and cry on his shoulder. But when he got up to move away from her, she couldn't lift a finger to stop him. Between her sobs she peeked from under her crooked elbow to see that he was getting his coat on to go out. Her spirits dropped to sub-zero and the paroxysms of sobbing increased.

Men were dreadful creatures, really. They spoiled your fun, they criticized you and admired other women, they were callous and unreasonable and generally impossible, and then, when all you wanted was to be petted and loved a little, they walked out on you.

And slammed the door.

The slam was such an alarming sound that she stopped sobbing to listen. Maybe she ought to run after him. Maybe she ought to call him back. But she couldn't.

It would be different if she were wrong. But she wasn't wrong at all. She couldn't help it if he was hopelessly dumb. He'd been unkind. He'd been downright cruel. If anybody owed anybody any apologies, he was the one. She wasn't going to crawl on her knees. Let him go for good if he wanted to. She had her pride too.

The apartment was utterly quiet now that she had stopped crying. No, it wasn't either. The clock made a hideous noise. Electric clocks didn't tick, but they hummed like dynamos when everything was still. That was Fran's present. Another wedding present.

Weddings. Marriage. They lived happily ever after. What a joke that was!

After fifteen looks at the clock she found that fifteen minutes had gone by. Why didn't he come back? If he came back, maybe she would go to him, get into his arms, and tell him what the matter was. Maybe he really didn't understand what he had done.

After a time she pulled herself to her knees and looked into the circular mirror that hung above the couch. Goodness, what a face! Tears had streaked the powder into a mess and her lipstick had gone smeary. But it was the hair-do she was interested in. Did it really look so very much like Irene's hair style? It was swept up the same way hers was. Gail had done a good copying job. But did it suit her the way it suited Irene? Was it the sort of hair-do that was meant for Marel Mallory?

She turned her head this way and that, trying to see herself as Chris might see her. Could he be blamed for not recognizing the similarity in styles when it made Irene look so very different from the way it made Marel look? Gail always wanted to stress sophistication. But perhaps sophistication wasn't meant for Marel.

She began to pull the pins out one by one, until strands of hair slid down her neck and the high-piled pompadour began to totter. She knew now what she meant to do. She'd go to the bathroom and wash the mess off her face. Then she'd brush her hair into the young, loose style that Chris thought became her. She'd get into the lovely negligee Gail had given her and when Chris came home she'd be sweet and forgiving.

The doorbell startled her so that she nearly fell off the couch. There was Chris now! She wouldn't have time for her plans, but it didn't matter. She was so glad to have him come back quickly that she knocked three books off an end table in her scramble to reach the door.

The lock stuck maddeningly, but somehow she got it to work and pulled open the door. Only then did reason tell her that of course it wouldn't be Chris. Chris had his own key. He wouldn't ring the bell.

The woman who stood before the door was plump and elderly. She was neat from her brightly polished oxfords to the smooth waves of white hair that showed beneath her hat. Marel felt as unkempt and untidy as she knew she must look. Even if this woman had just happened to ring the wrong doorbell, Marel hated to have a stranger see her like this. She made a futile attempt to hold back the tottering pompadour and managed a stiff smile.

"May I help you?" she asked. "Probably you misread the name on the door card. If you'll tell me who you're looking for——"

The woman broke quietly into her awkward words. "Are you Margaret Elizabeth Mallory?"

"Why—yes. Yes, I am," Marel said.

The older woman smiled. "Then perhaps you'll ask me in. I'm Chris's mother."

16

Unexpected Guest

Weakly Marel backed away from the door. The power of speech seemed to have left her entirely. Fortunately Mrs. Mallory waited for no invitation, but came past her into the apartment and Marel pushed the door shut after her.

Chris's mother paused a moment looking around the room, and Marel had the dismaying experience of seeing it as the older woman must have seen it. Books tumbled carelessly on the floor. The dinner table still uncleared at this late hour. Unscraped dishes piled in the sink. And her own tear-streaked face and untidy hair. She pulled what was left of herself together and made an effort to step into the rôle of hostess which had been thrust upon her.

"Won't you sit down? This is—is such an unexpected surprise. I'm sorry Chris isn't here. I know how happy he'll be. I expect him back any minute."

Now she felt she was talking too much, too breathlessly, and she cut herself off practically in mid-air. Mrs. Mallory walked to the couch and sat down. In contrast to the disorder of the room, she looked neater than ever.

Her eyes were bright and very blue—like Chris's eyes— and they missed nothing.

"You've been crying, haven't you? Wouldn't you like to go and wash your face?"

In spite of the directness of her words, her tone was kind. Marel needed no second invitation. She rushed away, nearly knocking a lamp over this time, and shut herself into the small bathroom. There she leaned weakly against the washbasin and turned on the cold water. Of all the dreadful, inopportune times for Chris's mother to arrive! There was nothing to do but see it through and try to live down the impossible first impression she was making.

She dashed cold water over her streaked cheeks, patted it against the puffiness of her eyes. At least she looked a little better with her face washed. She finished pulling the pins out of her hair and brushed it over her shoulders into a smooth, shining mass. Then she put on fresh make-up as quickly and neatly as she could. That wasn't for Mrs. Mallory, whose rosy cheeks were obviously natural, but for her own courage. A girl couldn't feel brave and able to carry off a bad situation when she was pale and washed-out and unappealing.

When she had done the best she could, she braced herself, summoned what few shreds of courage she had left, and went back to face Chris's mother. Mrs. Mallory had not been idle. She had taken off her hat and tied a big dish-wiper around her waist. So prepared, she was busily and cheerfully tackling the untidiness of the sink.

Marel rushed over to take a plate out of her hand. "Oh, no, please! You mustn't do that. I'm sorry you have to find everything in such an upset state. If we'd only known you were coming——"

"Then you'd have been ready for me," Mrs. Mallory said calmly. "I wanted to see how things were going when you didn't expect me."

She had picked up another plate, ignoring Marel's protest, and her daughter-in-law did not dare take that out of her hands too. For all her friendly cheerfulness, she did not look like the sort of person you could dissuade from a course of action she had decided to follow.

Marel fell to helping her, as a matter of second choice, trying unhappily to explain. "You mustn't think we're always like this about dishes. Tonight was unusual. We went to a party and then we had dinner late when we got home."

"And then you had a quarrel and Chris went off mad. Was that it?"

There was no denying that that was it, so Marel remained silent. She got the soap chips when asked for them, pulled the dishpan obediently out from under the sink, and wiped dishes while Mrs. Mallory washed. Whatever would Chris think of her when he got home? She hoped uneasily that they would at least have everything put away, so that he wouldn't have to walk in and find his mother doing dishes.

But they were still in the middle of cleaning up when Marel heard Chris's key in the lock. She waited anxiously, helplessly. What she cared about most was to see what expression he'd be wearing, so she could tell if he was still angry with her. She no longer had plans for being sweet and forgiving. She wanted only to be forgiven.

He was smiling good-naturedly and he carried a small green tissue-wrapped cone in his hand. The good-nature turned to surprise when he saw his mother. He put down the parcel and came across the room in a couple of long steps to put his cheek against hers and his arms about her.

She gasped and laughed over the force of his hug, and Marel knew by the look in her eyes how much she loved her son. When Chris let her go and turned to Marel, she knew the quarrel was over and done with.

"Hi, honey," he said. "What goes on here?"

"I didn't want your mother to do dishes," Marel explained. "I'm afraid she thinks I'm a dreadful housekeeper."

"Never try to keep Mom from doing what she decides to do," Chris said, leaning over to drop a teasing kiss on his mother's nose. "But if any cracks are made about the housekeeping in this establishment, I come in for my share. This is a co-operative marriage, Mom."

Mrs. Mallory dried her hands neatly on a towel which

Marel noted too late was in a grubby state. "That is what every marriage should be, of course," his mother approved. "But there's woman's work and man's work."

Chris shook his head. "Not here. We just call it Work and split it up between us. We've both got jobs, you know, to say nothing of ambitions."

Mrs. Mallory's smile offered no opposition to Chris's words, but Marel knew she was not in entire agreement with them.

"We didn't have problems like that in my day," she said. "I expect things are different now." She went back to her place on the couch and made herself comfortable. "I thought I'd like to come East without waiting any longer. I wanted to meet my son's wife and see just how everything was going. You're very crowded here, aren't you?"

"If you can find us a better place in the city of New York—that is, one we can afford——" Chris said, "we'll be in your debt forever. Don't they have an apartment shortage out in California?"

"I understand they do. But I'm sure, if you really want to work at it, something can be found. People give up too easily."

Chris winked at Marel. "Mother never gives up. Two bits she pulls an apartment out of the air under the noses of a million who are looking for one."

"If she can do that," Marel said, "she's every bit as remarkable as you've been telling me she was."

"Don't believe everything that son of mine says," Mrs. Mallory told Marel, but she looked pleased at the compliment. "I'm staying at Humphrey House for the time being. My train got in this afternoon. I'm a bit tired tonight, so I think I'll go back to the hotel and get some sleep. Suppose I see you both tomorrow night? Can you come to dinner at the hotel? Then we can spend the evening together and Marel and I can get acquainted."

Marel turned quickly to Chris. "I—I'm sorry, but I

must do the last polishing-up on the pictures tomorrow night. I couldn't work tonight because of the party, and——"

"I'd forgotten," Chris said. "Mother will understand."

"Of course." Mrs. Mallory nodded agreement, but she looked a little hurt.

"I'd love to come for dinner," Marel hurried to assure her. "But I hope you won't mind if I rush away right afterward. You see I have a deadline to make, and tomorrow is my very last night to finish the work I'm doing for this children's book."

"It's a pretty important job for Marel," Chris added. "Suppose we change the date to day after tomorrow? Then we can have dinner and spend the evening with you too."

"As you like," Mrs. Mallory agreed, but Marel had an uneasy feeling that she did not really understand. Oh, why couldn't she have got off to a better start with Chris's mother?

"I'll see you home, Mom," Chris offered, but she shook her head at him.

"Goodness, no! If you'll take me downstairs and get me a taxi, that will be fine. And I'll see you both night after tomorrow."

Marel wanted to say something friendly, something apt, but her mind had given up providing useful inspirations when they were needed. She managed an awkward "Good night," that did not sound as friendly as she wanted it to. She could only watch in relief as Mrs. Mallory went out the door.

Then she dropped limply into a chair to wait for Chris's return. She had reached a point of weariness where she could think sensibly about nothing. She could only wait in a state of inertia for whatever happened to her. On the couch across the room rested the green-wrapped parcel Chris had brought, but he seemed to have forgotten it in his surprise over seeing his mother, and she could not open it until he put it into her hands.

He must have found a taxi quickly, for he was back in five minutes' time. He came in breezily and picked up the neglected parcel.

"For you, honey," he said, dropping it into her lap. "I didn't want to give it to you in front of Mother because I had a special speech ready to go with it. But now I've forgotten the speech. Think you can just take it without trimmings and know what it means?"

She could easily. It meant that he was sorry about not understanding and about hurting her feelings. It meant that he loved her. She pulled the green tissue open to disclose the flowers inside. Three long-stemmed roses. Three creamy-pink roses whose fragrance brought a garden into the crowded little room.

"Three," he said. "Three because that's all the florist had of that shade. But three for another reason, too. One —because I'm sorry. Two—because I love you. Three— because I need you. Now for gosh sakes, don't cry *again!* This time you're supposed to smile."

So she did smile, though a little tremulously. And if there were tears this time, they were the happy kind.

"But you haven't asked why the color," Chris went on. "You're a most uncurious wench, if I do say so."

"All right," she said. "Why the color? Though I don't need to know. Just having them is enough for me."

He pulled her up and turned her to face the mirror. "There." He held the roses close to her cheek. "See what I mean? They're your very own kind of roses. Just your color."

That made the gift especially lovely, especially meaningful.

"And you've no idea how many doors I had to pound on before I found a place willing to sell me what I wanted out of hours," he went on. His hand touched the softness of her hair, smoothed it. "That's the way I like it. That way is *you*. But look here, Margaret Elizabeth, suppose you tell me just what was the matter. I know I blundered and said a lot of wrong things, but honestly, honey, I'm still in the dark as to what went wrong."

She held the comforting roses against her cheek, loving their fragrance and the velvety touch of the petals. It was easy to tell him now.

"You said Irene Allen looked wonderful with her kind of hair-do, and you said I ought to try wearing my hair that way. But Chris, that was exactly the way I was wearing my hair. Gail fixed it for me and she copied it from Irene's style."

He stared at her for a moment and then laughter wrinkles began to come at the corners of his eyes and the corners of his mouth. For a second she was almost angry again. Then the foolish indignation faded out and they laughed together, holding each other tight.

"Why didn't I see how funny it was?" Marel choked. "Why didn't I laugh first, instead of going all over dramatic?"

At least it was good to laugh now. To see how foolish she had been and how un-grownup the whole silly affair was. It was nice to have Chris's arms around her and know they had not moved apart one bit. Everything was going to be all right now.

Everything?

There was still the problem of Chris's mother. But even that could be met in time. Somehow it would work out. It had to.

17

Ordeal

Marel never dared to be lazy on a Sunday. That was a day for catching up on housework, for washing and pressing.

She pushed the carpet sweeper back and forth across the rug in time to the "tune" Chris was whistling in the shower. At least he was under the impression that it was a tune. But what popular number had been its original inspiration was impossible to guess. At least it had a sort of time to it.

Some day she was going to own a vacuum cleaner. Some day, some day. All their plans were made to that refrain. Anyway, Chris had had good news on his book. Two days after he had taken it up to Irene's office, he had come home one night and swept Marel into a hug that carried her right off her feet.

"She likes it!" he shouted, as if she had been a mile away.

"Ssh-sh!" she hushed him. "The neighbors! We'll get put out. Who likes what?"

"Irene," he said. "My book. What else? She thinks maybe she'll publish it."

Marel did a little shouting of her own at that. "There! I knew it was good. I knew you'd find a publisher. But what do you mean—she *thinks* she'll publish it? Doesn't she know?"

"It's not right in a few places, but it can be fixed up if I'm willing to work. And of course I am. I'm going up to the Allens on Sunday to talk it over with her."

"Sunday? Why on Sunday?"

"A lunch hour isn't long enough, or a good time to work. And there's no other time I can take off my job except in the evening or on Sunday. So she suggested this Sunday in the afternoon. You won't mind if I run out on you for a couple of hours, will you, honey? It's pretty important."

Of course it was important. And she knew from her experience at the Embree Studio that it wasn't unusual for people who worked in the making of books to carry their jobs over into their spare-time hours. In fact, some of the most successful ones seemed to have no life outside their jobs, and what was more they seemed to enjoy having it that way.

So she had said no, of course she didn't mind. But now that Sunday was here, she felt a little at loose ends. This would be the first Sunday since they'd been married that she had spent away from Chris. Not that she didn't have plenty to occupy her time. First the housework. Then an invitation from Chris's mother to spend the afternoon with her and be joined by Chris for dinner in the evening.

She had been dreading the ordeal a little, but she no longer had the excuse of a deadline to get her out of it. Ginger's book was done. Eric had taken it off her hands and by now his editor had it. So far no verdict had been given, and she and Ginger were in a state of suspense that had them holding their breath. It simply *had* to go over. Fran and Eric both thought she had done a good job on the pictures, and she knew they gave no praise that wasn't warranted.

But now she was in a curiously directionless state of mind. With no new work to occupy her time, it was hard to pick up a drawing pencil at all. Eric had warned her about that.

"Mustn't let down," he said. "Keep drawing. You don't have to have a job to keep you working. You don't know everything in this game by a long shot, so give yourself some assignments."

But after a real one, drawing without direction seemed dull. Chris had an advantage over her in his work. He could start a new free-lance story whenever he pleased, but in her case it wasn't possible to draw aimless pictures and hope to sell them.

The dinner a few nights before with Chris's mother had gone well enough. At least on the surface. Mrs. Mallory had been cheerful and friendly, and yet Marel had the feeling that she did not quite understand her daughter-in-law and her interests. Chris had remained undismayed when Marel had pointed this out to him.

"You wait," he said. "She's just never known a career girl before. Give her time."

With Chris present to give her support, it wasn't so bad. But this afternoon she would have to go through it alone. If it had not been for her desire to please Chris, she might have invented some excuse to release her. But it was natural that he should want her to be friends with his mother, and there was nothing to do but go through with it.

After lunch Chris went off, still cheerfully whistling, and Marel dressed carefully for the meeting. All the way to the hotel on the bus, she felt a little depressed, a little uneasy. She tried to tell herself that her feeling was without cause. She and Chris were married now. Nothing could change that. He himself had said, "It's me for you and you for me from now on," so what had she to worry about?

And, indeed, there seemed little to worry about when his mother greeted her at the door of her hotel room.

"Come on in," she said cheerily, ushering the girl into the small room. Once more it occurred to Marel that she resembled Chris a lot. That act was somehow reassuring.

Mrs. Mallory put her guest into the most comfortable chair, despite her protests, while she herself took the room's one other, straight chair. Marel watched her efficient movements as she took up the gray-blue softness of the sweater she was knitting for her son.

"I'm awfully glad to have this chance to talk to you when Chris isn't here," she said. "Two people need to be alone to get really acquainted. Don't you think so?"

Marel nodded, relaxing as she watched the smooth movement of the knitting needles. "I'm sorry you had to see everything the way it was the other night when you arrived. I did want to have things just right if ever you came to see us."

Mrs. Mallory smiled and nodded. "It wasn't fair of me to pop in on you like that. But now that we're getting to know each other, I don't mind admitting that I was a little upset over having my son suddenly marry a girl I hadn't even seen."

Marel thought: "But Chris is grown-up. And you were in California. You couldn't expect us to wait for your permission." But she did not speak her thoughts. Her own parents had been disturbed too. It was natural enough.

"But now that I've met you, I feel much better about everything," Mrs. Mallory went on. "You're young and sweet, and I like your willingness and eagerness to do everything for Chris's best interests."

"I do want that," Marel agreed earnestly. "I want his good more than anything else."

His mother nodded approvingly. There was an odd smile on her lips, as if she were secretly pleased over something Marel was not aware of.

"I've not been idle since coming to New York," she went on. "In fact, I've arranged a little surprise for you. I hope you'll be pleased. But I won't tell you about it just yet."

Marel waited, trying to shake off an odd sense of uneasiness that filled her.

The needles clicked on, and the quiet voice continued pleasantly: "Chris told me how good you'd been in moving out of that one little room every evening, so that he could work undisturbed."

"It wasn't so bad," Marel hurried to assure her. "And of course the studio was a much better place for me to work."

"Nevertheless, it must have been hard to do. It's bad enough to work all day at a job without going out evenings too. In fact, one of the reasons I was worried about your marriage was because you could not settle down to a normal life where Chris could have his wife home all the time."

"I don't think many young couples can manage that in the beginning these days," Marel pointed out. "We're not being different from anyone else. Most girls grow up expecting to work and help their husbands get their start."

Mrs. Mallory sighed. "I'm not sure I approve. When we married, my husband was earning enough so that he could make a home for me. And I could stay in that home and keep it for him."

Marel examined a fingernail on which the polish had chipped as if it were the most absorbing sight in the world. She had no answer for the things Chris's mother was saying. It was true, she supposed, that a girl ought to put home-making first in her married life. But how could it be managed when circumstances simply did not permit it? Later on, when her illustrating began to click, so that she could work at home, it would be different. But Chris understood that wasn't possible now. At least he expected no more than it was possible for her to give. But how to explain all that to an older woman, who felt that everything should be exactly as it had been in her own girlhood, was beyond Marel.

"I wonder," Mrs. Mallory said, with her usual directness, "if you could put aside this drawing hobby of yours for the time being? Don't you think that would be a wiser way?"

"Hobby!" Marel was startled into echoing the word.

"But drawing isn't just a hobby with me. I mean———"
It was so hard to explain what she meant to someone who
did not understand that she let her thought go unfinished,
unspoken.

Again Mrs. Mallory sighed. "I know young people
never want to take advice. Every generation has to make
its own mistakes."

"It isn't that I don't want to take your advice," Marel
said unhappily. "But Chris and I have already talked all
these things over. We're trying *not* to make mistakes. He
understands how I feel about drawing, just as I understand about his writing. It has to be like this."

Mrs. Mallory let her knitting drop into her lap. "I had
to try. I had to give my bit of advice. But if you and
Chris have thought this problem through and understand
it, then we needn't talk about it any more. There's nothing
worse than an interfering mother-in-law."

"Oh, you're not that!" Marel said quickly, and meant
her words. She liked Chris's mother better all the time.
She might be direct and quick to say what she thought,
but she never demanded that others agree with her.

"The main thing is that you and I are going to like each
other," Mrs. Mallory said. "In fact, I'm sure we're already
friends."

She held out her hand and Marel put her own into it to
seal the agreement. It was a relief to have all her fears
about this first visit alone with Chris's mother thoroughly
dispelled. The older woman was not a bit frightening or
managing, and she was completely reasonable.

"Thank you, Marel." Mrs. Mallory released her hand
and rose from her chair. "Now then! We've been much
too solemn and gloomy. Here—get your coat on. We're
going out."

She bustled into her own things, smiling mysteriously.
Something was certainly in the air and Marel wished her
rising curiosity was not tinged with uneasiness. She and
Chris's mother had just agreed that they were friends, so

what was there to be uneasy about?

They went downstairs and the doorman called a cab for them. All the way to the uptown address Mrs. Mallory gave, she chatted happily about impersonal matters, obviously enjoying Marel's unsatisfied curiosity.

The cab pulled up before a big square building with a green canopy reaching from its main entrance to the edge of the sidewalk. Mrs. Mallory led the way with assurance to a self-service elevator and they went up a half dozen floors. Marel felt more and more puzzled as she followed her guide out of the elevator and down a corridor. Mrs. Mallory stopped before a door, opened her handbag and took out a key.

"The Billings are out today," she said, "but Susan gave me an extra key."

Who the Billings were and why Susan had given Mrs. Mallory a key was all a mystery to Marel. Still puzzled, she walked into a big sunny living room, tastefully furnished, with windows overlooking the avenue below.

"Come along," Mrs. Mallory beckoned her across the room.

Off a small hallway opened a bedroom as big as Marel's one living room. From there they went on to a beautifully tiled bathroom, and next to a combination kitchen and dinette that was as roomy and attractive as the rest of the apartment.

Mrs. Mallory was beaming. "Well? How do you like it?"

"It's a beautiful apartment," Marel admitted, a little enviously. "Who are the lucky people who live here?"

"You," Mrs. Mallory said. "You and Chris."

Marel could only stare in bewilderment and her mother-in-law laughed happily, enjoying her astonishment.

"Perhaps you don't live here yet," the older woman went on, "but you'll be able to move in in a short time. You see, Susan Billings is the daughter of some old friends of mine. I went to see them the other day and was there when the unexpected news came. Susan's husband is being sent to Mexico by the company he works for. He will probably be stationed there for a year. She's going with him, but they don't want to lose their apartment entirely. As soon as Susan brought that up, I told them about you and Chris. They'd like to have nice people in it who would take care of their things and be willing to occupy it for just a year."

Marel looked about her at the shining little kitchen where they stood, and at the gaily curtained windows of the dinette. To live in a place like this with Chris—! But it was a dream impossible of fulfillment.

"We could never afford it," she said sadly. "The rent would be way beyond what we could manage."

"Wait," Mrs. Mallory said; "You haven't seen it all."

Again she waved a beckoning finger and led the way back to the hall, where a door opened into a room Marel had not seen. It was a small room, but pleasantly furnished, with a single bed, a chintz-covered chair, and a maple dresser.

"This is the maid's room, really," Mrs. Mallory said, "though Susan keeps it for a guest room. It will do nicely for me."

"For you?" Marel felt that everything was moving too fast for her and that she was behaving stupidly, but she could not help herself.

Mrs. Mallory nodded. "Yes—if you'd care to share the apartment with me. The rent I'd pay would make it possible for you to take the place."

"Oh," Marel said, wishing her tone did not sound so blank. Oh, I see. But I thought you liked California best and——"

Mrs. Mallory shook her head. "I don't see why I should go on living in California when I can help you out by moving here. I'd like being with you, and I'm sure a place like this would make life more pleasant for you and Chris."

She led the way back to the bright living room and

Marel followed, trying to see the apartment with new, realistic eyes. It was hard to believe that all this comfort might really be theirs. In a place like this there would be plenty of room for both her work and Chris's.

"I hoped you'd be happy about it." There was a faintly wistful note in Mrs. Mallory's voice.

Marel shook her head quickly, as if to shake away the cobwebs of bewilderment. "It's just that I can't get used to the idea. I can't quite believe it."

"Then you do like the apartment?"

"Oh, yes!" Marel breathed. "It's lovely. It's everything anyone could want."

"Fine! Now you can tell Chris this evening that you have a new place. I'll let you have the pleasure of springing the surprise. If you'll just let me watch."

"Of course it can't be really settled until we find out what he thinks," Marel said.

"Of course not," Mrs. Mallory agreed. "That is the way it should be. But I'm sure he'll want to get out of that place you have as much as you do."

"That place we have," Marel thought. It was natural that Chris's mother could not know the love and hope that had gone into fixing it up. Maybe it wasn't any palace, but it belonged to them. And they'd been happy there. She had a queer, unreasonable feeling that they might not be as happy in this bigger, more comfortable place.

But she knew such a thought was nonsense even as it went through her mind. She would do whatever Chris wanted her to, and do it gladly.

Later, when they were back at the hotel and Chris had joined them, he was so filled with a desire to talk about his afternoon that she made no effort to speak about the apartment for a while. At the dinner table in the hotel dining room, she caught Mrs. Mallory's gaze questioningly upon her, as if the older woman were wondering why she did not go ahead and break the wonderful news. But somehow she waited and let Chris run on about his own affairs.

"Irene is really terrific," he told them. "The way she has gone to work on that story of mine and hit all its weak places!"

"*I* read it and I didn't see so many weak places," Marel told Chris loyally.

"Honey, you're not an editor. Irene's right, and I'm going to follow her advice. It's going to take a heck of a lot of revision, but she thinks I can do it. Imagine a girl who looks like that having brains too!"

Marel looked at her plate. She did not want to remember Gail's sly remarks at the party. She did not want to think about Gail's warning to look out because Irene was such a special dish. She wasn't going to be the jealous type of wife. Chris and she had decided about that before they'd married. They *had* to trust each other.

Unaware of the faint quirk of doubt in his wife's mind, Chris went happily on. "Stuart was there too, and I got a chance to talk to him awhile. He's a quiet sort of bird, but I like him. In fact, he's given me an idea for another book."

"Another—what do you call it?" Mrs. Mallory asked. "Another whodunit?" She looked so pleased over managing a term that was strange to her that Marel had to smile.

"Sure thing," Chris said. "Irene thinks I've hit a gold mine and that I have a flair for writing this sort of thing."

"The kind you write," Marel added, "are psychological novels, not just blood-and-thunder."

Chris grinned at her. "It pays to have that kind of perception in my own family. Though as a matter of fact, that's about what Irene said. She wants my next one to be more serious, to get into the psychological angle more deeply. Stuart had an idea about using a college background and having a professor for a hero."

"That doesn't sound awfully interesting," Marel said. "Hasn't it been done already?"

"This would be different. The professor would be married to a spectacular sort of career-girl wife and———"

"Like Irene?" Marel broke in. "You mean he was suggesting that you write their story?"

"Irene suggested that part. She was sort of kidding, I think, but Stuart took her up on it. He said he could give me all the lowdown on that. So Irene said sure—go ahead. Of course I wouldn't use them at all. Just an angle here and there. And Stuart could help me on the college background from the professor's viewpoint."

"Maybe it's all right," Marel said, a little doubtfully.

"You ought to see their apartment," Chris went on. "Talk about comfort and room! What you and I wouldn't give to have a place like that!"

Marel caught the look Mrs. Mallory flashed at her and knew that she could hold off no longer.

"That's the spot for a commercial if ever I saw one," she said. "Chris, your mother has found a place for us to live."

Chris put down his fork and looked at his mother. "There! Didn't I tell you she was one for action?"

Marel hurried on. "We could just have it for a year, but it is a beautiful place. Nicely furnished and with lots of room."

"How much rent?" Chris asked.

"That is where I come in," his mother said quickly. "There is an extra room for me, and if I rent that from you you can manage the rest."

Chris looked at his wife. "Is the place what you want?"

"It—it's very nice," she admitted.

Mrs. Mallory reached out to give Marel's arm a friendly pat. "She wouldn't agree to take it till we had consulted you. If you like, we can go back there tonight. Then you can have a look at it."

"If you two like it, I don't need to look," he said. "I guess anything with more than one room would look good to us. It would be nice to have my wife home evenings, for one thing."

She would like that too, Marel thought. And yet—and

yet——— Somehow she wished he would not agree too quickly.

"Now you can have a pleasanter home," Mrs. Mallory said. "Both of you. I'll be able to take some of the house-work off your hands, Marel, and I love to cook. I doubt if either of you has been getting the proper food to eat the way you've been living."

Chris smiled dreamily. "That sounds good to me. Wait'll you taste Mom's biscuits, Marel. And oh, that pie! Any kind of pie! To say nothing of what she can do to just plain stew."

Listening, Marel found that the hotel dinner had gone tasteless and that it was becoming harder to swallow with every mouthful. Marriage had apparently been more of a hardship for Chris than she had realized.

But now it was settled and the hardships would be done away with. She and Chris and his mother were going to move into the Billings' beautiful apartment. Now Chris could have a comfortable, well-kept home and better food than two novices had been able to prepare for themselves. So she must cheer up and be happy about it for both Chris's sake and her own.

How foolish she had been to regard this meeting with Mrs. Mallory as an ordeal. Chris's mother could not have been more kindly and reasonable. She was not at all the storybook mother-in-law. She would be very easy to live with.

There was no sense at all to the nagging little voice inside her that kept insisting that this was the wrong thing to do. She must silence that voice as quickly as possible, not listen to it at all. She had said she would do cheerfully whatever Chris wanted. Well—this was what he wanted.

18

"No Vacancies"

Tonight Chris was at the Allens' going over more revision. He worked as hard these days as Marel had worked during the last few weeks. Every minute he was home he sat at his typewriter making the keys fly. Marel washed dishes, wiped them as quietly as she could, and then slipped out of the apartment to let him work in peace.

She had no assignment now to keep her occupied and the urge to draw seemed to have lessened. Sometimes she went to the studio and tried to work, but it was only a pretense to please Chris. Sometimes she took long walks about New York's streets. She found a bench in a small park along the river where she could sit and watch the boats go by when it wasn't too cold. Sometimes she dropped into a cafeteria and sat for an hour over a cup of coffee, reading a book or a magazine. Other times she went to an inexpensive movie and sat lonesomely through the picture, wishing Chris was there to share the experience when the movie happened to be good.

The Billings would not be out of their place for another month, so there was no use beginning to pack. Four more weeks of crowded quarters had to be got through somehow. Then everything would be better.

Often now Chris was with the Allens. Or at least with Irene. Once or twice he had asked Marel if she would like to go along, but she had felt she would only be in the way and had pleaded work of her own. At least, when he was out she could stay in the apartment instead of trying to kill time away from home.

Tonight when he'd gone, she tried to settle down with a book, but the story dragged, and she could take no interest in other people's problems.

She turned the radio dial listlessly, searching for a program that would suit her mood, finding none. What *was* the matter with her? Why couldn't she put up with the few remaining weeks before they moved into the new apartment without making herself miserable? It was silly that she should have felt better when an apparent eternity of living here had stretched ahead.

Her fingers clicked off a news announcer, and she jumped up from the chair, stood with her hands on her hips looking about the room. Maybe she *had* better have things out with herself. Maybe she had better face this and take a look at the thoughts she was trying to suppress.

Her gaze moved from one article of furniture to another. From the sofa Aunt Peg had given them—a cheerful splash of color along one wall; to the lamp shade she had painted herself. The shade was tipped, and she put out a finger to straighten it, loving the warm glow it gave to the room. It was a cozy room at night. Attractive and homey, for all that it was so small. The curtains Chris had chosen were exactly right, and the rest was nice too, and very dear to her.

The room looked different from the way it had at first. In the beginning it had seemed dressed-up, as if it were putting on its best face for company. Now it looked lived-in, and she liked the way Chris's things and hers had stopped being "his" and "hers" and had become *"Theirs."*

Now most of these belongings must go into storage because the Billings' place was perfectly furnished. A second-hand, home-made lamp shade would have no place in all that perfection. Nor would a coffee table, with a deep scratch across the top that had to be kept carefully hidden with a Mexican pottery ash tray. Or the chair, with the slightly wobbly rear leg that threatened to give way every time Mac Conway sat in it.

Nevertheless, she loved these things. They were *theirs*. They belonged to her and to Chris, not to some well-off family who was away on a trip to Mexico. What was more, she and Chris could enjoy them alone here. Within the limits of the demands their work placed upon them, they could do as they pleased. They did not have to consider the comfort or desires of a third person, no matter how sweet and pleasant that person might be. They were two—working together, tackling their problems side by side. Once they had moved into the Billings place, it would no longer be like that

Now it was coming out. This was what the matter was. This was the thing that took the drawing ability out of her fingertips and the ambition out of her soul.

"Oh, dear," she said aloud, while the little room seemed to listen with sympathetic attentiveness, "I want to live with just Chris. I don't *want* to share my home with a third person—even if she is Chris's mother. I want my own place. *Our* own place!"

Well, then—why didn't she do something about it? Why did she sit here mooning, dreading the move to the bigger apartment, neglecting her own work and brooding?

After all, what had she really done to try to find a place to live in New York? She had simply sat and let apartments fall upon her. There had been enough of that.

She pulled open the closet door and took out her coat. A scarf tied about her head would keep out the wind she could hear howling down the alley outside her window. Knitted mittens warmed her hands. Fall was fading into winter and the night was chilly and brisk.

Outside, she walked quickly and with purpose in her steps. She would do this with mathematical precision. No matter how discouraging the response, she would cover one block after another. There were millions of people in this town and some of them moved from time to time. If she really worked at this, she would meet with luck eventually. There was, after all, a law of averages.

She walked into the first building she came to a little breathlessly. The lobby was empty, but there was a desk in one corner with a small printed sign upon it:

NO VACANCIES

Marel looked the sign straight in the eye and made a face at it. She wasn't to be frightened off as easily as that.

She went over to the row of bells and mailboxes and searched until she found one labeled "Building Manager." She pressed the bell and waited. Nothing happened. Nothing happened after she had pressed it three times. Building Manager was apparently not home. Or else he had given up answering his bell because of people who wanted apartments.

Resolutely she went out on the street again and into the next building. This time the bell was marked "Janitor." She put a demanding finger against it and a raucous feminine voice came out of the tube at her ear.

"What you want?" it demanded.

"I want to speak to the janitor," Marel said into the speaking tube.

"He's asleep," the voice shouted back. "You looking for apartment? We don't got any!"

Well, that made two tries, Marel told herself, as she returned to the street. At least there was some variety to this experience. Sometimes people were not home and sometimes they were asleep.

In the next building she popped through the door in time to catch an elevator man about to shut the gate of his car. She made a dash for the end of the hall.

"Please," she said, "is there anyone around who could tell me about apartments?"

He looked bored with his job, bored with her. "Sure," he said. "I can. There ain't any."

"I know," she told him. "I think I've heard that some-

where before. But surely some of these places take names
and——"

"Oh, sure, sure," he said. "They take names. Hundreds
of 'em. Maybe you might get called in about fifty years.
Sorry, lady, there's my bell."

The gate shut her out relentlessly, and the car went off
to pick up some lucky occupant who possessed an apartment.

Well, that covered this block. Now for the next. She
would go six blocks on this side of the street, then cross
over and come back on the other side. At least things
were looking up. She had actually talked to somebody in
person this time.

The next two bells did not answer. At the ring of the
third one, a frowsy-looking woman came into the hall.

"I'm the manager," she said in response to Marel's
question. "And you're the fifth to ring my bell tonight.
Can't you read?" She pointed an irate finger at a "No
Vacancies" sign and disappeared down the hallway,
slamming her door expressively.

Marel looked at herself in the hall mirror. "Am I that
repulsive?" she inquired of her reflection. The girl with
the scarf tied under her chin looked back at her, nodding
solemnly. "You are if you're looking for an apartment,"
she said.

"Okay," Marel told her reflection. "So we're repulsive.
What are we waiting for? Let's go and repulse some more
people."

A young couple came through the door just then and
caught her talking to herself. They gave her a curious
look and a wide berth as they went by, and she returned
to the outside cold blushing. They needn't have looked at
her like that. People got that way hunting apartments.
Didn't they know? How had they got their apartment?
Perhaps she should have run after them and asked.

In the next place she really threw herself into the spirit
of the thing. A porter with a thick red mustache and

very red hair was mopping up the hallway. In answer to her question he said, "Second door down the hall," and went back to his mopping.

She knocked on the door and burst into words the moment a tall man in overalls opened it. She told him her story in heart-wrenching terms. All about how she was a bride and her life and happiness were about to be broken up because she would have to move in with her mother-in-law. She turned on all the feminine appeal she could muster, gave him her nicest smile and her saddest story.

He heard her through, mainly, she suspected, because the suddenness of her attack surprised him into listening. But when she was through, he said, "Lady, I got troubles of my own," and shut the door none too gently in her face.

A discouraged voice inside her suggested that she give up and go home. What she was doing was completely hopeless. But she was not ready to listen yet. The porter looked up as she went by.

"Your psychological approach is wrong," he told her.

It was Marel's turn to be taken by surprise. She stared open-mouthed while he sloshed a puddle of water around the floor.

"It's no good to talk mother-in-law to that guy," he went on amiably. "He's got two of 'em living with him. Besides, you'll never get anywhere telling people your troubles and expecting them to sympathize with you. Why should they care about *your* troubles? Come on, now— why should they? Do you care about mine?"

He had a nice wide grin beneath the furry mustache and she had to smile back at him.

"You're wrong," she said. "I'd be fascinated to hear about your troubles. You're the first person who has given me a kind word tonight."

He nodded his red head at her. "I'm a brightener. That's why. But you don't really care, because you've got too many troubles of your own."

"Brightener?" Marel repeated. "Oh, I know. You mean you brighten the corner and all that sort of thing?"

"Sure," he said. "That's it."

He was nice. He was practically the nicest person she had met in years.

"What about this psychological approach?" she asked him. "If I can't tell them my troubles, what can I tell them? I mean it's no go just to say I want an apartment. I have to figure out a way to get past their guard."

He swept a wide area of tile floor with the mop, talking as he worked. "I'll tell you, miss. I used to sell stuff myself. Door to door. It's a tough racket, but after a while you learn about human nature. Learn some of the tricks. Look, now—this is what you do, see?"

She listened while the red-haired porter leaned on his mop and outlined a course of attack for her. What he said sounded at least worth a try. And the words she had exchanged with him gave her new courage and hope.

In the next building, when the manager proved to be a more kindly-looking woman than the others she had met that night, Marel started in on her new tack.

"I wonder if I could speak to you for a moment?" she inquired.

The woman began to shake her head. "If it's about an apartment——"

"Oh, I'm not asking for an apartment," Marel said quickly. "What I want is advice."

She waited hopefully. People loved to give advice, her friend the porter had told her. Ask for what they wanted to give and seldom got enough chance to give, and you had 'em. So he claimed.

Her prospective victim looked a little startled. "Well— I don't know. Just what is it that you want advice about?"

Marel smiled at her brightly. "I know this seems queer of me—just ringing a stranger's doorbell and asking favors. But I thought there must be one friendly person in the city of New York who could tell me what to do."

No one could resist being called friendly, the porter had told her.

"I'll try," the woman said. "That is, if I can."

"The point," Marel went on, "is that you are on the inside in this apartment business. I know perfectly well that you haven't a thing and that you must have dozens of people waiting for whatever comes up. But suppose you had to look for an apartment in this town, how would *you* go about it?"

For a moment Marel feared she would wave her away like the others and refuse to bother. But she was a nice person. And she was ready to be a little sorry for Marel.

"I don't think I can help you," she said, "but come in for a moment and we'll talk it over. I'm Mrs. Jackson."

Marel introduced herself and followed her hostess into a small neat apartment. There was a bedroom door showing off a tiny hallway and Marel sighed.

"You're lucky. Room to breathe in. But I'd be so grateful if you'd give me any tips that occur to you. People must do awfully silly things when they are desperate for a place to live."

Mrs. Jackson agreed emphatically. "You've no idea the hard-luck stories I have to listen to. Every one is worse than the last, and people seem to think I'm mean and stony-hearted because I don't fish an apartment out of the air for them. You're smart not to pull any sob stories."

Marel hoped she wasn't blushing guiltily. "But surely there must be some way—I mean people do move out, and somebody moves in."

"Mostly it's somebody with a drag, or somebody who knows somebody. But I'll tell you what—why don't you try outside Manhattan? This is the toughest place of all to crack. If you'd try the Bronx, or Brooklyn, or Long Island, or Staten Island."

"But this is so convenient. I mean there's the matter of transportation. I'd hate to get caught in that subway jam every morning and every night."

"There're worse things. Anyway, some of these outlying districts have local newspapers. Sometimes they run apartment ads, believe it or not. You could even try advertising yourself."

Marel looked at her thoughtfully. "It's worth a try. And it's something we haven't looked into yet. Thank you for being so nice."

Nevertheless, when she was outside again, she followed her original plan through to the grim finish. She rang doorbells for the six blocks home, and whenever she could reach a listening ear she asked for advice, instead of for an apartment. At least there were some of these people who would remember her out of all the apartment-hunters who came their way. When she went back again, they'd know her. Perhaps she might even wear one of them down, or make friends so they might tip her off if anything came up. At least it would be a way to spend these lonely evenings, while Chris worked or visited the Allens.

When she got back to her own building, she found Eric Webb in the vestibule, pressing a finger against her bell. One look at him told her that he was in a ferocious mood.

"Hello," she said limply, wondering what was up now and how she could cope with any more problems.

He scowled at her. "About time you got home. I was afraid I'd wasted my evening. Well, don't stand there with your mouth open. Why don't you ask me in?"

"Why—of course." She stopped gaping at him and led the way down the hall to her own door.

In the apartment she switched on lights and got wearily out of her coat. She felt tired all over. Not only had she walked quite a distance on hard city pavements, but she had used up a lot of nervous energy as well. If Eric had a scolding for her, she wasn't at all sure she could take it.

"I'm tired," she said apologetically. "I've been apartment hunting. Is anything wrong?"

"I'll say it's wrong," Eric told her. "Your pictures have been turned down."

She waited blankly for him to go on. Somehow she couldn't feel anything. It was as if this were happening to someone else and she was merely an observer whose own emotions were not involved.

"Anita Johnson called me tonight," Eric fairly barked the words. "She's my editor at MacLane's."

"The one who thought she liked my pictures?" Marel asked.

"That's right. But now she doesn't want 'em. She'll take your friend's stories alone, but not the pictures."

Marel pushed a soft pillow up on the couch behind her shoulders and leaned back. After a while, she knew, she was going to feel something. But right now she was too numb.

"Tell me about it," she said. "Tell me what happened."

19

Storm

The story came out in a sputter of indignation. Eric was mad at everybody. At Anita Johnson. At Marel. At Ginger. At the world. But in spite of his fury, Marel pieced out the picture.

Miss Johnson felt extremely unhappy about the whole thing. She had not, however, actually commissioned Marel to do the pictures. Marel had understood it was just a trial. Now the publishing business was pulling in its horns everywhere, fearing a drop-off in sales. The heads of Miss Johnson's company had issued an edict that made the utmost thrift necessary. She was no longer in a position to take the risk of publishing two unknowns in as expensive a book as this would prove to be. She was still willing to bring out Ginger's stories, but she wanted to put a name artist to work on them—not to do color pictures like Marel's—but simple black-and-white line drawings that would not cost so much to print.

'She liked your pictures all right," Eric said crossly. "But that's the verdict. Ginger's in and you're out. That's the trouble with this screwy business. Why anybody is crazy enough to go into it, I wouldn't know."

She knew his irritation wasn't directed at her. It was a bluff, mostly, to conceal how sorry he was about her bad break. But it wouldn't be like Eric to be openly sympathetic.

"It was good of you to take the time to come and tell me," she said. "I know why you did it. You didn't want me to have to take it on the chin the first thing tomor-

row at work. This way I'll have time to pick up the pieces
before Gail and Fran know about it. Perhaps—perhaps
you don't have to tell them right away?"

I don't have to tell 'em at all," he said gruffly. "It's
none of their business."

"They'll have to know. Just so it's not tomorrow."

Eric rose. "I must say you're a cool one. I thought
you'd be one of these hysterical females who weep and
tear their hair."

She managed a smile. "I'm not being cool. It's just
that I haven't started to feel yet. I can't believe it yet."

"Well, it's true enough. Anyway, you can use those
pictures as samples of your work. Maybe they'll get you
another job. I'll leave it to you to break it to Ginger. At
least, she's not out altogether. And a name artist won't
hurt her sales any."

Eric put out his hand, doubled into a fist, and tapped
Marel under the chin. "Don't go to pieces over this. It
happens to everybody in one way or another. It's how
you take it that counts."

Just as he turned toward the door, Chris's key sounded
in the lock and Chris himself came in whistling jauntily.
The whistle broke off at the sight of Eric and he greeted
the artist without enthusiasm.

Eric said, "Be seeing you, Marel," and took his de-
parture.

Marel saw him to the door and then turned back to
Chris. It was beginning to hurt now. The numbness of
shock was going away and tears of sick disappointment
had started to burn behind her eyes. All she wanted now
was the comfort of Chris's arms about her and his shoulder under her cheek. Having him would make it hurt
less. It would be much worse to take it all alone.

"That guy!" Chris said the moment the door was
closed. "I don't like him. I don't want him here."

Marel paused on her way across the room. Chris had

his back to her, taking off his things. She blinked away the haze of tears.

"He came about the book," she told him. "Ginger's and mine. It was very kind of him to come."

"Hmph!" said Chris, dismissing the subject of Eric Webb as he took an envelope from his pocket. "Come over here, honey, and see what I've got."

He held out his arm, but she did not go into the circle of it. She stayed outside, waiting.

He glanced at her in surprise and then tossed the envelope onto the coffee table. "It's just the contract for *Fear on the Ferry*," he said casually.

She wanted to take up the folded paper eagerly. She wanted to sit on his knee and go over every word of it with him. In spite of her own hurt, she wanted to be big enough to be happy over success for him.

But some queer stubbornness held her back. Inside her was an ache she needed him to heal. And he had been so filled with his own success that he had not noticed how she felt. He'd been a little rude to Eric too. He didn't deserve to be applauded and hugged and praised. It apparently made no difference to him that his wife had just had her own career blighted, or that she had walked her feet off that evening to try to find an apartment for them. Little things like that he could brush off as being of no consequence. So why should she get excited about his book? The stubborn voice was stronger than her generous impulse.

"I know publishing a mystery story isn't much," Chris said stiffly, "but there'll be a three-hundred-and-fifty-dollar advance when I sign the contract. And if it hadn't been for Irene——"

If he had not mentioned Irene perhaps she could even yet have thrust away that frozen stubbornness inside her and behaved like herself, like the Marel Chris knew and loved. But Irene's name at this time was the last straw.

"I think it's very nice about the contract," she said,

and her words were like icicles clicking out, freezing in the air between them, "but if you don't mind, I'd rather not listen to any more about Irene tonight. I've had her served up for breakfast and dinner for weeks and the diet is getting monotonous."

She could see the flash of anger in his eyes and she remembered what Mac had once said about how mad Chris could get when he really got mad. Well, let him! She walked coolly to the door and opened it.

"I want to see Ginger for a minute. I'll be back."

She went out before he could explode and, though she had not meant to bang the door, it startled her with the sharp sound it made in closing. The sound relieved her feelings a little, even while she regretted it. By the time she reached Ginger's door, her own anger had died to some extent.

It was late and Mrs. Williams came to the door in her bathrobe. A moment later, Marel was sitting on Ginger's bed, pouring out her story. Ginger sat up aganist a pillow, looking plumper than ever in her butcher-boy pajamas, her eyes bright with dismay.

"You mean that awful woman doesn't want your pictures after letting you go to all that work?"

"It isn't her fault, really," Marel explained. "She feels bad about it too. Eric said she was very sorry. But there was nothing she could do. And she hadn't made any promises about the pictures, you know. It was something I knew I was doing on trial."

"If they were badly done," Ginger protested, "that would be different. But how could she turn down good work?"

Marel's shrug was limp. "It's a matter of expense. The expense of printing a color job like that. Anyway, I'm glad you'll get your chance, Ginger. At least this won't make any difference as far as your stories are concerned."

Ginger was plainly astonished. "Won't make any difference? What do you mean? Do you think I'd let her have my stories when she won't take your drawings? Don't be silly! We'll take the whole thing to another publisher. You and I are in this together."

Marel leaned over and hugged Ginger. This was such generosity as she had not expected, but she could not accept it.

"Of course you'll let her have the stories, Ginger. It will mean a contract right away and an advance. And you need the money to buy things you want for the future."

Ginger shook her head. "I don't need it as bad as that. Ken wouldn't want it that much either. Do you think I'd just walk out on you and let all the work you've done be wasted? There's no use arguing. We'll sell it and we'll sell it together. See?"

It was left at that. There was no swerving Ginger, and hope began to rise in Marel again. Not even Eric had expected Ginger to turn down her own chance in order to stand by. She was a real friend.

Marel went back to the apartment feeling better. She knew what she had to do now. She had to make it up to Chris for not being properly excited about his success. He couldn't know what had happened to her unless she told him. So now she would apologize about the door and tell him why Eric had come.

When she walked in, he was slumped in their one big chair with his nose in a book and he did not look up. The contract had vanished from the coffee table.

"Chris," she said, "I'm sorry I was bad-tempered and slammed the door. I want to tell you about what Ginger has just done."

His gaze did not lift from the page he was reading and his expression was not that of the Chris she knew.

"Suppose we let Ginger go till some other time," he said indifferently. "I guess I get as fed up with her sometimes as you do with my friends."

"Ginger's the swellest person ever!" In spite of her good intentions annoyance got into her voice again.

He gave her a long, unloving look. "As far as I'm concerned, she's a bore and a scatterbrain."

"That's just because she sounds silly sometimes," Marel protested. "And she does talk a lot. But you have to be big enough to look past things like that and see what's underneath."

"No, thanks," he said. "I like good qualities out where they show."

"Oh, Chris, I don't want to argue about Ginger."

"Then why do it? Why not drop the whole thing and let me read in peace?"

She let him read in peace after that. She left him strictly alone and busied herself pulling out the roll-away bed. Then she took a shower and tucked herself between the sheets. By turning on her side she could shut out the light to some extent. Usually Chris was considerate about turning off lights when she was ready for bed. But tonight he read on obstinately while she pretended to sleep.

It was the first time they'd ever gone to bed without a good-night kiss, without even speaking to each other. All her anger had seeped away. She felt hurt and sore. After a while the pillow began to get damp under her cheek. But Chris did not notice she was crying. All his interest was for his book.

She tried to fall asleep, but instead she kept remembering things. All sorts of things that belonged to happier times when there had been no Irene Allen to fill Chris's spare time. And maybe his thoughts? She remembered she had felt that, because she and Chris were going to be married, she would never have to feel lonely again. Foolishly she had thought that marriage solved everything.

But here she was married, and feeling more alone—with Chris right across the room from her—than she'd felt when they had lived under different roofs. Somehow they had gone so far away from each other tonight that there was no bridge across which either could walk to reach the other.

In the morning they were coolly polite, and there was none of the usual joking over breakfast, no talk about plans for the day. It was "Please pass the toast," or "Will you have another egg?" as if they were strangers who had just met and did not like each other very well.

Chris usually left earlier than she did in the morning and there was a moment before he went out the door when they might have got back together again. She still felt hurt and mistreated. He did not deserve to be let off easily.

She said, "Be seeing you. Don't spend your fortune all in one place."

He said, "I haven't collected it yet," and they looked at each other coldly.

Then Marel went into the bathroom and shut the door. How could Chris know that she put her ear against it, listening, half hoping he'd come over and tap on it, and say, "Look, honey, aren't we being pretty silly?" But, he did not. She heard the click of the apartment door and knew he'd gone.

So let him, she thought. If that was the way he felt, let him! It had been petty and small of him to make cracks about Ginger last night. Maybe he'd be ashamed when he heard what Ginger had done. She could never forgive him for that.

A voice inside her murmured: "*You* made cracks about Irene. He was just paying you back." But she thrust it aside. That was different. After all, she wasn't seeing a lot of another man the way he was of Irene. Maybe she could if she tried. But she didn't want to. She only wanted Chris. The old, understanding Chris. They had been married less than three months and everything was in a muddle. They rubbed each other the wrong way and said unkind things and grew further apart every minute.

20

Marel Dines Out

Marel was down on her knees sorting books in Fran's bookcase when the phone rang. Fran answered it and waved the receiver at Marel.

"It's for you. Your one and only."

Marel got up from her knees with no outward haste, but there was an eagerness in her she wanted to hide from Fran. Chris might be calling to make up, to say he was sorry, maybe to ask her to lunch. But she would put no warmth in her voice until he had apologized properly.

"Hello," she said coolly into the phone.

His greeting was no warmer than hers. "Hello, Marel. Mother wants us to have dinner with her tonight."

"Oh?" she said.

"Maybe we can meet at her hotel after work. She'd like to take us to a special place she knows."

"What's it all about?" Marel asked.

He hesitated just a moment. "I got my check today. And when I called Mom to tell her about the contract, she suggested a celebration. The party's going to be on her."

Marel regarded the telephone reproachfully. How *could* he have forgotten? How could he have called his mother first about the check? When all along they'd planned to go to the Blue Peacock together. Just the two of them.

She spoke carefully so that her voice would reveal no tendency to quiver. "I don't think so, Chris. I haven't felt very well today and I guess I'd rather get home to bed. You go ahead and meet your mother."

He might have offered some sympathy, or have protested that he wanted her in on the celebration, but he did not.

"Okay," he said, "if that's the way you want it. 'Bye now."

She said, "Good-bye," faintly and hung up the phone. She was aware of Fran's eyes upon her and she turned her back and dropped to her knees before the bookcase again.

The office was quiet for a while, except for the sound of books being moved and thumped together, and the rustle of a page as Fran read the morning's mail.

An exclamation made Marel turn to see Fran frowning at a drawing she had just taken from a big envelope.

"Drat it!" Fran said. "And if there weren't ladies present I'd use language. Will you look at this atrocity?"

She held the drawing up for Marel to see. It was a rough for the jacket of an animal story and it was a "busy" cover. Little animals swarmed all over it, leaving the eye weary at the first glance. There was nothing definite to follow. You jumped from here to there to yon, without being able to tell what the picture was all about.

"Good night!" Fran said. "This gal's genius, if any, doesn't lie in designing jackets. I'll bet you could do better than that."

She shuddered and put the picture face down on her desk. Then her gaze turned speculatively to Marel and there was an understanding in her look that had nothing to do with cover designs. Something that saw too clearly and went too far for Marel's comfort. She turned away from it quickly and began replacing books on an empty shelf. But when Fran spoke, her words were on safely professional ground.

"You know what? I'll bet you *could* turn out a better cover than this. You've been putting a few animals into your pictures for Ginger's book. You've got a feeling of the texture and anatomy. Why not? Want to try?"

Marel did not feel like trying anything. With her so-called career shattered by the rejection of her pictures, with Chris behaving like a stranger, she could not get excited about designing a cover—even if she could do it, which was doubtful.

She shook her head gloomily. "I guess animals aren't my line. I don't think anything's in my line." Fran had to hear the worst sometime—it might as well be now. "Mac-Lane had turned down my pictures. They can't use them, after all. They like Ginger's stories, but Eric says my drawings would be too expensive for them to print at this time."

Fran spent not a moment in wringing her hands or wasting sympathy. "Is Ginger giving them the stories?"

"No," Marel said. "Ginger's being swell. She wants her stories to be published with my pictures."

"Then what are you looking so woeful about?" Fran said cheerfully. "Get the manuscript back to me as fast as you can and I'll start looking for a buyer. In fact, I think I know a spot for it right now."

If she had not been in such a state of general depression, Marel might have cheered up over that. But as it was she could only say, "Thank you" bleakly, and turn back to her work.

After that, Fran left her alone until after lunch, though Marel was aware every now and then that she was being quietly observed.

"You've wallowed long enough," Fran announced finally. "Out you go for fresh air and some ideas for that jacket design. There's a bookstore a few blocks down the street—go have a look in the window. See what's cooking in book jackets this season and don't come back till you have an inspiration I can use."

When Fran decided on action, there was no use protesting. Marel smiled wryly as she got into her coat. "Okay, boss. But don't be surprised if you never see me again. I have a feeling this isn't my day for ideas."

It did help a little, though, to get outside and walk briskly along the sidewalk, lost in the crowd where no one knew who she was, and no one watched her covertly. She even put her nose against the bookstore window and looked at jackets as Fran had instructed her to do. But she did not really see them. Colors and designs blurred together as an indistinct background for her thoughts.

Maybe she should have said "yes" to Chris's invitation. Maybe men just weren't made so they saw as important the same things that were important to women. After all, going to the Blue Peacock was a sentimental notion on her part—not a life-and-death matter; yet here she was letting the fact that her husband had forgotten a promise made half in fun become serious enough to widen the uncomfortable breach that had lately grown between them.

Perhaps there was still time to undo what harm she might have done. She could still call Chris at the office and tell him she'd like to join his mother's party tonight.

With the making of that resolution, her spirits began to rise. Now that she felt better, the book jackets in the window made more sense. Those green leaves floating down a tan background looked good. Why couldn't something like that be adapted to little animal forms in a design that would be her own?

She turned away from the window with new courage growing in her. Everyone had failures. Eric said it was the way you took the bad times that counted. So now she would get busy on a new project and work at it as hard as she could. But first she would stop at a drugstore on the way back to the studio and phone Chris.

She felt almost happy as she dropped her nickel, and when she heard Chris's voice at the other end of the wire, she made her own sound as cheerful as possible.

"I'd like to change my mind," she told him, "and join you and your mother tonight for dinner."

The silence at the other end of the wire was not reassuring. After an uncomfortable pause, Chris said: "Sorry, but I've called off the dinner. Something unexpected has come up. I'll be home a little late tonight."

There was nothing she could do but say, "All right," and hang up. He had not offered to explain what the something unexpected was. He had not sounded friendly, or sorry, or anything nice. You couldn't close a breach all by yourself, she thought, as she walked back to the studio. It took two people to build that kind of bridge. Chris wasn't holding up his end at all.

When Fran asked, "Any ideas?" Marel shook her head. "Nothing good. Let me try some other day."

Fran urged her no more, and the rest of the afternoon crawled drearily along to a dull conclusion. Again it was a relief to get away from eyes that watched her. Marel put on her hat and coat and went downstairs.

It was one of those raw November evenings when the city vanished into dirty gray murk and the lights lost the washed brilliance they had when it was clear.

Cold dampness was sticky against her face as she went through the revolving door and out on the street. Silly to think of Chris every time she went through a revolving door.

The crowds on the sidewalk were all hurrying to get somewhere, and once more Marel had a feeling of being at odds with everyone in New York. Once more she had no urgent desire to go either east or west, or uptown or downtown. There was nothing to stay outside for, but there was nothing in particular to go home for either. A lonely dinner to get and eat by herself. Dishes to wash with no gay companion to make washing dishes fun. It *had* been fun at first. So what had happened? What had gone wrong in so short a time?

As she stopped to wait for a light to change, a mocking sign winked at her—a gay peacock's tail of red and green and blue lights.

The Blue Peacock.

She slowed her steps as she walked beneath the blue

canopy that stretched over the sidewalk. This was where they had promised each other they'd go to celebrate that first check. But Chris had never given the promise a second thought. She felt much less forgiving now about that than she had during the afternoon.

She walked past the restaurant and went down the block. Then, impulsively, she turned and walked back to the canopy. She knew now what she meant to do. Never mind if it was crazy—even a little reckless. Goodness only knew how much a dinner here would cost. But since she would probably never come with Chris, she might as well take herself. At least she'd have the experience without waiting till she was too old to enjoy it.

She checked the contents of her purse to make sure she had enough of the week's grocery money with her to pay the bill. She would replace it later when she earned an extra check of her own. For the rest of this week they could just eat out of cans. The head waiter was distant and haughty and Marel said, "A table for one, please," in a tone which she hoped would indicate that she was quite accustomed to dining in places like the Blue Peacock. But she suspected that he saw through her pose.

The table for one to which he led her was not the best in the room. In fact, it was in a crowded spot where waiters brushed by on their way to the kitchen, but she had neither the heart nor the courage to assert herself and ask for something better. She meekly took the chair he drew out and buried herself in a study of the alarmingly large menu he handed her.

She noted with a sinking heart that she and Chris could eat for days at home for what one meal would cost here. Well, she was in for it now, and she might as well enjoy every minute. Nevertheless, she ordered as cautiously as possible. No appetizer. No extras of any kind. The entrée would cost enough. As she gave the waiter her order, she sensed that he felt unfortunate to have her at his table.

When he had gone, she sat up very straight, sipping ice water and looking about. This was the Blue Peacock. This was where she had always wanted to dine. She was here to have a wonderful evening and never mind whether Chris was with her or not.

But when the food came, it tasted like so much sawdust in her mouth, and she found herself miserably aware of the fact that no one else was dining here alone. There were lots of women, happy, laughing women, each with her own escort. There were no foolish little wives who were using up the grocery money in an effort to pretend that dining out alone could be fun.

She remembered the time when she had waited at the ferry for Chris and every other man she saw had reminded her of him—just because she so longed to find him in the crowd. It was the same here, even though she had tried to fool herself into thinking she could have a lovely time without him. There was a man two tables away with his back to her. When he turned his head, there was a Chris look about him. But he wasn't Chris, and he was with a pretty blond girl who was having fun.

Even voices made her think of him. A man who had just come in was asking the waiter for a table by the window, and his voice reminded her of Chris. She turned her head to see the man who could sound so amazingly like her husband and her breath caught in her throat.

It *was* Chris! For a single crazy instant she thought he had come there looking for her; that suddenly in a miraculous flash everything was going to be all right. Then he stepped aside to allow the woman with him to follow the waiter to a pleasant table near a window. The woman was Irene Allen.

They brushed so close as they crossed the room that Marel could catch the fragrance of Irene's perfume, but neither one looked down at the single occupant of an awkwardly placed table on the aisle.

Marel continued to raise her fork automatically and

chew food that was tasteless. Irene and Chris. And he had brought her here to the Blue Peacock.

She wanted to look away, but in spite of herself she watched as he helped Irene off with her coat, and then took his place, smiling at her across the table. His chair was half turned toward Marel and she had a horrid feeling that at any minute he would raise his eyes and meet her own across the room. Then what would he do? Ignore her? Bow to her distantly like a stranger? Or perhaps come over and get her to join that intimate little party?

Whatever happened would be awful. To sit here without making her presence known would be spying, but to let them know she was here would be even worse. She had to get away as quickly as she could.

She signaled her waiter and asked for her check, no longer caring that his eyebrows rose a notch higher at the sight of the half-eaten food on her plate. What a waiter thought scarcely mattered any more.

Until the moment when she found herself beneath the blue canopy again, she was in dread lest Chris should look up and see her. But once on the sidewalk, she was safe and could walk miserably in the direction of home.

No matter how hard she tried to shake off the memory, the image of those two sitting at the small table together persisted in her mind. Why hadn't Stuart been with them? Why had they been alone? And why the Blue Peacock? How could he, how *could* he?

She let herself into the apartment, threw off her things, and curled herself in a corner of the sofa. The first numbness of misery was wearing off now and in its place came indignation, anger. Did he really think she would take this sort of thing from him? Did he think she would smile sweetly when he came home and ask if he had had a nice evening with Irene? Or that she would greet him happily, not dreaming where he had been?

It was high time, she decided, that Christopher Mallory had a lesson taught him. A lesson he would not forget in a hurry. But for all the stormy thoughts that thronged her mind, the time dragged and seemed endless. What fun those two must be having together that they should take so long over dinner! What——

And then she heard his key in the lock. A moment later he came into the room, grave and thoughtful now, no smile on his face.

"Well?" she said.

At her tone he looked at her quickly. "Well, what?"

She sniffed. "I hope you had a pleasant evening at the Blue Peacock."

He watched her quietly, not saying a word, waiting for her to go on. The way he looked made her angrier still.

"I suppose you thought I wouldn't know that you were out with Irene? I suppose you thought I'd never know that you took her to the—the place where you were going to take me when you earned your first check? Took her behind my back!"

"You're certainly well informed," he said, and the words had a clipped sound she had never heard before.

"It's too bad that I'm smarter than you think!" she cried. "It's too bad I had to find out and spoil everything!"

"I take it you must have been at the Blue Peacock too?" Again he clipped out the words.

"That's where I was. I saw you. I saw you both. I saw the way you smiled at her." Even as she spoke the words, she felt a little sick over their ugliness, regretted them, wished them unspoken. Yet perversely she allowed them to rush out anyway.

This time he did not answer. He had started to get out of his coat, but now he pulled it back on and crossed the room to the closet door. When he came into sight again, he had a suitcase in his hand. He set it down on a chair and began to put things into it. His pajamas and shaving things, his shirts and good suit. Marel watched in frozen fascination.

She had not expected this. Somehow, deep down inside her, she had hoped that in spite of everything he would come and take her into his arms, forgive her stormy words. That he'd tell her she was wrong and Irene didn't mean a thing to him. That Marel was the girl he truly loved. But he was doing none of these things. He was obviously packing to leave.

She put her cheek against her arm on the back of the couch. She did not turn her head to look at him again, but wept softly into the crook of her elbow.

After a while she heard him close the lid of the suitcase. The click of the lock had a frighteningly final sound. But still she did not look up. She heard him come to stand beside her and hoped with all her heart that he would lean over and gather her into his arms.

"Maybe our friends were wiser than we thought," he said quietly. "Everyone told us we were marrying too quickly without knowing each other well enough ahead of time. I guess it's beginning to show up now."

Marel blew her nose and cried harder than ever. But he did not seem to care how miserable she was.

"I'm going away for a while," he went on. "I think we both need to think things over and find out where we stand. Lately you've been finding in me someone you don't care very much about. And I'm afraid the same thing's been happening to me."

He did not say good-bye, but walked to the door. She heard it open and close again and knew she was alone.

After a time the tears stopped flowing, and except for a gulping sob now and then, she lay quietly, feeling limp and numb. It was hard to understand what had happened. Chris couldn't be really gone. Any minute she'd hear the familiar sound of his key in the lock and he'd come back to comfort her and tell her it was all a mistake, that of course he couldn't go out of her life, or let her go out of his.

But no step sounded in the hallway outside the door,

no key grated in the lock. When she sat up wearily and looked around, the clock told her how late the hour was. If she was going to be at work in the morning, she would have to get to bed, get some sleep somehow.

"And they lived happily ever after," she said to herself bitterly as she got undressed and ready for bed.

21

"I'm So All Alone . . ."

The following week at work she heard the surprising news about Irene Allen. Fran came into the office in a depressed mood, shaking her head. When Gail asked what was wrong, she said, "Irene and Stuart have separated. I've seen it coming for a long time, but somehow I always thought they'd have sense enough to work things out. Now it's definite."

Gail shrugged. "Marriage!" she said, and snapped her fingers eloquently.

Fran scowled at her. "There's nothing wrong with marriage. It needs a little more give than take, that's all. And from both parties."

"Oh, sure, sure," Gail sniffed. "The only trouble is that men think it's the other party who ought to do the giving."

"I wonder," Fran said. Then she braced her shoulders and turned to the work piling up on her desk. "Anyway, we can't solve other people's problems for them, no matter how much we'd like to try." She turned to look at Marel. "Just see that nothing like this ever happens to you, young lady. Be sensible ahead of time."

Marel bent her head over the book dummy she was pasting. She had told no one at the office about what had happened in her own life. She had a feeling that perhaps if she kept quiet Chris would come back and everything would be all right again. Then no one need ever know. So she stiffened her spine with a firm appli-

cation of pride and forced herself to smile when there
was nothing in life to smile about.

She felt a sense of shock concerning the news about
Stuart and Irene. Those two had seemed to have everything. Success, good incomes, a lovely place to live,
interesting work. What had parted them? What had gone
wrong? Had what had happened anything to do with
Chris?

She had not heard a word from him in the week he had
been gone. She did not even know where he was staying. A
dozen times she had been on the verge of going to a phone
and calling him at the office, but each time pride had held
her back. He was the one who was in the wrong, so he
must come to her. She could never go to him.

As day after day dragged by, until it was no longer one
week, but two weeks and three weeks, the frightened con-
viction began to grow in her that he was gone for good.
Wrong or right, he had no intention of coming back.

She tried to fill in her time with work. At the office she
seized on every odd job that offered. She was at Fran's
elbow ready to help almost before she was needed and
she worked overtime whenever the opportunity came her
way. It was better to sink herself in work and postpone
the unhappy moment of going home to the empty apartment until she was so weary that she cared about nothing
except to tumble into bed and fall asleep. When she wasn't
tired enough, it was too easy to lie awake and think. With
long, long thoughts in the dark came pain and loneliness.

She worked harder than ever under Eric Webb's direction, but she felt again and again the whiplash of his
tongue because her drawing would not come right. Her
fingers were willing, but the spirit that brought lines on
paper to life was gone. She could no longer care deeply
about her work except as a way to fill up the empty hours.

Once or twice Fran reproved her. "Don't turn yourself
into a work machine, Marel. It's all right to be ambitious
and try to get ahead and learn all you can. But you've

got a husband and a marriage to think about too. No man wants a wife who is nothing but an animated paintbrush."

She gave Fran a stiff smile and shrugged her words aside, but she winced nevertheless. An animated paintbrush! That was what Eric Webb thought she ought to be, but now that she was becoming just that he was less pleased than he had been before.

Once, in a gentler moment, he stopped beside her drawing board and it was not at marks on her papers he looked, but into her eyes.

"You must paint with the heart too," he said. "Not only with the fingers."

But the heart was lacking and nothing came right.

Later that same afternoon Chris's mother appeared unexpectedly at the studio to take Marel out to dinner. More than once Marel had been tempted to go to Mrs. Mallory with her problem, but each time she had drawn back in uncertainty. Probably she wouldn't be welcome. Of course Chris's mother would side with Chris. Such a visit would gain her nothing. But now that Mrs. Mallory had come to her, she found her heart leaping with unreasonable hope.

They went to a quiet restaurant on a side street nearby. Mrs. Mallory was friendly and cheerful, but once they were seated at a table, she wasted no time in going straight to the point.

"I'm leaving for California tomorrow," she said. "I wanted to see you before I left."

Hope died out painfully. "What about the—the apartment?" Marel asked.

Mrs. Mallory did not answer until she had sent a waiter away with their order. Then she smiled sympathetically at Marel, as if she knew that her news would hurt.

"Chris decided it was better to give it up, and I think that was the wisest way."

Marel could find no words. As long as the apartment

had been in the offing, there had seemed a possibility that she and Chris might get together again. Now the last slim chance was gone.

"I've been thinking over a number of things in the last few weeks," Mrs. Mallory went on, "and I've decided that perhaps I was not too wise to try to thrust that place upon you. If you and Chris were having difficulties, a change of setting alone wouldn't solve them. You needed to work out where you were and with what you had, without any third person present."

Marel looked away from her. "I'm afraid they're beyond solving."

"Nonsense! I won't believe that. I'm willing to admit that I objected to Chris's marrying you in the beginning. I felt you were too young and that neither of you had had time to get well enough acquainted with the other."

"I guess that was true enough," Marel said.

Mrs. Mallory went on as if she had not spoken. "But now that you are married, I think you both need to do everything you can to work this out. That's why I'm going back to the coast. I don't want to be where I might take sides. This is something for you two to work out yourselves. Too many marriages are broken up by well-meaning in-laws."

Marel had never liked Chris's mother as much as she did now. Always before, she had held herself back a little. Now a warm rush of affection rose in her and she reached impulsively across the table and squeezed Mrs. Mallory's hand.

"I think you're the most outstanding in-law any girl could have," she said.

The older woman's fingers returned her squeeze. "You'll be all right. You'll work this out somehow. I know you will."

But later that night, lying awake in the dark, Marel wondered if they ever would—she and Chris. And she wondered about the things that had gone wrong. She remembered the time Mac Conway had told her she ought to get out of Chris's way, so he could work in the evening. Her solution hadn't been too successful. To be away every evening was not to be much of a wife. Perhaps there was a better way, if only she had troubled to look for it.

Mac had called her a burbling brook because she hummed and he'd said Chris couldn't write in a public square. She could remember unhappily now the ways in which she had blithely interrupted Chris's work. Running over to put her cheek against his, reading over his shoulder, humming everlastingly. He had not wanted to hurt her feelings by telling her it was impossible to work with her in the room and she had done nothing at all to try to make it possible.

Mrs. Mallory was right when she said they ought to work things out with what they had and where they were. If ever she got the chance again, she would recognize and accept Chris's need for uninterrupted quiet. That was one thing they *could* work out together if they tried, and without Chris's fleeing to Mac's, or Marel's forcing herself back to the studio at night.

Another thing they'd never done anything about was the matter of social life. After that time at the penny arcade, they'd tried to make play a part of their program, but always they played by themselves. They had made no effort to develop mutual friends. There were people Chris liked and people she liked, but they had not found friends they could share. They had not tried.

Now perhaps there would never be another chance to try.

But in spite of her discouragement and depression, she kept plugging determinedly at her work. That, at least, was something to cling to. Fran wanted a cover design— Marel Mallory would prove that she could come across when she was given an assignment. Her first efforts went into the wastebasket, while time sped along. And then one day she was able to place before Fran a not too impossible sketch.

Fran seized upon it with alacrity. "Now you've caught it! And just in the nick of time, my girl. I think this will turn the trick. I'd about decided to use the design Janey Burns turned in. But I like this better. If you can give me a finished job by tomorrow morning, you'll be launched as a cover designer. I think this is a good enough job to bring other orders. Think you can manage it?"

"I'll manage it," Marel told her. But the old lift over a bit of success was gone. This was important to her, so she would do it. But without Chris to run to with the news that she had turned in a design that had met with Fran's approval, the whole thing was without savor.

That was the day she came home from work to find a letter from Chris waiting in the mailbox. When she recognized his writing, her hands trembled so that she could hardly get the door to the apartment open. Once in, she banged it shut behind her, dropping her bag of groceries on the floor and sat down on the couch, without stopping to remove hat or coat.

The glue on the envelope stuck maddeningly, and she tore it open untidily to pull out the single typewritten sheet and an enclosed check.

Dear Marel:

I am sending you a check for my half of the rent money.

I told Mother that we would not take the sub-lease on the larger apartment and she cancelled the arrangement. She returned to the coast the end of last week.

The larger apartment would not have solved our difficulties, I am afraid.

CHRIS

That was all. No indication that he meant to see her

again. No softening words of any kind. No hint of any conclusion he might have come to since he had been away from her. Not even a return address.

The check slipped to the floor and she did not trouble to pick it up. Somehow the curtness of the note hurt more than anything that had gone before. It made the possibility of his coming back fade into remote distance.

She looked about the little apartment which they had furnished with so much love and hope and courage, and everything in it brought some stabbing memory. The curtains they had argued over, the gay dishes, the coffee table with the scratch on top. How little any of it meant with Chris gone! How much it had all meant when he was here!

The ringing of the doorbell startled her. She picked up the check from the floor and thrust it into its envelope, stuffed the whole out of sight in her purse. Then she went to the door and opened it.

In the hallway outside stood Irene Allen.

At the sight of her, the feeling Marel had always thrust back before rushed up full force. How could she dare come here—this woman who had everything, and who wanted more!

"Hello," Irene said. "Just going out?"

Marel stared at her, not understanding at once. Then she remembered that in her excitement over Chris's letter she had not troubled to take off her hat and coat.

"No," she said stiffly, "I'm just getting home." She knew ordinary courtesy required that she step out of the doorway and invite Irene in, but somehow she could not move.

Irene took matters into her own hands. "Mind if I come in for a moment?" she asked, and stepped quietly past Marel into the room. "I was hoping to find Chris here."

Marel could feel the flush rising in her cheeks. She was wordless with indignation. She had never in her life disliked anyone so intensely as she disliked this poised, attractive woman before her.

"I suppose Chris will be home any minute?" Irene went on. "Would you mind if I waited? It's terribly important for me to see him."

"He won't be home." Marel felt the stiffness of her lips as she formed the words. What sort of game was Irene playing? What was all this about?

"He—he won't be home?" Irene repeated blankly. "You mean he's out of town? Then that explains—but he shouldn't have done a thing like this! I can't understand it. To throw over his responsibility concerning his book! A responsibility to his publishers as well as to himself."

Irene sounded as though she did not know Chris had left home. She sounded as though she had not seen him at all during the time he had been away. But that didn't make sense. Not after that night at the Blue Peacock.

Irene dropped into a chair. "This is terrible! We need another chapter written into the book. There's a gap that must be filled. He knows that. I told him the last time I saw him. If it is to go to press this month, we've got to have the new chapter quickly. If he wants to throw over the chance of writing another book, that's his affair, regrettable as it may be. But he can't let us down on this one."

Again Marel found herself stupidly repeating words. "Throw over—another book? I don't understand."

"You mean he didn't tell you about the foolish letter he wrote me saying that he wasn't going to try another story? That he was through as a writer?"

"I don't know anything about it," Marel said dully. "I don't know where he is. I haven't seen him in more than three weeks."

As the significance of Marel's words reached Irene, her eyes widened and she looked quickly about the room, as if she were registering for the first time the absence of masculine belongings. "You mean——?"

Marel nodded. It wasn't possible to say in so many words that Chris had left her.

"But why, Marel? Why? I thought Chris was the happiest, proudest young husband I'd ever seen. The way he talked about you and that talent of yours for drawing! There've been times when I've envied you two young people."

"*You* envied *us?*" That was something which had never occurred to her—that Irene Allen would envy Marel Mallory! The anger, the ugly feeling of jealousy, was fading out now. Suddenly it was easy to tell Irene. "We'd promised each other that when one of us earned a big check he'd take the other to dinner at the Blue Peacock. Chris's check came first. But he forgot all about the celebration. And he made another date for that night. I was hurt and sort of peeved, so I took myself to the Blue Peacock alone."

"The Blue Peacock?" Irene said. "That's where Chris and I had dinner the last time I saw him."

"I know," Marel said. "I saw you come in. That was the night I was there."

"I'm beginning to understand," Irene went on thoughtfully. "I wondered why he was unwilling to go there. I remember he asked if we couldn't go somewhere else. So I told him not to be silly—it was near-by and the food was good. I thought he might be worried about the steep prices, but of course it was *my* party. The publisher always pays when it's a business dinner. So I wouldn't take 'no' for an answer."

Marel leaned limply against the sofa. "And I—I thought ——" But she was too ashamed of what she had thought to say any more.

There was a little silence during which Marel looked at her hands and twisted her handkerchief. Then the other woman left her chair and came to sit beside her on the sofa. She put her arm around Marel's shoulders and gave her a little pat of understanding.

"You must never get ideas like that. They aren't worthy of you and they're not worthy of Chris. I don't need to tell you what a fine person he is, or how much he's worth all the belief you can put in him. For me he has been—not just another writer—but one of the most promising to come to me for a long time. It distresses me very much that he seems determined to give up his writing."

Marel straightened suddenly. "He shan't give it up! He mustn't give it up!"

"Good for you," Irene approved. "I think he needs you, Marel. Maybe just as much as you need him." She picked up her gloves and handbag and walked to the door. As she followed her, Marel noticed for the first time how weary she looked, how much older.

At the door Irene stopped and turned back for a moment. "I'm not the one to give anyone else advice, but I know where some of the ruts in the road are because I've stumbled over most of them. Don't be too much of a career girl, Marel. Take a little longer to arrive as an artist, so that you'll have time enough to be a wife. Otherwise—before you know it—it may be too late to be one."

Then the moment of seriousness was gone and she smiled her smile of artificial cheer again.

"See if you can get that chapter for me, will you?"

"I'll get it," Marel said firmly. "I'll call him at work the first thing in the morning."

Irene shook her head. "I tried that yesterday. He hasn't been at the store all week and the person I talked to didn't seem to know when he was coming back—if ever. That's why I came here tonight. I'm afraid you'll have to do a bit of detective work first."

Marel said "Good night" a little blankly and Irene went away. She closed the door after her and leaned against it, trying to sort out her thoughts.

Chris hadn't been at work all week. Chris had given up his writing, fallen down on his responsibility in meeting a deadline. It wasn't like him at all. Something had to be done right away. But what? His mother had left town, so that closed one channel of approach.

There was Mac Conway. Mac still had his old apartment —there would always be room for Chris there. That would be the most likely place for him to go. She had not taken off her hat and coat when she'd come home, so she was ready to leave without spending a moment on preparation. There was her cover design, but she could work on that later—even if she had to stay up all night.

The bus ride to Mac's seemed endless, and all the way there she kept running over the words that she would say to Chris. Perhaps Mac would be out. Perhaps Chris himself would come to the door. She'd tell him how ashamed and sorry she was and how completely wrong. There was no false pride left in her. She knew now that the fault had been hers.

She had been petty about the Blue Peacock and had not given him a chance to explain the spot he had been in. She had been envious of Irene and jealous of her. She had said unforgivable things for which she must now ask forgiveness. If only it wasn't too late!

It had been all very well to show Irene a front of determination; to promise to get Chris back to his writing. But as the bus drew nearer Mac's place, she became less and less sure she could manage it. She had no reason to hope that Chris would ever forgive the way she had behaved.

The time had come with Irene—for all her attractiveness, for all her success—when it was too late for her to be a wife. Was it already too late for Marel to be one?

22

Light in the Window

It was not Chris who came to the door when she rang the bell, but Mac Conway. When he saw who it was, he said, "Hello," with his usual lack of enthusiasm.

"H-h-hello," Marel said. "Is—Chris here?"

Mac stood looking at her in his maddeningly deliberate way, as if she were some sort of bug on a slide. "No," he said at length, "he isn't here."

"Do you know where I can find him?" Marel pleaded. "Have you seen him at all?"

Mac stepped out of the doorway grudgingly. "I suppose you'd better come in for a minute."

It was anything but a cordial invitation, but she accepted it quickly before he could change his mind. She looked around his living room for some mark of Chris's presence, but she could find no evidence that her husband had been there recently.

"Sit down." It was not an invitation, but an order, and Marel seated herself gingerly on the edge of a chair.

"Irene Allen stopped in tonight." She tried to make her explanation sound casual, but her voice had a tendency to quaver. "She needs another chapter for Chris's book and she can't get in touch with him."

"So that's why you're here?" Mac said. "You've been moved by a tender interest in your husband's work at last."

None of her old anger against him rose at his words. "I guess I deserve just about anything you want to say," she told him miserably. "If you'll help me to find Chris—that's all I want."

Mac snorted. "That's *all* you want! Well, it's more than you'll get from me. Chris was here for a couple of weeks, but he's gone now."

"Oh, Mac, tell me where! *Please* tell me!"

"So you can go trailing after him and interfere with his work again? Not a chance!"

"Then he *is* working? It isn't true what Irene said—that he wasn't going to write any more."

"It's true enough," he said curtly. "He's thrown over the idea of doing another book. But he's not the kind to let an editor down on one already taken. He's gone away to get that chapter written. It wouldn't come here in town, so he's taken a leave of absence from work till he gets it done. The kindest thing you can do is stay away and let him finish the job."

Was he right, she wondered? Was that the kindest thing she could do for Chris? Somehow she could not, would not, believe that. She left her chair and went to the door. There was no use staying here talking to Mac. He had never approved of her as a wife for Chris. And maybe he'd been right.

"I suppose you want to tell him you're sorry again?" he said. "That you didn't mean a word of it and you want to kiss and make up."

She did not turn to look at him and he went on quickly.

"Oh, don't think Chris has been crying on my shoulder. He's not that kind. He hasn't told me what it's all about. He didn't need to. Little girls like you go on being little girls for much too long a time. You think that every time you throw a tantrum all you have to do is say you're sorry afterward and the sun will come out and everything will be rosy right away. But being sorry isn't good enough. It gets monotonous."

"I know," Marel said. She pulled open the door and went out of the apartment into the cool city night.

Where would a man go to write a chapter of a book —a chapter that he couldn't write here in the clatter of New York? Where else but to a cabin in Connecticut where he could shut out everything but the sighing of pine trees in the wind and the crackle of a fire on the hearth?

There was that cover design she had to have ready for Fran Embree the first thing in the morning. If she threw that over now, Fran might not trust her again with another urgent assignment. That cover meant a real step ahead in the work of Marel Mallory.

She seemed to hear Irene's voice again: "Take a little longer to arrive as an artist, so that you'll have time enough to be a wife . . ."

There was a drugstore in the next block. She went into a phone booth and dialed Fran's number. When Fran answered, she told her the situation quickly and this time she held nothing back.

"I guess the people who say a woman can't manage a career and marriage at the same time are right," she finished. "I hate to let you down, but I have to choose the marriage. That is, if I have any marriage left."

"Don't worry about letting me down," Fran told her quickly. "I can use the Janey Burns jacket. It's not as good as yours, but it will do. Wish I could give you a few more days, but tomorrow's the final deadline. But on this marriage-career business—don't give up for good. That would be silly."

"If my wanting to be an artist gets in the way . . . I mean, after what happened to Irene——"

"Look, Marel," Fran broke in, "this is something you have to figure out for yourself. Nobody else can tell you what to do. But there *are* women who manage a career and a marriage at the same time. They have to be ʼart women. Are you smart enough?"

She wondered about that in the subway to Grand Central. Then she put the problem aside and checked the contents of her purse. She ha1 enough for a ticket, enough for a cab at the other end—if one was available. There would be no other way to get to a cottage in the woods.

By sheer luck she caught a train with just two minutes to spare and dropped into a seat by a window where she could turn away from people and watch the lights moving by outside. Not that she really saw them except in a flash now and then. Everything was like a dream—unreal, impossible.

What if this was a wild-goose chase? What if Chris had not gone to Connecticut at all? What if he'd left his job for good? Left New York for good?

All the unanswerable questions she could think of pounded through her thoughts, keeping monotonous time to the wheels of the train. Once when her fingers sought a handkerchief in the pocket of her coat, they met a queer little ball of something or other, and she drew it out to examine wonderingly.

It was a very shopworn bit of cleansing tissue, rolled into a tight wad around small things that were hard and sharp. She unwrapped the wad and looked at the bits of broken twigs it contained.

And suddenly she was no longer on a train bound for Connecticut. She was back in Central Park with Chris beside her. Chris—breaking bits of twigs and tossing them down, while Marel listed the marriage resolves they stood for.

Fran said you had to be smart. How smart had she been? She had gone blithely ahead putting her work first, not worrying about whether she might do more toward helping Chris to a better working setup for his writing.

Yet, in spite of what she had told Fran over the telephone, in spite of the way her work had not come right lately, she had a feeling that she would be unhappy if she really gave it up for good. All her life she would feel that she'd missed something and there would always be an empty place that not even loving Chris could fill. For women like herself, who had a strong urge to create, an either-or answer wasn't the right one.

Then how to be smart? As Fran said, she had to figure this out for herself. She poked a finger among the bits of twigs as if she might find inspiration there. But somehow, in their ahead-of-time figuring, they had not seen all the pitfalls, all the difficulties.

When there were two careers in the same family, one of them had to come first. The way things were in the world, it was right for the man's work to take first place. From now on, she would make haste a little more slowly. There would be other opportunities like this cover design, opportunities which wouldn't conflict with Chris's welfare. She could continue to be happy in the work she was fitted for, but, by being wise and not pushing too desperately, she could enjoy a successful marriage too. She *would* be smart enough to have both.

If only there was still time to be smart!

When the train pulled into the station and she stepped down to the platform, she had a moment's fear that she would not be able to carry through what she had come to do. Then a taxi of ancient vintage rolled up to the curb and she rushed across the platform to hail it.

Her directions were not very clear, but her determination was terrific. The driver understood the latter, if not the former.

"I hope you know where you're going, lady," he said, as she dropped into the back seat, "because I sure don't."

But she wasn't an artist for nothing. She had a trick of registering all sorts of things at a glance and finding them useful for picture details later on. Sometimes that faculty came in handy in other respects, as it did now. She remembered photographically the turns of the highway as it led out of town, remembered the look of fence and field and a dark hillside above the road.

When she saw the white fence again, she knew she was right, and though the cab driver did not approve, he turned up the narrow woodsy road that cut into the hills.

They took one wrong turn and the unfamiliar look of the road in the car's headlights warned Marel, so they turned back. The next turn was right, and her heart began a tattoo beneath her ribs.

Any moment now and Mac's little cabin would come into view. It should be up around that hill on the right. If it was dark—then her trip was futile. But if there was a light in the window—!

"Stop here!" she called to the driver. "I can't see from inside the cab."

She got out of the car and walked through dead leaves on the road, her eyes searching the hillside above. And then she saw it—set there beyond the tall trunks of the pine trees. A square of light shining through the darkness, and most wonderful of all, she could hear the clattering sound of typewriter keys.

"This is the place," she told the driver, and paid him as quickly as she could. "No, you needn't stay. I'll be all right now."

She waited while he drove ahead to a clearing and swung the car around. When he'd gone and her eyes had become accustomed to the faint starlight, she found the path that was a short cut up the hill. The sound of those clattering keys grew louder—incongruous in this quiet world of pines, but a symphony to Marel's ears.

The typewriter went steadily on. The sound of the car had not penetrated the clatter. Chris did not dream that anyone was near.

Her teeth were chattering a little, and it was not entirely from cold. She was frightened, now that she was here. What if he were angry when he saw her? What if he would not want her here? What if Mac was right, and she'd only be interrupting his work again?

But there was no going back now. Always, she thought, always and forever from now on, when she caught the spicy odor of pine trees she would be transported back to this shadowy hillside, this moment of anticipation that had in it both fearfulness and hope.

When the typewriter suddenly stopped, the silence was startling. Marel held her breath, waiting for what might happen next, but the silence continued unbroken. No one came to the cabin door and flung it open to look out into the night. The rough bark of the tree beside her felt as if it was making a pattern on her hand. She pushed herself away from the tree and climbed toward the cabin, stepping carefully lest the crackle of a twig beneath her feet warn the man in the cabin that someone was near-by.

She reached the veranda quietly and stood before the door, her breath coming quickly as if she had run all the way. This was it. This was the moment when she had to carry through what she had come to do. She raised her hand to knock against the wood of the door, but before her knuckles touched the wood, she let it fall to her side again. The silence in the cabin kept on.

This time she made no effort to knock. She put her hand on the knob and turned it softly, pushed the door panel gently with her shoulder. The door was not locked. It swung open, and the fragrance and warmth of burning wood in the fireplace rushed to meet her. Swiftly, softly, she closed the door behind her.

Across the room before the fire the man at the typewriter did not stir. There were wads of crumpled paper on the floor about him and a sheet in the machine with a few lines of typing on it. Her hands were so cold and shaky that she thrust them into the pockets of her coat to still them and warm them. Beneath her fingers she felt again the small wad of broken twigs.

Abruptly the man at the typewriter stretched out a hand and ripped the paper from the machine, crumpled it with an impatient gesture, and tossed it to the floor to join the others cluttered about his chair.

"Chris!" Marel cried. "I can't draw either!"

He pushed his chair back with a clatter and stood

there looking at her across the width of the room. She did not wait to see what was in his eyes. She did not wait for him to hold out his arms or turn away. She flew across the room and put her own arms about his neck, hid her face against his shoulder.

"I'm so sorry, Chris. So ashamed. I—I just don't know how to tell you."

The words were nearly muffled against his shoulder, but he must have heard, because he put his two hands on each side of her head and tipped her face so that he could look down into her eyes.

"I'm glad you came," he said. "I'm so very glad you came." And she knew that no more words were needed just then.

He discovered how cold her hands were, discovered she had had no supper. Quickly he bundled her into a blanket and tucked her cozily onto the couch before the fire, busied himself with warming food, making hot coffee.

Words could come later, as they would need to come, but now she need only sigh contentedly in her comfortable cocoon as the food warmed and strengthened her.

Things were right between her and Chris. It wasn't too late. Marriage was just like anything else. You had to learn how to make it good and right, and you learned by trying, by practice. Sometimes you failed, but when you stopped taking the "ever after" part for granted, then you learned how to be a good wife, just the way you learned how to be a good artist, or a good anything. She was going to be a good wife and a good artist too. But she was going to be the first one first.

She stretched herself lazily. "I'll do the dishes," she offered, yawning.

"Tomorrow," Chris said. "Tomorrow while I'm getting that extra chapter done for Irene."

"I'll be so quiet while you work," she said. "I won't go outside. I won't go away, but I'll stay and I'll be quiet, just to show you I can."

She didn't need to ask him if he really meant it about not writing another book. Of course he hadn't meant it —any more than she had meant that she would never do anything with her drawing again. He had been discouraged and depressed, just as she had been. They needed each other.

He came over and sat down on the couch and took her onto his knees, blanket and all. And the soreness and loneliness went away. It was good to be together and not just one alone.